BE

Ben the tramp, with his usual genius for trouble, runs into danger when he finds a dead body and decides to help out.

Son of novelist Benjamin Farjeon, and brother to children's author Eleanor, playwright Herbert and composer Harry, Joseph Jefferson Farjeon (1883–1955) began work as an actor and freelance journalist before inevitably turning his own hand to writing fiction. Described by the *Sunday Times* as 'a master of the art of blending horrors with humour', Farjeon was a prolific author of mystery novels, with more than 60 books published between 1924 and 1955. His first play, *No. 17*, was produced at the New Theatre in 1925, when the actor Leon M. Lion 'made all London laugh' as Ben the tramp, an unorthodox amateur detective who became the most enduring of all Farjeon's creations. Rewritten as a novel in 1926 and filmed by Alfred Hitchcock six years later, with Mr Lion reprising his role, *No.17*'s success led to seven further books featuring the warm-hearted but danger-prone Ben: 'Ben is not merely a character but a parable—a mixture of Trimalchio and the Old Kent Road, a notable coward, a notable hero, above all a supreme humourist' (Seton Dearden, *Time and Tide*). Although he had become largely forgotten over the 60 years since his death, J. Jefferson Farjeon's reputation made an impressive resurgence in 2014 when his 1937 Crime Club book *Mystery in White* was reprinted by the British Library, returning him to the bestseller lists and resulting in readers wanting to know more about this enigmatic author from the Golden Age of detective fiction.

J. JEFFERSON FARJEON

Ben on the Job

COLLINS
CRIME
CLUB

COLLINS CRIME CLUB

An imprint of HarperCollins*Publishers*
1 London Bridge Street
London SE1 9GF
www.harpercollins.co.uk

This paperback edition 2016

First published in Great Britain for The Crime Club Ltd
by W. Collins Sons & Co. Ltd 1952

A catalogue record for this book is
available from the British Library

ISBN 978-0-00-815603-9

Set in Sabon by Palimpsest Book Production Limited, Falkirk, Stirlingshire

Printed by Clays Ltd, St Ives plc

MIX
Paper from
responsible sources
FSC™
www.fsc.org
FSC® C007454

Contents

Misbehaviour of Two Thumbs

When Ben had got up that morning—getting up with Ben was mainly the process of changing from a prone to an erect position and peering into a mirror, if there happened to be one, to work out whether he'd washed last week or the week before—he had been quite sure that something would happen to him before the time came to lie down again. He knew it by the infallible sign of itching thumbs.

Whenever his thumbs itched, something 'orrible always happened. His thumbs had itched on that never-to-be-forgotten foggy afternoon when he had stumbled into a house numbered 'Seventeen', to die a hundred deaths before he stumbled out again. They had itched before he had advised a bloke leaning over a low stone parapet not to jump into the Thames—'I wouldn't, mate, if I was you,' he'd said, 'it looks narsty!'—to discover that the bloke was already dead. They had itched before a peculiarly unpleasant meeting with an Indian. Ben 'ated Injuns. They had itched before a shipwreck that had hurled him into a situation so completely and fantastically impossible that he still didn't believe it.

And now, here they were, itching again! Lummy, what was it going to be *this* time?

Well, there was nothing to do but to wait and see. What was was, what is is, and what will be will be, for once. Fate puts the spotlight on you there's no slipping out of it. And so, resigned but alert, Ben paused at a morning coffee stall to fortify himself for whatever lay ahead.

'Mornin', guv'nor,' he said, 'wot's the noos terday? 'Ave they started the Fif' World War yet?'

'Wouldn't surprise me,' grinned the stall-keeper.

'Nor me neither,' answered Ben, 'but let's 'ope they stop at 'arf a dozen. Cup o' corfee.'

'Did you pay for the last?' inquired the stall-keeper good-naturedly.

'On'y by mistike.'

The stall-keeper laughed as he pushed a thick cup across. Ben took a cautious sip.

'What's the matter? Think it's poisoned?'

'Well, there's no 'arm in bein' careful,' returned Ben. 'See, this ain't goin' ter be my lucky day. Coo, call this corfee? Am I s'posed ter fork aht threepence fer *this?*'

'Not if you can give me a tip for the two-thirty?'

'Saucy Sossidge.'

'That's a new one on me.'

'Go on, wot higgerence! I'm ridin' it meself!'

Warmed by the coffee—warmed but not ruined, for the stall-keeper said he had had three penn'orth of fun and allowed his comic customer to depart with his last shilling intact—Ben shuffled off to face the day, and the morning passed, most surprisingly, without any shocks. It was indeed a remarkably successful morning, for it produced seven fag-ends, one almost half its original length, and twopence for helping a nervous old lady across the road.

At one o'clock he partially filled a neglected void with two substantial sandwiches. They were so substantial that you couldn't taste what was inside them. Thinking it might be a good idea to find out, Ben opened one to see, but as he found nothing he supposed he had opened it in the wrong place. Nevertheless, they did their job, and half an hour on an Embankment seat put him right again.

He might have stayed longer on the seat, for Ben liked sitting down, it was comfortable, if an old man with fuzzy white hair had not suddenly darted towards him and sat down by his side. The old man was breathing heavily, and his tongue kept shooting out to moisten his lips. 'If this is It,' thought Ben, 'I ain't stoppin'!' And he got up and departed.

To his considerable relief, and even more considerable surprise, the old man did not get up and follow him. False alarm! This was not It!

'I wunner if me thumbs was wrong this time?' reflected Ben, as he resumed his way to nowhere. The day was passing too smoothly to believe. 'Arter orl, I expeck yer *can* get a nitch wot's jest a nitch, even in yer thumbs?'

There was yet another theory that might explain his strange immunity. Perhaps Fate *could* be dodged if you were nippy enough? Suppose, for instance, that nasty old man, and he *was* nasty, the way his tongue was working overtime—suppose Fate had sent him along, but Ben had beaten Fate on the post? With sudden hope Ben grinned. 'That's wot it is!' he decided. 'I've given Faite the KO!'

Before long, however, he found his self-faith weakening.

Here came the mist! That was a second sign of trouble. In rather surprising obedience to a weather forecast, a thin, depressing mist began to weave through the streets; and half Ben's woes took place in fog. He had even been born in one, birth being the initial woe that preceded all the rest. A fog in the street and an itch on the thumb formed a combination to kill all hope.

A minor drawback of foggy weather was that it made fag-ends harder to find. In order not to miss them you had to keep your nose well down, which often made you bump into people . . .

And then Ben did bump into someone. Or someone bumped into him. He couldn't say which. All he knew was that he suddenly found himself sitting on the pavement.

'Oi!' he bleated.

The man with whom he had collided was also on the pavement, but he was up again before Ben had begun to think about it. 'Tork abart bounce!' thought Ben. ''E must be mide o'rubber!'

There was no time to find out whether he was indeed made of rubber, because the next instant the man was gone.

'Corse, don't say "Beg pardon," or "Are yer 'urt?" or anythink like that! Jest buzz orf, like I didn't matter!'

Still sitting on the ground, Ben gazed indignantly after the vanished man. Then all at once his emotion changed from indignation to anxiety, as the unmistakable form of a policeman materialised out of the fog.

Was *this* going to be It?

'Hallo, hallo!' said the policeman.

'Sime ter you,' replied Ben.

'Had a tumble?'

'No, I jest thort I'd sit dahn in the sunshine.'

'Oh! Well, how about finding a seat somewhere else where you won't be in people's way?'

''Ow abart you givin' me a 'and hup first, and then findin' me one?'

The constable stooped and helped Ben to rise, and then stood watching while Ben groped about himself for bruises. You did it by pressing various parts of your anatomy to see whether any of them hurt.

'Feeling all right?' inquired the constable.

He seemed friendly enough. Perhaps, after all, this was not going to be It? That might or might not be an advantage, because after you'd screwed yourself up to it like, there was something in getting it over.

'Dunno,' answered Ben.

'Well, no one else can tell you.'

'I feels a bit groggy. Things is goin' rahnd like.'

'Then hold on to me until they stop going round like. You'll be all right if you just take it easy, sonny.' Funny how policemen seemed to like calling him sonny when he was often old enough to be their great-grandfather! This 'un didn't look more'n twenty. P'r'aps it was because they was generally big and he was only a little 'un? 'You haven't told me yet how it happened?'

'Eh?'

'Did you slip?'

'No. Bloke bumps inter me.'

'Oh.'

'Yus, and never stops, like them motor-cars they arsks for on the wireless. Fer orl 'e knoo, I might 'ave broke me blinkin'—wozzer matter?'

'Nothing,' replied the constable, 'only you've dropped something.'

'Eh?'

'On the ground there.'

'Not me—I ain't got nothin' ter drop!'

'Well, if you'll let go my arm for a moment I'll pick it up.'

Ben relaxed his grip as the constable stooped. Dropped something? He had spoken truly when he had said he had nothing to drop. His shilling had gone for his sandwiches, and the change had gone through a hole in his pocket. (One does need a wife for holes.) And that was all he had, apart from himself. So he couldn't have dropped anything, could he?

But the policeman had found something, and as he came up from his stoop and slowly straightened himself, Ben saw what he held in his hand. It was a jemmy.

'Yours?' inquired the constable.

Perhaps if Ben's thumbs had behaved themselves that morning he would have acted differently, and the course of events for himself and for several other people during the period ahead would have followed a very different pattern. For himself, undoubtedly. He would never have met the other people. But those thumbs had become far more of a superstition to Ben than spilling salt or walking under ladders, and the sense of impending trouble was increased by a sudden movement of the constable's hand towards Ben's shoulder. And so, instead of denying ownership—to be believed or not as the case might be—he decided that This Was It, wriggled away, and ran.

Nothing could have been sillier. Of course the constable ran after him. To a constable Ben, running, was as irresistible as an electric hare to a greyhound, but when it came to making the pace the electric hare wasn't in it, and although policemen are experienced in pursuing, Ben was far more experienced in being pursued. From all of which it may be deduced that our present policeman, with the added handicap of fog, had no chance.

There was, however, one serious flaw in Ben's defensive process. He could run fast, but he could not run for long, and although he always got away the first time he did not always get away the second. No legs could last indefinitely at the pace Ben's were driven, so when his legs and his breath gave out he was forced to seek the nearest sanctuary in the hope that heaven would be kind and send him a good one. If heaven had given Ben his desserts it would always have been kind to him, because strange though this may seem in a difficult world where poverty can be so sorely tempted, Ben had never performed an illegal act for which God might not have forgiven him, and never a mean one. But the luck varied.

This time the luck seemed good. Appearances, unfortunately, can be deceptive. Having evaded the pursuing bobby and vanished temporarily out of his life, Ben's knees went back on him, or down under him, outside the kind of building that he loved above all others. An empty building, useless to all save human derelicts. There were other empty buildings on either side, but at the moment Ben did not know this, for when you are running away all you see is where you stop, and on a misty afternoon you don't see even that very clearly. But what Ben saw was enough to satisfy him, and after crawling through two tall gate-posts that had lost their gate, he slumped behind one of them as hurried footsteps grew into his drumming ears.

The footsteps came closer. Lummy, 'ow many was makin'

'em? More'n one? Voices soon proved this point. Policemen don't talk to themselves.

'Are you sure he turned down this street, sir?'

'Well, you can't be sure of anything in a fog.'

'That's a fact, but I had an idea he took the other turning.'

'He may have done, but I don't think so. It was because I thought I saw somebody bunk round the corner that I spoke when I saw you running.'

The speakers were now just on the other side of Ben's post. Thank Gawd it was a thick 'un! One of the speakers was the constable; the other, assumedly, a passer-by. Unsporting blokes, passers-by, turning even odds into two to one. There ought to be a law agin' 'em!

Crumbs! They'd stopped!

'Wonder if I was wrong?'

('Keep on wunnerin'!' thought Ben.)

'No sign of him, sir.'

'Think we ought to go back?'

'I think that's the best idea.'

('Don't lose the idea,' thought Ben.)

'What was he like?'

'Oh—smallish chap. Put him on a stick and he'd make a good scarecrow.'

'What's he done?'

'That's what I'm after finding out, sir.'

'Then what are you chasing him for?'

There was a tiny pause after that, and then a low whistle.

'Where did you find *that*?'

'On the ground, where I picked him up. He dropped it. He spun some yarn about somebody bumping into him.'

'Then perhaps—'

'No, sir, he bunked the moment I showed him this jemmy. There's been a gang working the district—'

'Hey! Isn't that someone?'

'Where?'

'End of the road! Now he's gone! But I swear—'

The next moment they were gone, too.

For a few seconds Ben remained motionless behind his post, enjoying the blessed silence, and grateful to the red herring that had started them off again on a wrong scent. But he couldn't remain motionless for long, in case they came back. And, lummy, *wasn't* that somebody coming back? Or was it just a tree dripping? Trees often played tricks on you like that! Yes, it was a tree dripping? No, it wasn't! A tree goes on dripping in the same place, and this wasn't sticking to the same place, and he couldn't be quite certain where the place was, anyhow. Of course, it mightn't be the copper . . .

The new approaching sound ceased, then came on again. Ben hesitated no longer. He twisted round and shot up a side path to the back of the building.

2

Strange Partnership

At Ben's next stop, after hitting a back wall—his progress was rather like that of a billiard-ball bouncing off cushions—he found himself facing a back door. Behind him was the back wall off which he had bounced. It was a very high wall, but as it was behind him and he had seen nothing but stars when he had hit it, he did not know that. What he did know was that the back door, set in prison-like bricks, was just ajar. A thin, dark, vertical slit, contrasting with the filmy white mist, indicated the fact.

He could not decide, as he fixed his dizzy gaze on the door, whether the fact was a comfortable or uncomfortable one. A door that is ajar may always be useful to pop into, but you have to remember that before you pop into it, something may pop out of it. There was that time, for instance, when a Chinaman had popped out. And then there was that time when four constables had popped out. And then there was that time when a headless chicken had popped out. Or had that one been a dream? Yes, that one had possibly been a dream, but even so it only went to

10

prove that, waking or sleeping, you could never be sure with a door that was ajar.

The great question of the moment, therefore, was, 'Do I go in or don't I?' He certainly felt very queer, and was quite ready to sit down again. 'Wunner if them sanderwiches 'as anythink ter do with it?' he reflected. Perhaps he ought to have explored a bit longer and taken out whatever was inside 'em. You couldn't be sure with sanderwiches, either. Life teems with uncertainties.

He did not have to wait long to make up his mind. It was made up for him by a sound like a pail being kicked over. He did not know that he had just missed that pail himself—occasionally he was spared something—as he had shot through the side passage, but since the sound came from outside and not from inside, the inside now proved the preferable location, and once more Ben shot and bounced.

But this time he went on bouncing, with the object of bouncing as far away from the back door as possible. He bounced across a dim space, through another doorway, across a black passage, up eight stairs, into a wall, down eight stairs, and then after a dark interval which left no memory, down a stone flight to a basement.

Finally, just to round the incident off, he came to roost on the body of a dead man.

This was an obvious situation for a further bounce, but by now Ben was beyond it. Instead, he removed himself carefully, and then gazed, panting, at the thing he had removed himself from.

It was a well-dressed man lying flat on his back. He had pale cheeks—whether they were normally pale it was impossible to tell—and across one was a very ugly mess.

Without this mess, as far as one could judge, the face would not have shown any special distinction. The lips were rather thick and loose, the features rather characterless, though here again judgment could not be final since the spirit behind the features had departed. Light hair sprayed untidily over a bruised forehead . . . Oh, yes! The man was dead. No doubt whatever about that. Ben was an expert on corpses. They just wouldn't let him alone.

He recalled the first corpse he had ever come across. He had jumped so high he had nearly hit the ceiling. But now—though, mind you, he still didn't like them—they usually had a less galvanic effect upon him. He could feel sorry for them as well as for himself. They must have been through a nasty time. This bloke, for instance . . .

He heard somebody coming down the stairs. The some-body from whose footsteps he had been flying. The somebody who had barged into the pail outside. But Ben did not move. He wasn't going to run no more, not fer nobody. Not even fer the ruddy 'angman. You get like that, after a time.

'Hallo! What's up?'

It was a constable's phraseology, but it wasn't a con-stable's voice, nor was it the voice of the passer-by who had been with the constable. Someone new. All right, let 'em all come! Ben turned his head slowly, and in the dimness saw a tall, bony man descending towards him. His big boots made a nasty clanging sound on the cold stone. His trousers were baggy. Not neat, like the trousers on the corpse. He had high cheek-bones, which looked even more prominent than they were as they caught the little light that existed in the basement. The light came through a small dirty window set in the wall at the foot of the stairs.

His eyebrows were bushy. His hair was black. His nose was crooked. A boxer's nose. That was a pity.

'What's up?' repeated this unattractive individual.

'Doncher mean, wot's dahn?' replied Ben.

Anyhow, it was easier to talk to this chap than to a bobby.

The newcomer regarded the prone figure on the ground with frowning solemnity. Having reached the bottom of the flight he did not move or speak for several seconds, and suddenly conscious of the length of the pause Ben blinked at his companion curiously. He was not reacting to the situation in a quite normal manner, although Ben could not have put it in those terms. What he would have said was, ''E don't seem ter be be'avin' nacherel like, if yer git me?'

'Looks dead,' the man said at last.

''E more'n looks dead,' replied Ben. ''E is dead.'

'Oh! You know that?'

'I won't stop yer, if yer want ter find aht fer yerself.'

The man removed his eyes from the dead to the living.

'Did *you* kill him?' he inquired.

'I wunnered when that one was comin',' answered Ben.

'Well, did you?'

'Corse I did. I pops orf anybody 'oose fice I don't like. That's why I carry a pocket knife.'

The bushy eyebrows shot up.

'Bit of a comic, ain't you?'

'Fair scream. 'Aven't yer seen me on the telervishun, Saturday nights?'

'I must look out for you. Meantime, suppose we stop being funny. What would you do if I went for a policeman?'

'Well, there's nothink like tryin' a thing ter find aht, is there?'

13

'True enough, but I reckon I'll find out a bit more before I try! What did you kill him for?'

'You carn't learn nothink, can yer?'

'Meaning you didn't kill him?'

'Corse I didn't!'

'You told me just now that you did.'

'Well, fancy you arskin'. Wot abart me arskin' if *you* killed 'im?'

'How could I, as I've only just come?'

'Sez you!'

'What's that mean? All right, all right, let's get on with it! If you didn't kill him, what are you doing here?'

Now what was the answer to that one? Ben pondered.

'Come along! Out with it! You've been running like a bloody hare—'

'Well, wasn't you arter me?'

Ben thought that quite good, but it did not seem to satisfy his interrogator, who thrust his face closer to Ben's. It was a nasty face, you couldn't get away from it—and you wanted to get away from it!

'You're a queer cove, if ever I've seen one,' grunted the man. 'Is anybody else after you?'

That was a teaser, but Ben evaded it. 'Ain't one enough?' he retorted. And then to divert further questioning on the point and to clear himself generally, he burst out, ''Ave a bit o' sense! Yer chaised me in 'ere, didn't yer, so if I've on'y jest come in 'ere 'ow could I of 'ad time ter kill that bloke, let alone 'ow I did it and why? Orl right! Now yer know why I'm 'ere, but yer ain't said yet why you're 'ere—'

'I'm here because you're here, you fool!' exclaimed the man impatiently. 'Haven't you just said yourself I chased

14

you in? Or would the right word be "back"? If you'd been here before you'd have had plenty of time, wouldn't you?'

'Yes, and so'd you,' returned Ben, 'with nobs on!'

Now, of course Ben knew *he* had not been here before, but—yus, come ter think of it serious like—he did not know that this unpleasant bushy-browed individual had not. Suppose he had? After all, in regard to the reason for their presences here at this moment, both were lying. Ben was not here through being chased by this man since it was not this man who had chased him. Therefore the man must have accepted Ben's version for his own convenience, and his presence must be due to some other cause! Lummy, it was a fishy business from the word go! Because—another thing—here was a deader on the floor, and neither of them was making any move to get a policeman!

Suddenly the man's mood changed. Or seemed to. 'Don't let's lose our wool,' he said. 'Let's find out who this fellow is, shall we? And how about picking up that broken chair?'

He moved forward and began to stoop over the victim of the as yet unsolved tragedy. His large hands groped about the dead man's clothes. Ben glanced at the broken chair but did not pick it up. A piece of rope lay near it.

'You wanter be careful,' Ben warned his companion.

Ben's mood was changing, also, although he could not decide just what it was changing to or whether the change would last. Bushy Brows had not become any more lovable, but his mood certainly seemed less threatening.

'What do I want to be careful about?' asked Bushy Brows. 'He's not going to jump up and bite me!'

'Yer never know—I seen a chicken run abart withaht its 'ead,' retorted Ben, 'but I wasn't thinkin' o' that. Wot I meant was—well, seein' as 'ow this ain't like jest stealin', but a bit more serious like, and seein' as 'ow you and me ain't done it, sayin' we ain't—'

'Do you know what you're talking about?'

'Yes. I'm torkin' abart not bein' supposed ter touch the body, that is, not afore—'

Bushy Brows interrupted with a laugh, and then looked at Ben hard.

'You're a caution, and no mistake,' he said. 'Do you know, I don't think I've ever met anyone like you before!'

'Tha's right—nobody 'as,' agreed Ben.

'I believe it! In fact, old boy, I'm beginning to think this meeting may turn out a good thing for both of us—but we won't go too fast, eh? It's nice and quiet here, and there's plenty of time, and you've only just come in, and I've only just come in—that's how it is, isn't it?—so we've nothing to worry about while I find out what's in this fellow's pockets! Have we?'

Nice and quiet—plenty of time—nothing to worry about? Hadn't they? 'Tork abart fishy!' thought Ben, unhappily. 'Lummy, wot's this leadin' ter? I—wunner—?' He tried to stop wondering, for wondering can be exceedingly troublesome. It leads to thinking—or is it the thinking that leads to the wondering? Whichever way it is, just when you're wanting peace and rest it comes along and throws a spanner into the works. Gives you—what do they call it?—a sense of responsibility like . . .

And there was something else that Ben was wondering, though this had nothing to do with Bushy Brows. He was wondering why there was something familiar—or seemed to be—about the dead man on the ground? He'd never seen him before, he'd swear himself pink he hadn't, and yet—

'Ah! Here's something!' said Bushy Brows.

'Wot?' asked Ben.

Bushy Brows did not answer at once. He was counting coins and notes. When he had finished he reported, 'Five pound eight and six. Would you like the eight and six?'

'Nah, then, none o' that!' replied Ben.

Bushy Brows grinned.

'You're not going to tell me, Eric, you've never made a bit on the side?'

''Oo's Heric?'

'He was a good little boy.'

'Was 'e? Orl right. I'm Heric.'

'As you like. Then I'm to have the lot?'

'Oi!'

'Well?'

'You better put that back!'

'If I did, what would be the good of having found it? It's no good to him any more, is it? Come off it, Eric! We're getting to know each other, and you can't pull that stuff on me!'

He grinned again as he pocketed the money.

Getting to know each other? Again Ben wondered. Was this a trick to catch him out? He'd known it played before. A 'tec comes along, mikes yer think 'e's crooked, cheats yer orf the stright, and 'e's got yer! Not that anybody had ever got Ben that way, because by that odd kink in his character Ben *was* straight, but he'd seen it done, and orf goes the poor bloke to the lock-up, and orf goes the 'tec to promotion . . . Lummy, here was an idea, though! Why shouldn't *he* play the trick? Beat Bushy Brows at his own game, if it was a game, and if it wasn't, see how far he could make him go? Corse, it'd be a bit of a risk if things went wrong, but this bloke on the floor was getting on

17

Ben's nerves, and 'e must of 'ad a 'orrible time afore 'e got lookin' like 'e did! Blarst this wunnerin'! Fair blast it! But Ben knew he would not learn anything from Bushy Brows unless he won his confidence, and what he had to decide was whether to play for dangerous knowledge or to cling to the bliss of ignorance.

'What's going on behind your film face?' asked Bushy Brows. 'You and I wouldn't do anybody in, would we? We're not the murdering sort—but didn't you say yourself just now that stealing was a different thing? Even if stealing's the right word for taking a bit of loose change from a man who won't need it any more! After all, in this naughty world, there's no saying how *he* got it!'

Bushy Brows was smiling, but Ben detected a note of uncertainty in his voice. In a flash, his friendly mood might change again. This was the moment when Ben had to give up the game or continue it, and to go on playing it harder.

'Bit slow, guv'nor, ain't yer?' he responded.

'Meaning?'

'Well—fer one thing, when *I* meets a bloke wot I ain't never seed afore, I don't put me cards plump dahn on the tible!'

'Ah!'

'Yer've said it!'

'And for another thing?'

'Fer another thing, yer gotter be careful wot yer tike orf a bloke wot's been killed. See, even if yer didn't do it, it might mike some think yer did!'

'Quite a brain, Eric!'

'Oh, I got one, even if sometimes I keeps it dark!'

'And for another thing? Or is that the lot?'

'There's another.'

'Let's have it.'

'Eight and a tanner! I arsk yer!'

Bushy Brows laughed.

'Not enough?'

'Wot do *you* think?'

'How about this, then?' He dived into his pocket and brought out one of the pound notes. 'Will that do for the moment?'

'If yer mike it a short moment!'

Ben snatched the note, donning an expression intended to convey the fiercest greed. As it was entirely spurious, and occurred on a face surprising enough even without it, Bushy Brows had never seen anything like it before.

'After you're hanged, Eric,' he commented, 'there'll be a three-mile queue outside Madame Tussaud's! Now let's see what else we can find?'

He continued his search, while Ben watched him closely. That Bushy Brows was a wrong 'un was now beyond all possible doubt, and this confirmed Ben's determination to maintain his pretence of being a bird of the same feather. But just how much of a wrong 'un Bushy Brows was remained in doubt. Murder was not yet proved.

'Ticket for the Odeon,' said Bushy Brows. 'Or, rather, the counterfoil. Best seat. Hallo!' He gave a low whistle. 'Now, this *is* interesting!'

'Wot is?' asked Ben.

'The date. What's today?'

'I never trouble.'

'It's the thirteenth.'

'Corse it is.'

'Why?'

'Look wot's 'appenin'!'

19

'I get you, but superstition never worried me. Anyhow, where's the bad luck? Aren't we making a bit?'

''E's 'ad the bad luck.'

'But we're not him! What I'm interested in is the date on this counterfoil. It's today's date, so it looks as if our friend was at the Odeon this afternoon.'

Ben considered the point.

'Well, why not?' he replied. ''E 'ad ter be somewhere!'

'You—don't—say!' retorted Bushy Brows. 'You know, Eric, we'll get on faster when you drop your pose of being a mug! It's a good wheeze—I've used it myself—but there's no need to keep it up with me!'

'Orl right,' answered Ben, 'I'll work it aht fer yer if yer want ter see me brine. 'E goes ter the cinema, and 'e sees a fillum, and then 'e comes on 'ere ter think abart it, and when 'e's 'ere 'e bumps inter somebody 'oo murders 'im but wot we've agreed atween us ain't you or me. Is that orl right or ain't it?'

Bushy Brows narrowed his eyes, as though all at once considering Ben again.

'You're quite, quite sure it wasn't you he bumped into?' he said.

'It wern't me if it wern't you,' returned Ben. 'So was it?'

Bushy Brows looked exasperated, shrugged his shoulders, and bent down over the body again. He came up next time with a letter-case.

'Nah we'll know,' said Ben.

'If there's a card in it,' answered Bushy Brows. 'Or a letter.'

There was a card. Bushy Brows slid it out of its special little space and contemplated it with thoughtful eyes. He contemplated it for so long that Ben took a peep over his shoulder, and although the light was so dim he could just make out the name inscribed upon it:

GEORGE WILBY

18, Drewet Road
S.W.3.   Southern Bank

Then something else attracted Ben's attention, something that had fallen out of the case while Bushy Brows had extracted the card and that now lay near the dead man's foot. Ben stooped and quietly picked it up. It was a photograph of a woman. Rather a good-looker. Not one of your film stars, but a face you didn't mind looking at, that was a fact. Indeed, the more Ben looked at it, the more he didn't mind, without exactly knowing why. She was smart, and he was more at home with holes and patches. She had dark hair, and as a rule he preferred 'em blonde—if it was nacherel, mind, and not on one o' them tarts. This wasn't no tart! You could tell she was the sort that would draw away quick if she saw Ben coming. There was nothing to suggest that the admiration would be mutual.

One reason why the face appealed to him was that behind the photographic smile there was a hint of trouble which neither the photographer nor his subject had been able to eliminate. Possibly neither was aware of it. But Ben had a subconscious sense for trouble, and an instinctive sympathy for all who encountered it. Lummy, didn't he know?

Bushy Brows' voice brought Ben's head up from the photograph.

'What have you got there?'

'Pickcher,' answered Ben.

'Oh! Where did you get it?'

'Fell aht o' the case, I reckon.'

'Let's have a look.'

Rather reluctantly Ben held it out, and the man took it. He seemed as interested as Ben, if from a different angle. When he had finished examining it he slipped it back into the letter-case.

'Did yer put the card back, too?' inquired Ben.

'Don't worry. You shall have the chap's name and address if you're good.'

Deciding not to let on that he already knew them, Ben asked innocently:

'Yer know 'oo it is, then?'

'I know more than that, Eric.'

'Oh! Yer do?'

'I know who put the bullet through his head.'

'Oh! It was a bullet wot done it?'

'I never really thought it was a penknife. But you're not going to pretend now, are you, that you never guessed he's been shot?'

'Where's the gun?'

'If you'd shot him, would you have left the gun behind?'

'Tha's right, and as I ain't got no gun on me that shows I didn't shoot 'im, so now yer can tell me 'oo did?'

But Bushy Brows laughed softly as he shook his head.

'For the moment, if you don't mind,' he said, 'I think I'll keep that to myself.'

Ben grunted. 'Yus, yer keeps a lot to yerself, doncher? The corpse's nime, the corpse's address, the bloke wot done 'im in, not ter menshun four pahnd eight and six! P'r'aps

22

yer dunno orl yer sez yer does—people 'oo doesn't tork doesn't always 'ave anythink ter say!'

Bushy Brows laughed again.

'Believe me, Eric, I've plenty to say, and if I told you the lot those pretty little eyes of yours would grow as big as the moon! Now, listen! You and I have been here as long as is good for us, and it's high time we said good-bye—or, rather, *au revoir*. Do you know what that means?'

'Orrivor? I sez it every night ter meself afore I goes ter sleep.'

'Really? I'll have to come and hear you one time, but we've no time now to be funny any more, so just attend and get down to business. You've got a pound, haven't you?'

'And you've got four pahnd eight and a tanner, aincher?'

'Would you like the chance of making even more than that?'

'I ain't 'eard meself say no yet.'

'Very well, then. Let's agree on certain points. You haven't seen me here, and I haven't seen you here. Okay?'

'Okay.'

'And we've neither of us seen this fellow on the floor. Okay?'

'Okay.'

'Just the same—as we're getting on so well together—I am now going to tell you what was on the visiting card.'

'Yer don't 'ave ter. George Wilby, 18, Drewet Road, SW3, and 'e works at the Southern Bank.'

The bushy brows rose.

'I got eyes, sime as you,' said Ben.

'And use them, eh? Very well. What's your own address?'

'Wotcher want ter know for?'

23

'Make up your mind quick, for I'm not waiting here any longer. Are we together or aren't we? If not, I leave you to stew!'

Bushy Brows began to look ominous again.

'We're tergether,' answered Ben meekly.

'Then act as though we are, or I'll pair up with somebody else! You see, I've got to go away—up north—and what I'm needing is some guy who'll keep an eye open this end—and particularly on No. 18, Drewet Road—and report when I get in touch again. Got that clear?'

'As mud.'

'So what's your address?'

'I ain't got none.'

'Couldn't be better, because I can give you one.'

'Where's that?'

'No. 46, Jewel Street, SE. Can you remember it, or shall I write it down?'

'I can remember it.'

'No, I'd better write it down. Where's a bit of paper?' He examined the wallet again, and tore a blank sheet off the back of a letter. 'This'll do.' Taking a pencil stump from his own pocket, he wrote rapidly for a few moments, and then handed Ben the sheet. 'Read it.' He grinned.

Ben read: '"Mrs Kenton, 46, Jewel Street, SE. This is to introduce Mr Eric Burns, a pal of mine. As you know, I have to go away, and I want him to occupy my room till I come back. Ask no questions, etc. Love to Maudie. O.B."'

'Well?'

'I'm on.'

'Then you're on to a good thing—yes, and you can consider yourself damn' lucky, Eric, because if it had been a policeman who found you here instead of me you'd have been on to a very bad thing. And I'm not saying you're out of the wood yet if you don't behave! Meanwhile, you're in Easy Street. All right, that's fixed. You've got your note to Ma Kenton, she'll feed you, and you have a pound to take Maudie to the pictures. That's the lot. So long—till you next hear from me!'

'Oi!' exclaimed Ben, as Bushy Brows turned to go.

'Yes?'

'It ain't quite the lot! Wot abart this bloke 'ere?'

'He's nothing to do with us. Are you forgetting? We've not seen him. Someone else will find and report him—you and I certainly don't want to!'

The next moment, Bushy Brows was gone.

3

Step by Step

Well? Now what?

That was Ben's perplexing question when he found himself once more alone—because of course you don't count a corpse as company—and for a few moments he could not find the answer. Then all at once the answer occurred to him with such simplicity and force that he wondered why there had ever been any doubt about it. It was to follow Bushy Brows' example and to clear out!

But after he had cleared out, and by zigzagging through foggy thoroughfares had put three or four blocks between himself and the block he had started from, the question, 'Now what?' reverted to him in an even more perplexing form. He had dealt with the problem of his own immediate danger. The problems of the corpse, of the woman in the photograph—funny how that photograph stuck in his mind—and of Bushy Brows remained.

Corpse. Woman. Bushy Brows. He considered them in that order. Fust, the corpse. You couldn't leave even a dead man to himself once you'd found him. Well, could yer? I mean ter say! Especially when he was in an empty house and mightn't be found by anybody else for days and days. There'd be people worrying. That woman, for instance. P'r'aps an old muvver. And then the police. The longer they didn't know, the longer the murderer would have to get away. Maybe he was getting away at that moment—up north! But somehow, though he could not explain why, Ben did not think the murderer was Bushy Brows. Though, mind yer, he might be. And setting aside all else, if you left a corpse too long in an empty house, the mice might get at it!

All right, then. The police must be reported to. And a nice job *that* was going to be! A bloke who is being chased by one constable goes up to another and says, 'Oi, there's been a murder!' No, thanks!

How about sending a telegram?

But another solution was right at hand, and suddenly Ben realised what he was leaning against while he cogitated. A telephone booth!

'Lummy! That's the idea!' he muttered. 'Give 'em a ring!'

He did not put the idea into practice at once. Two women came out of a house nearly opposite, and he wanted them out of the way before he entered the box. A movement might attract their attention. Fortunately, they turned in a direction which took them away from the booth, and soon they had dissolved into the mist. Nobody else was in sight.

Quickly he slipped inside, and quickly he lifted the receiver to get it over. But nothing happened. 'Oi!' he called hoarsely. ''Allo! Oi!' Then he remembered that nothing would happen until he did something himself. Lummy, where was two pennies?

He recalled that the change he had received from his

last shilling had been lost through a hole in his pocket, and a pound note was no good in a 'phone box. 'I'm sunk!' he thought dismally. Then he suddenly remembered something else. The old lady who had given him twopence for helping her across the road. Hadn't he put those pennies in another pocket? To his relief he found that he had, and that by a miracle this pocket was intact. Extracting them carefully and holding them tight in case they jumped away, he prepared to part with them for the doubtful benefit of a conversation with the police, when yet another snag came into his mind. He didn't know the name of the street or the number of the house in which lay the body he was about to report!

There was only one thing for it. He would have to go back.

The prospect was so unpleasant that he nearly weakened and gave up the whole affair. Why not drop it, and keep the twopence? Arter orl, 'e 'adn't done nothink! Why not remove himself as far as possible from this unhealthy district, and end the day in serenity and peace? But he had a pound note as well as twopence, and the pound note had been less innocently earned. There was only one way to square *that* account! And wouldn't the eyes of that woman haunt him? Not to mention the less attractive eyes of the late George Wilby, of 18, Drewet Road, SW3?

With a grunt of misery he left the booth and unwound his way back to the danger zone, and now he blessed the fog which, when you wish to avoid publicity, is so preferable to sunlight. It made the unwinding process a little more difficult, but Ben was good at groping, and when he came to the turning down which he had dived to escape the constable he immediately recognised it. Ah, there was the name! Norgate Road. Now he only had to go down it as far as the gate-posts without a gate. Not this 'un. Not this 'un. Not—yus, this 'un. Nummer Fifteen. Nummer Fifteen, Norgate Road . . .

As he peered through the gate-posts at the side-path along which he and Bushy Brows had gone round to the back, it seemed that it had happened years ago instead of only a few minutes! But there was the pail on its side, just as Bushy Brows had kicked it . . . And down in the cellar was the corpse . . . Or was it?

Suddenly assailed by the itch of doubt, Ben paused in the act of leaving. Suppose—it *wasn't* there? It wouldn't be the first corpse to walk off while his back was turned, and in that case there would be no object in reporting it! He hesitated between fear and curiosity, and the curiosity won, drawing him against his will along the side-path, past the overturned pail, round the corner of the building to the back yard, and in through the back door—still wide as he had left it. Or had he left it as wide as this? He couldn't remember.

Inside the doorway he stopped for a moment to listen. Reassured by the silence, he crossed the dim space to the top of the basement stairs and descended to the cellar. Narsty sahnd yer boots mike on stone—there don't seem no way ter stop it.

Something darted towards him as he reached the bottom. He struck out wildly, and just missed a large cat. Swearing at it as it vanished, he advanced a step farther and turned his head towards the shadowed spot where the body had been, uncertain whether he wanted it still to be there or not. He could not see it, but this was not conclusive, because he found he had closed his eyes to shut out the unpleasant sight.

He opened his eyes . . . Ah! Yus—there it was! Lyin' near the wall, with its feet sort of crumpled like, and with its arms . . . with its arms . . . His heart missed a beat. Several beats. Both arms had been outstretched before. Now only one was! . . . And the chair had been righted . . . And where was the rope?

'I'm goin' ter tell yer somethink,' Ben informed himself. 'You ain't stoppin'!'

The information was correct. Ben was out in the street again almost before he had given himself the news. He had no recollection of the journey from the cellar to the street. Nor, when he found himself back in the telephone booth, did he remember much about that. He must have come back here, because here he was back here. Funny 'ow sometimes wot yer did seemed to of been done by somebody else!

All right! Now, then! Get it over! But, first, a little check up. Nobody visible outside through the glass. Good! Two-pence—out it comes. Good! Address—address— lummy, *what* was the address? Sweat increased on a brow already wet. 'Ad 'e fergot it? His dizzy brain strove to recall the name of the street and the number. 'If I can't, this is the blinkin' finish!' he decided. 'I ain't goin' back, not fer nobody!' Ah—of course! 18, Drewet Road. No, was it? Yus. No! That was the address on the deader's visitin' card! Blarst. Then what—ah—of course! 46, Jewel Street. No, was it? Yus. No! That was the address of Ma Kenton where he was supposed to go and stay till Bushy Brows let him know. Lummy, what was this other? Like some seaside, wasn't it? Brighton—Eastbourne—Ramsgate? Ramsgate—that seemed a bit closer. Ramsgate—Margate. Ah! From Margate it was an easy jump, and all at once he saw the black letters against a misty white oblong—Norgate Road. That was it—Norgate Road. Nummer 15.

Even at the best of times Ben was not 'telephone minded', and this was by no means the best of times, but he must have done all the right things, because after he had parted with his two precious pennies he found himself being invited by an unmistakably official voice to inform the speaker what he wanted.

''Allo,' replied Ben.

'You've said that before,' came the reminder, patiently.

'Tha's right,' agreed Ben.

'Who is it speaking?' asked the official voice, not quite so patiently.

''Allo,' said Ben, and just saved an outburst at the other end by adding, 'Oi! Do yer know Norgate Road?'

'What about it?'

'Yer do? Well, see, there's a dead body on the floor of the cellar at Nummer 15.'

Then he slammed down the receiver.

The next five minutes were devoted to separating himself as widely as could be done in the time, and in the fog, from both the telephone booth and Norgate Road. His next stop was a pillar-box. He liked things to lean against. Indeed, this afternoon he needed them.

Well? Next?

The corpse had, so to speak, been ticked off, and second on his list was the woman in the photograph. Bushy Brows came third—a matter perhaps for longer consideration. But rather to Ben's surprise the woman in the photograph did not seem to require any consideration at all. He *had* to know a little more about her, and as the only place where he had any chance of this was the address of the murdered man—sayin', mind yer, 'e 'ad been murdered and 'adn't committed suissicide—well, there he would have to go. But the finger with which Drewet Road beckoned to Ben was a very sinister one! Was Drewet Road, as a health resort, likely to prove any more salubrious to Ben than Norgate Road?

Perhaps none of us are complete fatalists. We rebel against the idea, even if we cannot disprove it, that we are mere movements in a flow that started before the world was born—that never started at all, in fact, since Time is limitless, with neither beginning nor end. It is humiliating to feel one is merely the ephemeral shape of a wave in a permanent sea.

But Ben was as near to a complete fatalist as you could get. In fact, if he could have explained his own position, he would have said that he spent most of his life in a fruitless attempt to avoid doing what he was compelled to do. In his own lingo, 'Yer tries not ter but yer finds yer 'as ter.' Take, for instance, the last fifteen minutes. He had tried not to go back to Norgate Road, but he had had to. He had tried not to revisit the cellar, but he had had to. Sometimes, of course, Fate gets caught as well as you, and you're out of a house before either of you had bargained for it. That had happened after that very nasty shock in the cellar. But after such moments the flow goes on again, and he had tried not to telephone to the police, but he had had to, and now he was trying not to go to Drewet Road, but he knew he would have to. 'Once yer in it, yer in it!'

But although Ben put it down to Fate, there might be others, with individualistic ideas, who would have argued that Ben had a soft spot inside him that was all his own, and that it was his own self that made him leave the pillar-box, where he could have remained in quite nice comfort, and turn in the direction of SW3.

It was not going to be so easy to get there, for all the workings of destiny. In the first place he had never heard of Drewet Road, although he had heard of SW3. In the second, fog didn't help. In the third, even if he found the right tube or bus—and his knees felt a bit too wobbly for a long walk—could you pay for your fare with a one-pound note? It was while he was pondering over these snags that he was handed an opportunity for solving all three. A taxi loomed out of the mist, and before he knew it he had hailed it. Ben taking a taxi! Lummy, wot did yer know abart that?

The taxi stopped, and he jumped in quickly before the driver could refuse so unpromising a fare.

'Drewet Road,' he called.

As he sank in the seat the driver's face twisted round and peered at him through the glass window that divided them. Sliding the window aside, the driver called back through the aperture, after a squint at his passenger.

'Can you pay for it?'

This was a repetition of the coffee-stall keeper's scepticism that morning. Nobody seemed to think Ben could pay for anything. Quite often they were right.

'If yer can chinge a one-pahnd note,' replied Ben.

'Let's see the note?'

Ben fished it out and held it up.

'Oh,' said the driver. 'Well, which Drewet Road do you want?'

'The one in SW3,' answered Ben.

'What number?'

'Eh?'

'What number Drewet Road?'

Ben hesitated. Taking this taxi was a bit of a risk, and it was a pity the taximan was having such a long look at him, though Ben hoped the corner he was sitting back in was too dark to reveal his features plainly. One of these days the driver might be asked to describe his passenger!

'There yer've got me,' said Ben. 'I know the 'ouse but I dunno the nummer. Stick me dahn at one hend, and I'll find it.'

'Okay. I hope you ain't in a hurry?'

'Tike yer time.'

'I'll have to in this fog. You wouldn't be slipping out on me, would you, at the traffic lights?'

'Yer can 'old the stakes if yer like,' retorted Ben, and thrust out his hand with the note.

The driver looked at the note, smiled, and shook his head.

'That's all right, chum,' he said. 'But we get some funny fares sometimes, and have to be up to their tricks.'

The journey began. Ben closed his eyes, and decided to make his mind a lovely blank. He was so successful, and the blank was so complete, that aided by the soporific comfort of the cab he went to sleep, and did not wake up again until the driver's voice again called to him through the window.

'We're there, chum.'

Ben opened his eyes. Lummy, so they were! The taxi had stopped.

'Sorry to wake you,' grinned the driver. 'You can sleep on, if you like, at five bob an hour.'

34

'No, thanks, I wants a bit o' change aht o' me pahnd,' retorted Ben. ''Ow much do I tip yer?'

'Oh, nine bob'll do.'

'Mike it pence, and add it ter the bill.'

The change amounted to fourteen and threepence, and as Ben poured it into his pocket it all came out on to the pavement. Most of Ben's pockets were mere passages. It was a nuisance, because the friendly driver insisted on getting down from his seat and helping to recapture the coins, which further stamped Ben upon his memory. It was unlikely, however, that even without this addition Ben would have been forgotten.

'All right now?' inquired the driver. 'I'll take you along to your house, if you like?'

'No, I can manidge,' answered Ben, the coins now secure in a pocket that functioned. 'Good 'ealth!'

The driver got back into his seat, gave Ben one more glance to make sure he hadn't been dreaming, and drove off, Ben filling in the time by inserting a fag-end he had found with the coins between his lips and sucking it. That is all you can do when you have used your last match.

Alone again at last, and trying not to feel anxious and depressed—an impossible effort—Ben began to walk slowly along Drewet Road. He found himself at the low-numbered end, which meant that No. 18 was not far off. He came to it, in fact, in less than a minute, and as he turned his head to the front door it opened, and a lady came out.

It was the lady of the photograph.

4

The Lady of the Picture

There was no mistaking her. Ben recognised her at once, not only by her dark hair and smart appearance, but by that indefinable 'something' in her atmosphere which he had discerned even in the photograph. This was all the more surprising since her mood at this moment was entirely different. There was a hardness in her expression, her lips were tight, and some inner excitement seemed to be causing the rapidity with which she slammed the door behind her and ran down the front steps. In her hand was a small suitcase.

As she came to the bottom of the steps she looked quickly up and down the road. Then she caught sight of Ben.

'I wonder if you could get me a taxi?' she exclaimed.

Ben's taxi by now was completely out of sight. For this he was doubly grateful. It wasn't going to help if she popped off the moment he'd opped along.

'I ain't seen one, mum,' he answered.

'No, but could you get me one?'

'Well, mum, that ain't goin' ter be easy in this fog—'

'All right, don't trouble,' she interrupted, with a slight frown. 'I only thought you—I'll get one myself.'

She was about to move when Ben stepped in her way.

'Beggin' yer pardon, mum—' Her frown deepened. 'Could I 'ave a word with yer?'

'I'm sorry, I'm in a hurry!'

'Yus, but—'

With a quick shrug, she began to open her handbag.

'No, mum, it ain't that,' said Ben. 'I ain't arskin' fer nothink.'

'Then what do you want?' she exclaimed. 'And please be quick—you heard me say I was in a hurry!'

'Yus, mum, and I wouldn't stop yer, not if it wasn't himportent. Yer—yer ain't goin' off like, are yer?'

Her dark eyes blazed with indignation.

'You're impudent,' she cried. 'Please don't stand there in my way. Ah—there's a taxi!'

'Oi! Don't tike it!'

In the stress of the moment Ben placed a grubby hand on her sleeve, but as the neatness of the sleeve emphasised the grubbiness of the hand he hastily whipped it off, while the indignation in her eyes changed to utter astonishment. The astonishment was so utter that the taxi which had suddenly grown out of the mist went by, and was now beginning to get lost in the mist again.

'Taxi!' she called.

But she was too late. Now her indignation returned in full force.

'You've made me miss it!' she cried, wrathfully. 'What's the meaning of all this? In a moment I won't be looking for a taxi, but a policeman!'

'I wouldn't do that, mum!' muttered Ben.

'*Wouldn't?*'

'No, mum. And—and p'r'aps it was a good thing yer didn't git that taxi!'

She moved a step closer, and stared at him hard. Then she asked shortly:

'Who are you?'

'Well—if I told yer me nime, that wouldn't git yer nowhere.'

A sudden idea seemed to occur to her. Still regarding him with searching eyes, she demanded:

'Are you a friend—an acquaintance of my husband?'

The change of word was made with scorn, a scorn which Ben had no means as yet of understanding. Indeed, at this moment he was not attending to the change. It was the word 'husband' that had pinned his attention.

''Usband,' he repeated, in a mutter.

'Answer me at once, or go!' she blazed.

'It—it ain't so easy, mum. I ain't wot I think yer think, on'y—well, see, I got some noose fer yer, and I'm afraid it ain't good.'

Now she looked puzzled.

'Have you come from my husband?'

That was a nasty one. Ben replied to the question with another.

'Beggin' yer pardon, mum, but might I arsk—are yer Mrs Wilby?'

'I am.'

'Oh! Then—in a manner o' speakin'—I 'ave come from yer 'usband. Don't fergit—on'y in a manner o' speakin'.'

'Then you'd better come in,' she said, with a little shrug which was an attempt to conceal anxiety. 'You've obviously got something to say that can't be said out here. Only, if I find you've been wasting my time—'

'I ain't goin' ter waiste yer time, mum. Do I look as if I was?'

She shook her head and, turning, led him into the house, and into a small drawing-room. When he had awkwardly accepted her invitation to sit down, he was wondering how to make a start when she made it herself.

'Before you say anything, and I haven't the least idea what it is, *I'm* going to say something. I'm not interested in gossip, and there's nothing whatever to be got out of me. I want to make that quite clear. But if what you've got to tell me is really important—and true—and if your reason for telling me is genuine—' She looked at him with sudden curiosity, as though trying for the first time to read what kind of a man he was. She went on: 'If your motive is good, then I'll listen. Not otherwise. Do you understand all that?'

Ben nodded. He understood, and he felt sorry for both of them. But he still couldn't get started, and while he was fishing for the right words his troubled confusion brought a new expression into her eyes.

'Is it as difficult as all that?' she asked him, almost kindly.

'Yus, mum,' mumbled Ben. 'Yer see—'

'Yes?'

'Well, I ain't sure as 'ow yer'll tike it.'

'There seems to be a lot we're both not sure about.'

'Yus, mum.'

'Would you like to begin by telling me just what your motive *is*?'

Her tone was still kind—very different from her tone at the start of their interview—and he almost wished it hadn't been. Somehow it made his job all the harder.

'This is orl wrong,' he complained. 'You're tryin' ter 'elp me, when I come 'ere ter try and 'elp you!'

'Did you? Is that true?'

'Corse, mum. Wot other reason would I 'ave?'

'I could think of others, but if I thought them about you I see now I'd be wrong. You must forgive me if I'm completely baffled! What do you want to help me about—and why should you want to help me?'

Here was a possible lead in.

'Well, see, mum, it was the photo.'

'Photo?'

'Yus.' Lummy, he was in now!

'What photo?'

''E 'as it on 'im.'

'Who?'

'Your 'usband. Mr George Wilby. That's right, ain't it?'

'Mr Wilby is my husband. And this photo, I suppose you are going to tell me, was of—some woman?'

Her tone was getting cold again.

'Yes, mum, it was of you,' answered Ben. 'That's why I come. That and the address. 'E 'ad it on 'im, and I—well, I dunno zackly why, but seein' the photo—corse, that's 'ow I reckernized yer comin' aht o' the door—and, well, things bein' like they was, I felt a bit sorry fer yer, like, if yer git me, so I thort "I'll come along and tell 'er fust sort o' quiet like," espeshully knowin' orl I does and thinkin' she orter know that, too, lummy, that's goin' ter tike a bit o' time, but mind yer it was a risk, in fack I nearly didn't come, 'cos, see, if the pleece find me 'ere I'm for it, I'll swing, doncher worry, though it's Gawd's truth I never done it, but jest found 'im like 'e was in that hempty 'ouse—'

He paused, breathless, as a car stopped outside. There followed a few moments of deathly silence. Mrs Wilby sat rigid, her eyes staring, her cheeks pale, the knuckles of her tightly clenched hands showing white in her lap. Then came steps, and then the front-door bell.

Neither had to look out of the window to feel convinced it was a police car.

5

Ben Gets a Job

The bell rang again, followed this time by the sound of the knocker. Mrs Wilby got up from her chair, steadied herself at a little table beside it, and then walked out of the room, closing the door behind her.

'This is the finish,' decided Ben. 'Well, when yer on the hend o' the rope, it's quick!'

He heard the front door open. Mug he'd been to take that pound note. What help was it going to be that Bushy Brows had all the others? Bushy Brows had vanished and would never be heard of again, and if Ben mentioned him to the police they'd say he'd made him up. Corse they would! That was what murderers did, wasn't it? Made somebody up! And here were the policemen who wouldn't believe him, here in the hall just the other side of the drawing-room door, He could hear their voices, though not their words. He was glad she had closed the door, but it wouldn't stay closed for long. In a moment it would open, and then . . . Yus, he ought never to of took that note—and he ought never to of took that cab! That fair made him the mug of mugs, because of course the police would get on to the taximan, and was the taximan going to forget he'd received a clean new one-pound note from a bloke like Ben? If he didn't have the note on him he'd know who he passed it on to, and seeing Mr Wilby probably got it from the bank where he worked you could bet it would be easy pie to trace the number . . .

Why didn't the door open, and get it over? Ben's eyes were glued on it, but it remained shut. Was they still torkin'? He listened, but now he could hear nothing. Lummy, that was queer, wasn't it? Where'd they gone?

A minute went by. Then another. Unable to bear it any longer he tiptoed to the door. Not a sound came from the hall, and after a moment of hesitation he turned the handle and softly opened the door an inch. Peering cautiously through the crack he saw that the hall was empty, but faintly-heard voices sounded behind a door on the other side of the hall.

'She's took 'em in there fust,' he decided, 'ter 'ear wot they say, and then they'll come along ter me, and good-bye, Ben!'

A few feet to the left of his projecting nose was the front door, and he nearly succumbed to its temptation, but two reasons dissuaded him from a dash for liberty, and as he closed the drawing-room door again and returned to his seat he could not have told you which of the reasons had been the dominant. One was the police car outside. There would probably still be the driver in it, in which case he'd be caught before he'd begun, and would be self-convicted. He had already had one example that afternoon of the trouble you could get into by running away before you were charged. Of course, there might be nobody in the car (he did not go to the window to look, lest temptation should return, or his own face be seen), but even so they'd probably catch him in the end, with all their clues, and then ask, 'If you were innocent why did you bunk?'

The second reason that had brought him back into the room was, perhaps, less explainable—but there it was, you couldn't get away from it. Mrs Wilby must have known that, by leaving him alone, he would have his chance. So—well, she'd sort of trusted him like not to take it. Unless—another thought suddenly intruded—she had *meant* him to take it? Had she led the police into the room across the hall to give him this opportunity to escape? Well, even so, he couldn't work it. He'd got a lot more to let her know, and he couldn't do that from five miles off.

Four or five minutes must have gone by before he heard sounds in the hall again, and at last the door opened. To his surprise, only Mrs Wilby came in, and she only stayed for an instant. She gave him a quick glance, revealing nothing by her expression, took a handkerchief from the table beside the chair she had been sitting in, and then left him once more to himself.

'Well, I'm blowed!' he thought. 'Wozzat mean?'

Another period of waiting had to be endured. It lasted about as long as the first. Then the door across the hall opened, the fact revealed by the renewed audibility of the voices—one was saying, 'Very well, Mrs Wilby—in half an hour'—footsteps moved towards the front door, and the front door opened and closed.

Ben listened in surprised relief to the sound of the departing police car, and the sound had not died away before Mrs Wilby returned to him. She looked pale, but composed.

'Well—they've gone,' she said.

'Yus. I 'eard,' answered Ben. 'Why didn't yer bring 'em in 'ere?'

'Did you want me to?'

'Gawd, no!'

'Then I expect that's why I didn't. You've got some more to tell me, haven't you?'

He nodded. 'Tha's a fack!'

'I want to hear it—and of course you will want to hear what the police said. I didn't mention you—'

'Go on!'

'Surely you must realise they'd have come in here if I had?'

'Yus, only I thort p'r'aps you'd menshuned me but jest said I'd come and gorn, like?'

'I see. Yes, I could have done that. And if you *had* gone I *might* have mentioned you. I came back in the middle of our interview to find out whether you were still here or not.'

'Oh! Not fer yer 'ankerchiff?'

'That was just my excuse. Tell me, why didn't you go?'

'There was a police car ahtside, wasn't there?'

'Nobody was in it.'

'Oh! Well, I didn't know that.'

'You could have seen from the window.'

'I dessay, but—well, there was hother reasons, too. If I'd done a bunk, yer might of thort, "'E done it arter orl, or 'e wouldn't of bunked." That's wot the pleece'd of thort, any'ow, so it seemed it'd be best ter stay 'ere—you 'avin' trusted me, like.'

In spite of the distress she was controlling, she smiled faintly.

'What's your name?'

'Eh? Ben.'

'Just Ben?'

'Nobody never troubles abart the other part.'

'Then I won't either. Yes, I do trust you, and perhaps I rather need somebody I can trust at this moment. I—I'm grateful that you caught me before I—before I left the house just now.' He noticed that her eyes wandered for an instant to her suitcase, which she had put down on the floor beside the table when they had first entered the drawing-room. 'Before you tell me what you have to say, would you like to hear what the police said?'

'Yus, mum.'

'They said somebody had 'phoned from a public 'phonebox, telling them to go to a house in Norgate Road where they would find a—a dead man. Do you know who that was?'

'It was me, mum.'

'I guessed so.'

'Did *they* guess?'

'How could they, if you didn't tell them?'

'Tha's right. Funny wot silly questions yer arsks sometimes when yer mind's goin' rahnd. But if yer'd brort 'em in, I hexpeck they'd of knowd me voice.'

Again the faint smile appeared, though it was very faint.

'I expect so, but so far they have nothing to go upon— oh, yes, they have,' she corrected herself, 'and perhaps I'd better tell you. They found fingerprints on the receiver at the telephone booth.'

That was nasty.

''Ow do they know I didn't wipe mine orf?' he said.

'Did you?'

'No, but I might of, and then wot they found'd be some'un helse's, wouldn't they?'

46

'Have you ever had your fingerprints taken—or is that a rude question?' she asked.

'I've never been copped fer nothink, if that's wot yer mean, mum,' he answered.

'That's fortunate, because they've also found fingerprints on some of the things on my husband's body.'

Ben nodded gloomily. 'There yer are! And I told 'im not ter touch it—'

'Told who?' she interrupted sharply.

'Eh? Oh! A bloke 'oo come along jest arter I fahnd it in the cellar. See, that's wot I've got ter tell yer abart.' She stared at him. 'Was one o' the things a letter-caise?'

'Yes!'

'With a visitin' card in it, and that photo of you, but no money?'

'Yes, yes, but who is this person you're talking about?' she exclaimed, with a new anxiety in her voice. 'Tell me quickly! I have to go and identify my husband—they're coming back to take me there—and I must know everything before I go! Somebody came to the house after you did? Who was it? And what took *you* there?'

Once more Ben noticed the direction of her glance. This time it was towards a photograph on the mantelpiece, a photograph of a good-looking man with a small dark moustache. But the glance meant little to Ben, and his mind was too occupied with other details to associate the photograph with the suitcase on the floor by the table. There was no reason why he should do so, although there was something in Mrs Wilby's attitude he could not quite understand. You'd have thought she might have shed a few tears like?

'What took me there, mum,' be began, 'was—well, I

47

better go back ter the start, didn't I? If yer've got ter 'ave it, I was runnin' away from a cop arter a chap bumps inter me wot drops a jemmy, see, it wasn't mine but the cop thort it was so I 'oofs it and slips inter this hempty 'ouse ter git away from 'im. And it was there I fahnd—wot I fahnd, and then this other bloke comes along, and we each thinks the other done it. If yer git me.'

'What was he like?'

The question was asked quietly, but Ben was too absorbed in his story to note its tenseness.

'Well, mum, I ain't much good at dessercripshun, but 'e was a big feller with big 'ands and feet, and a crooked nose, and 'e 'ad black 'air and heyebrows like a couple o' birds' nests. I don't suppose you know 'im, do yer?'

'No,' she answered, and as he had missed her anxiety, so now he missed her relief. 'Go on! What took him to the house? Was he running away, too?'

'No, mum.'

'Then he wasn't the man who dropped the jemmy—'

'Lummy, no, I never saw no more of 'im, but I don't know why this hother feller come. Corse we both begun with a pack o' lies, and when 'e tikes the money orf the body, yus, and hoffers me one o' the notes—well, then I gits proper suspishus, and seein' as 'ow 'e was a wrong 'un I thort I'd pertend ter be a wrong 'un, too, ter see wot more I could git aht of 'im—not meanin' more notes, o' corse, but infermashun. Mind yer, it was a risk, but then that's life, ain't it? If yer git me? Yer born ter die. Any'ow, that's wot I done, and when 'e sez 'e knoo 'oo done the crime—'

'What!'

The anxiety that had been quelled by Ben's description

of the man returned. She tried to recover her composure while Ben blinked at her.

'But, of course,' she suggested, 'he might—he could have said that just to put you off!'

'Ter put me orf thinkin' 'e did it 'imself? Yus, I thort o' that,' agreed Ben, 'on'y sometimes yer can sorter smell when yer 'earin' the truth, even when it's liars wot's tellin' it, and I smelt 'e was torkin' the truth that time. 'E knows, that I'd swear ter, but 'e didn't go no further with it, 'e didn't say 'oo it was, but soon 'e gits torkin' abart some gime 'e's got on, and 'ow if I went in with 'im I could do a bit o' good ter meself—and so—well, yer see 'ow it was?'

Mrs Wilby did not answer for a few moments. She was sitting very still, staring rigidly across the room, as though afraid to move.

'Or doncher?'

'I think it will be best to tell me,' she answered at last. 'What did you do then?'

'Well, see, mum, wot I 'ad ter decide,' replied Ben, 'was if ter brike with 'im, or if ter go on pertendin'? I'd never learn no more if I said "Nuffin' doin'," but if I didn't I might, 'speshully as 'e gives me an address ter go to where 'e'd been stayin' and where I was ter stay meself till I 'eard from 'im agine. 'E said 'e 'ad ter go away fer a bit.' Ben dived into a pocket. 'This is the address wot 'e give me. 'E wrote that. And so I sez okay, and then arter 'e went I telerphoned ter the pleece, like I said, and then I come on 'ere ter you.'

He held the paper out to her, and she took it and read its message: 'Mrs Kenton, 46, Jewel Street, SE. This is to introduce Mr Eric Burns, a pal of mine. As you know I have to go away, and I want him to occupy my room till I come back. Ask no questions, etc. Love to Maudie. O.B.'

She read it through two or three times, as though to memorise it, and then handed the paper back.

'I thought your name was Ben,' she said.

'That's right,' answered Ben, 'but 'e got callin' me Heric fer a joke, though I never knoo wot the joke was, and then 'e tacks on Burns ter mike it complete like.'

'And he is O.B.'

'That proberly don't mean no more on 'is birth certifikit than wot Eric Burns does on mine. Well, mum, there we are, so wot do I do?'

'What do you want to do?'

'Well, come ter that, I s'pose wot's best.'

'Best for—'

He filled in her pause.

'Fer you, mum, wouldn't it be?' he said. 'I mean that's wot I come 'ere for, ain't it?'

'I don't understand you.'

'It's a waiste ter try. I was tryin' ter work it aht meself once when somebody said it couldn't be done.'

'I believe they were right. But let us forget ourselves for the moment—what do you think we *ought* to do?'

He noticed that it was 'we' this time, not 'you'. He thought hard, so he would make no mistake.

'I expeck it's like this, mum. If we was ter go by the copybook—you know, "I must be good," "I mustn't tell no lies," "I must wash arter meals," then p'r'aps I orter tike this bit o' paiper ter the pleece, tell 'em me story, and let 'em git on with it, never mind the risk. I'll do that if yer say so—on'y, some'ow, I don't think yer want ter say so.'

'Why wouldn't I?'

'Ah, there yer are! I'm givin' yer feelin's, not reasons.'

After an instant of hesitation she asked: 'But—don't you

think I would want the person who killed my husband to be caught?'

Ben's eyes opened wide. 'Well, nacherly, mum,' he answered. 'But arter wot I've told yer, yer may think—like me—that p'r'aps I got a better charnce o' bringin' it orf than the pleece—things bein' like they are like?'

She nodded, then suddenly glanced at a clock on the mantelpiece and jumped up from her chair.

'Wait a moment!' she exclaimed.

She ran out of the room, and Ben got an impression during her short absence that she was telephoning. He thought he heard a faint voice coming from some other part of the house, and although he could not hear any words the voice had that odd, telephonic quality as though the speaker were talking to a wall. When she returned, something had changed in her mood. She spoke swiftly and urgently.

'We must hurry!' she exclaimed. 'They will soon be back for me. Would you go to that address?'

'Yus,' he answered. 'Okay.'

'There may be some risk—'

'Well, it's gotter be one kind of a risk or another, ain't it?'

'Perhaps—I don't know. But—if you learn anything— well, what would you do?'

'Come ter you with it.'

'You'd do that? Whatever it was?'

'I carn't see why not, mum? See, if we git on ter 'im defernit like, you could pass it on ter the cops as well as me, couldn't yer?'

She regarded him uncertainly, then said: 'Yes—I could. And now you must go quickly—Ben. But there's one more thing. How are you off for money?'

Ben blinked rather sheepishly.

'Well, mum, strickly speakin', I got fourteen shillin's and threepence, and that's more yourn than mine. See, it's the chinge I got orf the taximan arter givin' 'im your 'usbin's pahnd note fer the fare.'

'You must keep that for expenses. But is that all you've got?'

'Tha's right.'

'You must have more. Now that—now that I've engaged you, you'll need something to carry on with your job.'

'Oh! Yer engaigin' of me?'

'Yes. You're my private detective.'

He watched her while she opened her bag and took out her purse.

'I see,' he said. 'On'y—I wasn't doin' this fer money, if yer git me?'

'I know that, but you've got to have money if you're going to be of any use to me. It's because you haven't been doing this for money that I trust you. Take this, and if you need any more you must let me know.'

She handed him five pounds in notes.

'Go on!' he exclaimed, incredulously. 'Mike it a couple!'

But she insisted, and he stowed the notes away anxiously in his one sound pocket.

Then, in a sudden panic in which he joined, she packed him out of the back door while a car drew up at the front.

6

The Kentons at Home

In spite of the glittering name of its thoroughfare, the front door of 46, Jewel Street had less appeal to the visitor than the front door of 18, Drewet Road. In fact, it had no appeal at all. It was in the middle of an unbroken row of a dozen front doors which were equally spaced in a long low width of depressing, time-worn bricks. Each door had a small square window beside it and a smaller square window above it. In some of the windows were uncheerful birds and gasping plants. The door of No. 46 had once been red, but had now faded to a pale and indeterminate hue, like the lips of an ill, disillusioned girl who no longer had the energy or interest to use a lipstick.

But, as Ben discovered the moment the door was opened, a very vivid lipstick was used on the other side of the door. Indeed, for an instant he was conscious of little else in the dimness of the narrow passage. Then two bright hard eyes bored inquiringly into his from beneath a glow of blonde hair. It was the lipstick's triumph that the blonde hair had not been first noted.

This, Ben guessed, would be the Maudie he was supposed to take to the pictures!

'Good evenin', miss,' he began, summoning the best smile he could manage. But what were Ben's smiles going to signify to a girl like this?

Maudie responded coldly, without any smile at all: 'Are you sure you've come to the right house?'

'Number 46, ain't it?'

'That's right, but we're not in need of any carpet-sweepers.'

Hardly a beginning likely to end up at the pictures! But Ben refused to be cowed.

'And I ain't sellin' any,' he answered, 'but I know where to find Nylong stockin's fer people I tike a fancy to.'

'Nylons?' repeated the girl, with a slight change of tone.

'*And* they don't 'ave ter pay through the nose fer 'em.'

She peered at him a little more closely.

'I don't see your little case,' she said. 'Do you get 'em out of a hat like rabbits?'

'Oh, I ain't brort 'em,' returned Ben, 'they'll come laiter if yer good. It's yer mother I wanter see this time. Mrs Kenton, ain't it?'

'That's my mother. But who are *you*?'

'Oh, I got a note that'll say that. It's signed O.B., if that means anything to yer?'

'O.B.?' she repeated, and then suddenly her expression changed completely. 'Come in! Why didn't you say so at once?'

She backed and pushed a door open at her side. Behind her was a dark flight of stairs, and she turned and called up as Ben went through the doorway.

'Ma! Someone to see us! Come down!'

Then she turned again, and followed Ben into a living-room which seemed to be under the control of a baleful parrot in a large cage. The cage was in the middle of a red-clothed table, which had room for little else.

'Where is he?' asked Maudie.

''Oo?' replied Ben.

'Oscar—the man who wrote your note? Let me see it!'

'It's fer yer mother.'

'Same thing here! Don't be the limit! Where is he?'

'Yer've got me instead.'

It was only the arrival of Mrs Kenton that prevented an explosion. Maudie Kenton had a temper. So, Ben guessed, had the parrot.

Mrs Kenton was a large untidy woman, as careless of her appearance as her daughter was particular. She looked as though she had just got up, and then not completely, or as if she had come off second-best in an encounter with the parrot. She moved slowly, with an almost swaying motion; but whether this were due to the amount of flabby flesh she carried or to the fear that too rapid movement might cause some of her clothes to come off, was a debatable point. As a household to live with, Ma Kenton, Maudie and the parrot would not have been everybody's choice. They were not even Ben's. But, he reminded himself, he had not come here for personal enjoyment.

'And who is this?' she breathed as she entered.

'This'll tell yer,' replied Ben, and fished out his note.

'It's from Oscar!' exclaimed Maudie.

'Oh! Oscar?'

'Yes, and he won't say where Oscar is. Do read it, and then let me see it! What's happened?'

Ma Kenton took the sheet of paper. Like Mrs Wilby, she

55

read it through twice, while her daughter watched her impatiently; and although it was to her daughter that she spoke when at last she laid the sheet down, Ben felt that her little pig-eyes were watching him closely out of their corners.

'Oscar's had to go away, lovie,' she said. 'He told me he'd have to before he went out.'

'And why didn't you tell *me*?' cried Maudie. 'What's the matter with everybody today?'

Her shrill voice penetrated to the parrot, and as she snatched the note and began to read the bird fluttered its feathers as though sharing her indignation.

'You've only been home a few minutes, dearie,' her mother reminded her. 'I should have told you. But he's coming back, and till he does—'

'Yes, I'm reading it, I'm reading it, can't you see?' snapped Maudie.

For the first time Ma Kenton turned to Ben directly and they exchanged understanding glances, although Ben had not the least idea what he was supposed to understand. When Maudie had finished reading she crunched the paper up and threw it into a corner. The parrot, growing more and more interested in the drama outside its bars, fluttered its feathers again, and eyed the scrunched paper balefully to see that it did not come back.

'Mr Blake was going to take her to the pictures tonight,' said Mrs Kenton.

Ben made a note of the name. Blake. Oscar Blake. In his mind he added: 'I *don't* think!'

'Wot abart me tikin' 'er?' he suggested.

Maudie swung round and stared at him open-mouthed. The parrot made an uncomplimentary sound. Then, all at once, Maudie laughed.

'Why not, Eric?' she replied. 'But you wouldn't mind washing your neck for me?'

'If that's orl, it's a date,' grinned Ben, and then addressed the mother. 'Well, mum, 'ow do we go? Can I 'ave this 'ere Oscar's room, or 'as 'e arsked too much of yer?'

'Oscar could never ask too much of us, could he, dearie?' said Mrs Kenton. 'Any friend of Oscar's, I'm sure, is a friend of ours. Er—where did you meet him, Mr Burns?'

'Mr 'Oo?'

'Wasn't that the name? Have I got it wrong?'

'Oh, no, that's me,' exclaimed Ben quickly. 'Burns. See, I thort yer said another one.'

'Where did you meet him? Have you known him long?'

'Wot, Oscar? 'Ave I knowd 'im long? Yer might prackertally say we was born tergether!'

'He has never mentioned you to us—'

'Ah, there's plenty Oscar and me don't menshun—but that don't surprise yer, does it, Ma?' He winked at her. ''Aven't yer fergot somethink? Wot was wrote at the hend of 'is letter? No questions arst?'

He winked at her again. Did the parrot wink at Maudie? Ma Kenton winked back.

'Oh, yes, of course! That's so like Oscar! Isn't it, dearie? A man of mystery! But then—well—you're rather that way yourself, aren't you, Mr Burns?'

'Yer've sed it,' agreed Ben darkly.

'But—' She paused, and glanced at Maudie, who was playing with her over-ripe lower lip as though it were a guitar-string. 'Wasn't there any message? I mean, besides what he wrote? Wasn't there—surely—wasn't there anything else at all to tell us?'

Maudie came back into the conversation like a boomerang.

'You bet there was!' she cried. 'And he'll tell it to *you*, Ma, the moment my back's turned or I'm out of hearing! And that's nice for me, isn't it, after all I've done for him! Could he have got on *without* me! Oh, but of course, I've done nothing—nothing at all. What an idea, I must have dreamt it!'

Ben discovered himself growing more and more interested in Maudie. Clearly, he must keep on her right side.

'You got it orl wrong,' he said soothingly. 'I ain't got nothink ter tell yer Ma that I ain't tellin' *you*.' Mrs Kenton looked disappointed. 'Yus, and yer can tike it from me *I* ain't fergittin' wot yer done fer 'im—'

He paused at her sudden searching expression.

'Do you mean, you *know*?' she asked.

He tried to work out the right answer quickly. If he said he knew he wouldn't be able to ask what it was, but if he said he didn't that would imply that his alleged friend-from-birth, Oscar, had not possessed the confidence in him to trust him with the knowledge. Wisely he adopted a middle, non-committing course, and responded:

'We'll 'ave plenty ter tork abart, I reckon, afore we're finished, missie, but the fust thing I want if I'm goin' ter tike yer ter the pickchers is that wash! Do I do it in the kitching, or would yer like ter tike me ter me room?'

Maudie accepted the situation. 'Come on, I'll take you up,' she said sharply. 'And what about our meal, Ma? P'r'aps you'd start it while I show Mr Burns our castle!'

Mrs Kenton accepted the situation with less enthusiasm.

'So I'm to do the meal! A lot of help one gets these days from one's daughters!'

'Well, I'm showing him up, aren't I?' retorted Maudie. 'I can't cook on the stairs!'

She jerked her golden locks at Ben and ran from the room, while Ma Kenton frowned. Feeling it necessary to keep in with both, Ben asked:

''Ave I your permish?'

'Who am I?' she demanded. 'All I did was to bring her into the world!'

'Doncher worry, Ma! I can see you and me'll be 'avin' a 'eart-ter-'eart one o' these days!' answered Ben, and escaped.

As Ben followed his blonde guide up the dark staircase at the back of the passage he realised that though he might need a wash it was less for looks than for the refreshment of it. Arter orl, when you was tired like he was, there was something in soap and water, and he wondered whether he'd feel fresher like if he patronised them more often? He certainly was tired now, not only in body but in mind, for his mind was simple and here he was trying to play a subtle game. These two women, he could see, were going to play old Harry with what was politely called his brain if he was going to get what he wanted out of them! What he wanted most at this moment was half an hour on a bed looking up at a ceiling. He liked ceilings. They were nice and quiet. Nothing happened on 'em. And sometimes you found sort of maps . . .

'This door's yours.'

Maudie's voice brought him down from the ceiling.

'Oh, this 'un?'

She shoved it open, entered a small bedroom before him, and then turned for his comment.

'It's nice,' he lied.

'I'm glad you think so,' replied Maudie. 'I call it the Black Hole of Calcutta.'

'I never bin there.'

'Or to school, p'r'aps?'

'Oh, yus, I bin ter school—whenever they was watchin'!—but yer don't learn so much from the corner.'

She gave a short laugh, and then frowned at herself, as though it were against her policy to be amused.

'Would you like to tell me something?' she asked.

'If I git somethink back fer it,' he replied.

'What?'

'Well, I ain't flirtin'.'

'You'd get something else if you were! Are you a fool, or aren't you?'

'You ain't!'

'Thanks, but sometimes I wonder. If I weren't a fool, would I still be living here, do you suppose?'

Ben nodded, and decided to take the question seriously to see whether it led anywhere. No let-up for him just yet. Maudie, with her arms akimbo in the middle of the room, and that watchful, purposeful look in her eyes, seemed too full of conversational possibilities.

'Wotcher doin' it for?' he asked. 'A good-looker like you?'

'Yes, you'd say I had looks, wouldn't you?'

'Venus ain't in it. 'Ow's that fer schoolin'?'

'We can leave Venus out of it, but I'll say I'm as good as some of them film stars—'

'Corse yer are, missie. And I'll bet my pal Oscar's told yer that!'

The mention of Oscar changed her expression.

'Yes! Let's talk about Oscar!'

'I wanter tork abart a lot o' things!'

'*Do* you? Well, one at a time's my motto. What's all this about? Tell me! I don't like mysteries, except in books!'

'Wotcher want me ter tell yer?' inquired Ben innocently. 'Yer don't mean as I know more abart 'im than *you* do?'

She considered the question, studying him as she did so. 'She don't know everythink,' Ben decided; 'but she don't like ter admit it.' Her answer, when it came, was a good one.

'How can I tell you that until you tell me what you *do* know?'

'Ah! There's somethink in that!'

'There's a lot in that.' She pressed her advantage. 'So suppose you talk first? Where is he?'

'Ah!'

'And why's he gone off suddenly like this—'

'Ah!'

'Without a word to me? And if you say "Ah" again I'll take that jug and pour it over you! You say you know what I've done for him, p'r'aps you do and p'r'aps you don't, but I wonder! I mean, all of it, including even three days ago, at that night club, where I was photographed in—'

She stopped short.

'In what?' asked Ben.

'If you can't finish it, tell me why I should?' she retorted.

From below came her mother's voice, floating complainingly up the stairs.

'Maudie! Where did you put the marge? Have we run out? I can't find any—do come down and help!'

Maudie swore under her breath. 'I suppose I'll have to,' she muttered in exasperation. 'There'll be no rest till I do! There never is when mother's around!'

'Would we 'ave ter tike 'er ter the pickchers?' inquired Ben.

'Pictures! You didn't mean that about the pictures?'

'Well, I've give yer the hinvite.'

'It's an idea.'

'And I'm washin' me neck fer yer, though I carn't see the sense when yer sittin' in the dark.'

'Maudie! Do come!'

Once more the complaining voice floated up, now closer, suggesting that in another minute Mrs Kenton would be floating up herself.

'Coming! Give us a moment!' Maudie shouted back. 'Goodness, you'd think the house was on fire!'

She turned to Ben.

'Okay, Eric—it's a date!'

She turned and departed, running heavily down the stairs. How blessedly quiet the room now seemed!

Ben walked to a cracked mirror on the wall and gazed at his neck.

'I can't see nothink wrong with it,' he said.

So he went to the bed, lay down on it, and stared peacefully at the ceiling.

7

Conversation on a Doorstep

Lying on the narrow little bed previously occupied by Oscar Blake—its dimensions were just sufficient for the smaller frame of its new occupant, but how Blake had managed to occupy it was something of a puzzle—Ben worked out a little sum. The sum that engaged him, however, was not corporal but temporal.

It took fifteen minutes, he calculated, to prepare a meal. It took two minutes to wash a neck. That meant that he had thirteen minutes to lie on the bed and think of nothing but the ceiling. Wonderful! He had not enjoyed such luxury since his snooze in the taxicab.

But unfortunately even the simplest sums do not always work out to rule, and the simple rule Ben had hoped to follow was ruined by both minor and major interferences. The minor interference was that the ceiling at 46, Jewel Street refused to oblige. It bore countless cracks and smudges and outlines and graduations of hue, but none of them would form into maps. This seemed unreasonable, because a map can be any shape, but there it was. Or, more correctly speaking, there it was not. No map would come, and instead he saw Questions. They streaked in shadowy writing from every dingy corner, and while some of them were trivial, like 'Do parrots think?' or 'Could you mend holes in pockets with paper fasteners?' others were disturbing like 'Who was Mrs Wilby telephoning to?' or 'Did I leave my fingerprints on that photograph?' These were the questions he wanted to be free of for thirteen minutes, but they wouldn't let him alone.

He was just wondering whether to try his device of escaping into a cave of cheese—you imagined the cave, and you imagined yourself going in, and if you imagined hard enough you could imagine the smell and the taste till all else was blotted out—when the major interference occurred. It was a loud rap on the front door, and it brought him bolt up into a sitting position.

Of course, it might be anybody. Doubtless the Kentons had their ordinary circle of visitors. But there was something in that knock that spoke of trouble, and Ben listened with tense anxiety to the sounds that followed it—low murmurs, footsteps coming out of the front parlour into the hall, and then, after a little pause, the front door opening. And then, voices:

'Good evening, miss.' A man's voice.

'Good evening.' Maudie's.

'I think you have a lodger here—'

Ben's heart gave a jump.

'Of the name of Terry Jones?'

'Terry Jones? Oh, no!'

'That's not your lodger's name?'

'No, sergeant, that's not his name, we've never had a lodger of that name.'

'But you have a lodger, I see.'

She had fallen into the little trap. Ben knew that one.

'What?'

'Perhaps the name might be Oscar Blake?'

'Oh, you mean another one—'

'That's as may be. Have you a lodger here of the name of Oscar Blake? I'm sorry to have to trouble you, but—'

'I'm sure you are, you look heart-broken, but you've come at a most inconvenient moment, we're just going to sit down to a meal. Doesn't it matter if it gets cold?'

Ben knew that one, too. Maudie, over her first panic, was fighting back, and trying to make time so she could think. Ben pictured the scene below. It was not difficult. Maudie striving behind her agitation to look composed, feigning indignation when she found this was not an occasion that could be helped by vamping (for although policemen are human you can never vamp them on duty), and seeking for the right answers to bring to her overpainted lips. Unseen behind her, with nose plastered to door-crack, Mrs Kenton straining to gather what was happening in the hall. And, still on the doorstep, the police, probably a couple, determined to get the information they had come for.

The voice continued:

'We've called on a serious matter, miss, but there'll be no need for your meal to get cold if you'll answer my question. It's not you we're here to see. It's Oscar Blake.'

'Well, he's not here for you to see.'

'You mean, he's not in?'

'No, he's not.'

'But you know him, I take it? He's staying here?'

She was caught again. She could not deny her knowledge of him now. Ben slipped from his bed, crept softly across the floor, and opening the door a crack emulated the behaviour of Mrs Kenton below.

'No!'

'He's not staying here?'

'Haven't I just said so? So now can I get back to my meal?'

'But he has been staying here.'

'You seem to know!'

'As a matter of fact, we do know. When did he leave?'

'A week ago.'

'A week ago?'

'Do I have to say everything twice?'

'I think I'd better remind you, miss, of what I said just now, and I'm not going to say this more than twice. We're here on a serious matter, and if you don't want to get involved yourself you'll give us truthful answers. I don't want to get you into trouble unnecessarily, so I'll forget, if you like, your answer to my last question, and so will my constable. The question was, when did Oscar Blake leave this house? Let's try it again. We're going to remember your answer this time.'

A short silence. Then:

'Do I get into trouble for trying to help—I mean, for not giving personal information about our lodgers to anyone who asks? All right, all right, don't fly off the handle . . .'

It was Maudie who was flying off the handle, which is not a habit of policemen.

'I know you're the police, but have you the right to come and ask questions, I mean, where's your authority, and do I get clapped into prison if I don't care very much about answering questions about other people?'

'You're not forced to answer any questions here, but you will be if, through our failure to get the answers now, you are asked them again at a police station. But I'll help you with this one, if you like. The man I'm inquiring about was here last night—'

'How do you know?'

'We have our methods. So, if it is true that he has left—'

'It is true! He's not here, I tell you. You can search the house, if you like!'

Ben's heart gave another leap. Idgit! Wot did she wanter go and say a thing like that for? P'r'aps it jest slipped aht, and she's cussin' 'erself hinside, sime as I am!

'I'm not saying I won't take your word for it—'

('Ooray!)

'But it's up to you to give me cause to believe you. When did he leave?'

'Today.'

'What time?'

'What time? How am I expected—oh, all right, it was after lunch, but I can't tell you the exact minute like they do on the BBC!'

'Did you see him go?'

'If it's of any interest, I did!'

'And was that the last time you saw him?'

'Of course!'

'You might have seen him later somewhere else?'

'Where would that be?'

'That's what I'd be asking you.'

'Then you'd be wasting your breath. Do you think I've got no work to do?'

'No, you work at Woolworth's, but you saw him leave

this house after lunch, you tell me, so I suppose you came back here for lunch. Why did he leave?'

'You seem to know everything!'

'Has he got a room somewhere else?'

'I wouldn't know.'

'I should have thought you would, miss. Where are you forwarding his letters?'

'If you mean what's his present address I can't tell you.'

'Rather odd he didn't leave it, isn't it?'

'There are plenty of odd people in the world—as *you* ought to know!'

'I know all right. You saw him leave, you say. How did he leave?'

'I don't get that.'

'Car? Taxi?'

'Oh! No, he walked.'

'I see. How did he manage about his trunk?'

'Trunk?'

'Did that go separately, or would he be coming back for it?'

'He didn't have a trunk.'

'Oh, only small luggage, eh?'

'That's right.'

'Which I suppose he carried in his hands?'

'It would hardly be on his head.'

'What luggage did he have? Bag? Suitcase? Could you describe it?'

'Really, I must say! What can that matter?'

'I am not asking anything that does not matter. If you don't know, say so.'

'No, I don't know!'

'Then you can't tell me if he took away with him a

dark-brown suitcase with the initials A.C.—or possibly A.O.—upon it. The letter C can quite easily be changed to look like an O.'

There was a pause after this.

'I think I see I am right, miss,' said the policeman.

'Are you suggesting—?' began Maudie.

'Whatever I may be suggesting, it is no news to you, is it, that this is no social call?'

'No, anyone can see that! And I'm not going to stand here any longer with the fog coming in answering a lot of questions, as if one of our lodgers was a common thief! I'm fed up with it!'

'I have called on a matter much more serious than theft, and there would have been no need to stand here if you had asked me in. I am afraid I must now ask myself in. I should like a word or two with your mother, Mrs Kenton, and if I do require to search the house I have a warrant. Stand by at the front, Smith, and send Williams round to the back.'

Then Ben heard the front door close, followed by a firm, heavy tread towards the parlour.

8

Vanishing Act

History was repeating itself, although in an environment very different from the previous occasion in Drewet Road, and once more Ben found himself considering the idea of escape from police temporarily diverted to another room. To be discovered here in Jewel Street would probably be more disastrous than discovery in Drewet Road would have proved, for the situation he would now have to explain would be far more complicated. It was so complicated, indeed, that Ben had yet to work it out for himself. All he felt certain of at the moment was that should the police search the house and find him in Blake's stead, he would be hauled off to the police station, and his chance of helping Mrs Wilby would be gone for ever.

Why this desire to help Mrs Wilby persisted he could not say. He had never seen her before that afternoon, and she had never seen him, and they were as widely separated as the poles, yet a queer sort of sympathy seemed to have been established between them, and—well, there it was. We are moved in life by many things beyond our comprehension, and in Ben's limited comprehension their number was legion.

But escape this time seemed even more impossible than last, for while an already suspicious sergeant was in the house, presumably with his ear well cocked, constables were stationed at both back and front, and there was no conceivable way in a house joined on to its neighbours of slipping out sideways.

This thought, flitting dismally through Ben's brain as he still stood uncertainly by the bedroom door, produced another slightly more cheerful. If there were no side path from the front to the back of a house, as there could not be to a house in the middle of a solid terrace, the constable deputed for duty in the rear would have to go to one or other end of the row to get round, and that would mean a bit of a walk—well, wouldn't it, with no easy matter to find out which back fitted which front when you got there? It was unlikely that the constable could have got there yet, and saying there was a water-pipe . . .

Ben slithered to the little back window, took a swift peep, and then swiftly withdrew. The water-pipe he wanted was not there, but the constable he did not want was! ''Ow the blazes?' wondered Ben. ''As 'e jumped over the chimbley?' Then the solution dawned, humiliating him by its simplicity. If you wished to pass from the front to the back of a house, why go out to do it when there was a way through the inside?

Well, flight being barred, there was nothing to do but to wait and hope, and he waited and hoped for some three minutes, till sounds began again below and the interview with Mrs Kenton was presumably over. He listened anxiously for the direction of the footsteps, praying they would fade away towards the front door, but his prayer was not heard. Instead of fading away, the footsteps grew more distinct, and a complaining mutter from Mrs Kenton confirmed his fears. 'He's gone, we tell you, but if you insist on going up to see for yourself, I don't suppose I can stop you!'

'If he's gone, there's nothing for you to worry about,' came the sergeant's voice, 'but there's something I've not mentioned that makes me wonder.'

'What's that?' It was Maudie's sharp question.

'I noticed in there you'd laid for three,' replied the sergeant, already on the stairs.

Ben should have learned by now the value, in extremity, of standing your ground, but in spite of the vast number of extremities he had been in he had never got used to them, and as the sergeant's steps mounted higher and higher he suddenly dived into a cupboard. In the blackness, with his face pressed against a dust-choked coat, he heard the bedroom door pushed open. Then followed a few moments of silence, saving for the sound of somebody else's footsteps accompanied by a faint rustle.

The sergeant's voice sounded again.

'Doesn't seem to be here.'

Maudie answered, 'What did we tell you?'

Even in his panic Ben was able to admire the way she concealed her surprise, for she must certainly have expected him to be here!

'I suppose that third place was laid for the parrot?'

'If you must know, it was laid by mistake.'

'Oh! You forgot he'd gone? Force of habit?'

'You'd have heard that, too, if you'd waited.'

'Mind if I look in the other bedroom?'

'A lot of good if I say no!'

'But I think I'll have a look in that cupboard first.'

To this Maudie had no immediate reply, and it did not come until the sergeant was crossing the room. Then she called, her voice now less confident:

'And don't forget the chimney afterwards!'

Ben's heart thumped. Now he was dished proper! Pressing harder against the coat he found himself toppling through to the space at the side, now coming up against what appeared to be a skirt. He kept going—for why stop any movement that carried him farther from the door?—and passed beyond a succession of other suspended and unidentified garments. It was an amazing journey, on account of both its speed and its unexpectedness, and the end of it was even more amazing than the beginning. A breeze played against his nose. It came through a long vertical crack. Pushing with his nose in obedience to its desire for air, he opened a door at the end of the cupboard and swayed out into another bedroom. It was a larger bedroom than the one he had left, and it had two beds. He stood in dizzy wonderment.

This stroke of extraordinary luck would not have served him, however, but for another stroke which delayed his pursuer. On the point of looking into the cupboard, when Ben was merely at the commencement of his journey, the sergeant thought of the window, and decided to have a peep out there first. Changing his direction, he went to the window, saw the man on duty there, opened the window, exchanged a few words, and returned to the cupboard. By this time Ben had reached the adjoining room.

One further point militated in Ben's favour. The sergeant was not enamoured of the unsatisfactory couple he had been interviewing and was very ready to conclude what appeared to be a fruitless call. He had ascended the stairs convinced that the wanted man was not on the premises, and he was not motivated by any hope of catching him here. His present actions were just a routine performance, enlivened by a certain satisfaction in giving annoyance to the unhelpful occupiers of No. 46, Jewel Street, and when at last he did open the cupboard door and look in, he did not consider it necessary to do more than grope to the wall behind the hanging coat and to the skirt at its side.

When he closed the cupboard door, satisfied, Maudie received her second surprise. She had believed the cupboard would reveal its secret.

'So what?' she jeered, concealing her astonishment.

'We'll just have a look in that other bedroom,' answered the sergeant.

But they found nothing in the other bedroom. Ben heard them coming, and returned via the cupboard to the point he had started from, and he remained plastered to the coat while the sergeant thumped down the stairs again. Then, feeling very wobbly in the stomach, he came out and waited till the front door reawakened into welcome life and he heard the sound he wanted most of all—the glorious little *plop* of its closing.

'Why ain't I bein' sick?' he wondered.

To be on the safe side, he went to the basin and waited. He seemed to have spent most of the day waiting for this, that, or the other. When nothing happened it occurred to him that a basin had other uses, and that life having returned momentarily to semi-normal he might get on with it and wash his neck. He did so, and to his astonishment enjoyed it. He must do it more often. Then he lowered his head into the basin, and found that pleasant, too. 'Nice,' he thought, still immersed. He came up to breathe, and went down again. How peaceful existence had become, all of a sudden! A few moments ago it had been horrible. A few moments hence it might again be horrible. Life went up and down like a temperature chart. But at this moment it was cool and lovely. You could imagine the bottom of the basin was the bottom of a pool in fairyland. A sudden memory came to him as he rose to breathe and descended once more. Funny 'ow them memeries kep' croppin' up out of nowhere. Most were narsty, but some were nice, and this 'un was nice. When he was little, he used to lower his head in water and see how far he could get with *Annie Laurie*. 'Wunner 'ow fur I could git now?' he thought, and decided to have a try. But he found he couldn't get anywhere, and he came up spluttering.

This little failure brought to an end his brief and somewhat unique respite. He could not remain in the room for ever, and difficulties would recommence the moment he went outside. If he did not descend to them, they would ascend to him. Heigho!

He went down quietly.

No need to proclaim yourself before you were there! And perhaps a spot more listening—he had done plenty lately—might come in handy?

The parlour door was ajar, and while still standing on the bottom stair he could hear Ma and Maudie talking, though their voices were subdued. They were evidently in a mood for quietness, too.

'I don't understand it!' Ma was saying.

'You've only said that five times,' came Maudie's answer.

She was not made up of sweetness, though she could smile like sugar when she wanted to.

'Well, I don't! How could he have not been there?'

'Don't ask me! All I can say is that he wasn't, and that it was a damn good thing! What did you let that policeman go up for?'

'Don't talk nonsense, and don't snap. If you couldn't stop him, how was I to? As soon as he's finished asking me questions, up he goes—'

'Yes, it was a pity he didn't begin with you!'

'Well, dearie, who kept him at the door?'

'You know why I did it! I thought I could make him leave without coming in at all! The way he tackled you, when he did, about why Oscar went, and why you didn't find out, and if it was sudden or if you'd known he was going yesterday! He must have thought you every sort of a fool—or lying!'

'He caught *you* lying at the door—'

'I know he did, I know he did! Lies to the police are one thing, but there's no need for 'em between you and me! Is it the truth you don't know why Oscar left?

'Maudie?'

'Yes?'

'I only lost my temper with your father once—'

'What of it?'

'I never had to lose it again. I don't know why Oscar left. He didn't tell me. I don't know any more than you do. I don't know where he's gone, or what he's done, or what the police want him for. Perhaps it's just as well. But I know *this*! It's a good thing he's gone, and you've done as much for him as is good for you, and you can be thankful the police aren't after *you*! Yes, and it's a good thing that other one's gone, too, though if I were you I'd run up again yourself to make sure, and then we can heat up our meal again and eat it!'

'What's the good of going up?' retorted Maudie. 'There's only the two rooms, and he's not in either of them. Don't mind about my legs! I haven't been on them behind a counter all day, have I?'

Then something happened which caused Maudie to change her tone, though Ben had no idea what it was.

'Oh, all right, all right, I'll go!' she muttered.

Ben twisted round, leapt up half a dozen stairs, and then descended them heavily. He had just got to the bottom again when Maudie's head appeared from the parlour, and she stared at him in stupefaction.

9

Ben v. Maudie

'Wozzer matter, miss? Yer ain't seein' no ghost,' said Ben, responding innocently to Maudie's astonished gaze.

'Then—you *haven't* gone!' she gasped.

'Gorn? It don't look like it! But I 'ope that copper 'as?'

'Where have you been?'

'Eh? Hupstairs. I've jest come dahn.'

She shook her head incredulously. 'You—you couldn't have been upstairs, it's impossible.'

'The himpossible ain't nothink ter me.'

'You weren't there when the sergeant and I went up. He looked in both rooms! I know he did because I was with him—'

'Yus, but 'e didn't look in 'em both at the same time. When 'e looked in one I was in t'other, and then when 'e looked in t'other I was in the one. But I don't git yer? Yer must know 'ow I done it?' This time Ben spoke genuinely. People know their own cupboards, and he didn't see why Maudie hadn't guessed. 'Are yer pertendin' or somethink?'

Before she could respond, Mrs Kenton's head appeared in the doorway behind her daughter's. She had got over her first moment of shock on hearing Ben's voice, and she was frowning.

'Don't stay out there talking!' she ordered shortly. 'Come in, and keep your voices down—for all we know there may be policemen around yet!'

Back in the parlour, where a cooling meal for three still waited to be eaten, Ben informed them how he had performed his vanishing act, and after the two women had exchanged perplexed glances Maudie turned suddenly towards the door.

'Yes, and have a look out of the windows at the same time,' said Mrs Kenton.

When she had departed and was heard racing up the stairs—this was the third time she had been up them since Ben's arrival, and for a young woman who complained that she had been on her feet all day behind a counter she was still amply active—Ben turned to Mrs Kenton and asked:

'Yer don't mean yer didn't know them cupboards 'adn't no wall atween 'em?

'There is a wall between them,' replied Mrs Kenton. 'Or there was!'

Then they fell silent, each busy with thought, till Maudie's racing steps were heard again and she returned breathless.

'It's gone—the partition!' she exclaimed. And then realising the loudness of her voice, she lowered it almost to a whisper, and repeated: 'It's gone!'

Mrs Kenton received the news grimly, and addressed Ben in a tone of accusation.

'That would be your friend Mr Blake's doing,' she said. 'It was only a thin partition. He must have got it down one day while Maudie was at work and I was out—and it must have been quite recently. Yes, yesterday, I shouldn't wonder, when I was out in the afternoon to tea with my sister.'

'What sauce!' muttered Maudie. 'I expect he did it in case he had to play the trick *you* did—Eric! You knew, of course? He told you, didn't he?'

Ben shook his head. 'As far as I was concerned,' he admitted, 'it was jest a bit o' luck, but it orl goes ter show, don't it, as 'e hexpected the pleece might come 'ere lookin' fer 'im?'

'Do you think we needed any proof of that?' snapped Mrs Kenton. 'Did you remember the windows, Maudie?'

'Yes. I took a squint out of both . . .'

'Well?'

'There's somebody back and front. I couldn't see them very clearly, the fog's getting thicker, but they're there all right, so *isn't* that nice for us!'

Ma Kenton threw up her hands. 'I've had about enough of this!' she cried. 'Why did you ever bring that man here? I didn't bargain for more than just . . .' She broke off, at a sharp look from her daughter. 'What's he done this time?' she demanded fretfully. 'Killed someone?'

Ben hesitated for an instant, realising that he ought to have come downstairs armed with a policy and that he had wasted valuable time up in the bedroom trying to gargle tunes in a basin of water. Cautiously he answered:

'S'pose 'e 'as?'

Both women sat very still. The temperature of the room seemed suddenly to have dropped several degrees.

'I didn't say 'e 'ad,' went on Ben. 'I sed s'posin'?'

A heavy little silence was broken by Mrs Kenton. She spoke with decision and determination.

'I don't want to hear anything,' she said. 'Not anything at all. He's gone, and the sooner you follow him the better pleased I'll be. We'll have our supper now before it's quite stony!'

'Well, I'm ready fer a bite, wotever the temperchure,' said Ben, as they took their seats round the table. The parrot had been relegated to a space on the sideboard. 'But I ain't doin' no follerin' while there's coppers waitin' ahtside.'

With her fork suspended, Mrs Kenton asked: 'Does that mean *you're* wanted for something, too?'

'Never mind wot it means,' replied Ben, 'not till I've got somethink inside me.'

It was an uncomfortable meal from every angle. If the food was cold the atmosphere was colder, and not a single word was spoken until the unsocial business was over. Ben always disliked silent meals when he was eating in company, though meals at which he participated were never completely silent, and it was because of the noise his food made when it went down that he welcomed drowning conversation. It wasn't his fault. His tubes were twisted or somethink.

At last the gloomy meal ended, and Maudie started the ball rolling again with a sarcastic laugh.

'Time to get ready for our film, Eric?' she inquired.

'That's orf,' replied Ben. 'If it was ever hon!'

'Oh, it was on all right, but the weather's turned a bit nasty, hasn't it?'

'Yer don't say!'

'So now what I want to know is—where do we all go from here?'

Mrs Kenton fixed Ben with a compelling eye.

'I don't know where you're going from here—all I know is that you're going!'

'Yer wouldn't like that no more'n I would,' answered Ben darkly.

'Why not?'

'I thort yer didn't want ter 'ear nothink? Do I 'ave ter tell yer?'

And then, all at once, he decided that he would. It might be wise, it might be not, but the situation was getting beyond him, that was a fack, so he'd spit it aht and see wot 'appened.

'Them bobbies was 'ere on a murder job,' he said.

The effect was electrical. Mrs Kenton, who had just begun to rise from her chair, remained suspended. Maudie gasped: 'My God!'

'Yer've sed it,' agreed Ben.

'You—you don't mean—?'

'I mean they wanter arsk 'im questions abart it, but whether 'e done it or not—well, we can leave that fer a bit. But there's one thing we won't leave so's ter git that stright at the start—*I* ain't done no murder, and that wasn't wot I was dodgin' the pleece for—'

'I won't hear any more, I won't hear any more!' interrupted Ma Kenton in a rasping voice, now completing her movement of rising and pushing her chair back. 'It's no concern of ours who did it, no concern at all! Maudie, I'm going into the kitchen and I'll be waiting for you there to bring me the things for washing up, and when we come back I want to find *you* gone. Do you hear? Don't let me

82

have to say it again! As far as we are concerned, you have never been here at all!'

'It ain't as easy as that,' returned Ben. 'I'd wait afore goin' inter the kitchen, if I was you.'

'What do you mean?'

'I *'ave* bin 'ere.'

'No one will know, if no one mentions it.'

'But 'ow do yer know I won't menshun it? That'd git yer inter a bit o' trouble, p'r'aps?'

'Wouldn't it get *you* into more, Eric?' interposed Maudie, her mother momentarily speechless.

'I ain't worryin', lied Ben, 'and even if I was, miss, trouble loves company. Yer ma sez orl this ain't no concern o' yourn, but wot'd the pleece think if they 'eard I was 'ere, bringin' yer a messidge from the bloke they was arter, and nobody sed nothink abart me or the messidge? And lettin' me alone, s'pose they ketches the bloke they're arter, you've worked with 'im, aincher? But p'r'aps yer wouldn't mind orl that comin' aht?'

'Is—is this blackmail?' demanded Mrs Kenton, in a splutter.

'Now, there's a narsty word!' complained Ben. 'I'd call it more like orl stickin' tergether—yus, and with a nice little nest-hegg at the hend of it, p'r'aps, if we orl keep steady.'

'That's right, ma,' said Maudie, suddenly taking control, and speaking sharply. 'We mustn't lose our wool! Let's get rid of these things, and afterwards see what. I'll clear away if you'll make a start in the kitchen.'

Mrs Kenton wavered, then gave a helpless shrug and left the room. Maudie followed, to reappear a few moments later with a tray.

'Ma's proper upset over what you've told us,' she remarked, as she began clearing the table. 'You'll get something if you're playing a game!'

'Wot'd I do that for?' demanded Ben.

'How do I know? Everything's phony from the word go! What about lending a hand instead of just looking ornamental?'

He helped with the tray. Queer girl, this. She'd need a bit of handling unless you got her on the hop. Had he been wise to let out about the murder so soon? Well, it was too late to retract now.

'We'll have the parrot back,' said Maudie, when the table was clear.

'Don't it never say nothink?' inquired Ben, as he lifted the cage across.

'Only once in a blue moon,' replied Maudie; 'but when it does it's good. Wait till I come back—next time it'll be for keeps.'

She went out again with the tray, was absent a little longer this time, and returned as Ben was coming away from the parlour window. The room was in darkness.

'I wouldn't show myself,' she commented.

'Teach me somethink I don't know,' replied Ben. 'I know orl abart winders.'

'Well, I see you had the sense to switch off the light.'

'I got sense, miss, as yer'll find aht.' Mustn't let this girl get on top of him.

'Did you see anything?'

'Yus.'

'What?'

'Fog.'

'And that's supposed to be funny—'

'Well, wotcher hexpeck me ter see through pea-soup? Churchill shavin'?'

'In that case, why waste time looking?'

'Lummy, yer got ter look ter see yer carn't see, ain't yer? Where's yer muvver?'

'Still in the kitchen,' answered Maudie, discovering that she was meeting her match in back chat. 'I've left her to it, and if you ask me, she's happier there than here and we'll get on better without her. Now, then let's straighten things out.' Her greenish eyes hardened. 'Someone's been murdered, you say?'

'Yus,' answered Ben.

'Who?'

'We'll leave that.'

'Oh? Why?'

'P'r'aps I prefers ter arsk the questions!'

'We don't get all we prefer in this world, smartie!'

'That goes fer both of us!'

She took a breath, and started again.

'All right. Someone's been murdered, and we're leaving who it is and who did it. We're getting on like a house on fire, aren't we? Is it anybody I know?'

'"Oo?'

'God! The one who's been murdered!'

'Well, yer might of meant the one 'oo murdered 'im—'

'Him?'

'Eh?'

'I've got the sex, anyhow.'

'Yer thort it might be an 'er?'

'If you want the truth, I did think it might be.'

She looked annoyed with herself the next moment and Ben made a note of it.

'Wich 'er?' he asked.

'Nothing doing, Eric!' she retorted.

'Ain't there? Well, 'ow can I tell yer if yer right afore I knows 'oo yer torkin' abart?'

'You've already told me I'm right by letting me know it's a man, you born idiot! Or aren't you? I think I've asked you that one before!'

'I ain't no idjit, miss,' replied Ben, against his own conviction, 'but I'll give yer that one. I didn't mean ter let on it wasn't a woman, and you didn't mean ter let on yer thort it might be. Well, that's fifty-fifty, ain't it? Wot abart gettin' aht the slate and keepin' the score?'

'I can't make you out.'

'I've 'eard that one afore terday, so don't try. The way I look at it is, once people can mike heachother aht, they're finished. Best go on as we are, miss, and we'll do fine. Nah, then—this bloke wot's bin done in. Yer arsked me if 'e was anybody yer knoo. Orl right. 'Oo do yer know?'

'The list wouldn't take a month of Sundays, would it?'

'It wouldn't, not if yer was ter keep the nummer dahn like ter blokes yer got ter know through my pal Oscar Blake.'

Her eyes narrowed. He saw that he had scored again. He guessed that, whereas she had been thinking of some definite woman before, now she was thinking of some definite man, and with more chance of being right, this time. He would have given a sack of buns, buns full of currants, for a picture of the man in her mind at that moment.

But Maudie, in spite of her own limitations, was shrewd enough to watch her step after its preliminary stumbles, and like Ben was beginning to profit by experience. Before answering she went through a little performance for which Ben in secret took off his hat to her. It was the only way he could ever take off his hat, because in public he never had one. She went quickly to the door, which was ajar, looked out into the tiny passage, exclaimed, 'Ah, *there's* my handkerchief!'—it was in her hand—stooped to the floor, returned into the parlour, and closed the door. Then she moved casually towards the window, looking like a dark ghost, for the light had not been switched on again and now the door was closed no light came from the passage, yawned as she adjusted the torn net curtain against the panes—there were no other curtains—and returned to the chair she had been sitting in. It was an over-elaborate performance, possibly as much to impress her guest as to achieve any other object; but apparently it impressed the parrot even more, for suddenly the bird woke up and screeched, '*Bloody good!*' and then went to sleep again. It may, of course, have been applauding some incident in a dream.

'Now, listen,' said Maudie, after they had both got over the parrot's effort to unnerve them. 'You may be a fool, I still can't say, but *I'm* not, and you're not going to get anything more out of me than you already know—if you really know anything, and I'm still not sure about *that*!— until I know just what the position is. You seem to think you're fixed up here for good and that we couldn't turn you out if we wanted to, but we could, and then you'd lose whatever you've come here for, which is another thing I'm waiting to hear.'

'You 'ave 'eard,' Ben reminded her. ''Ave yer fergot that note I brort from our pal Oscar? I expeck yer know 'im well enough ter know 'is 'andwritin'? I'm 'ere becos 'e's comin' back and 'e wants ter see me. I knows that much, any'ow, and so do you.'

'Do you know why he wants to see you?'

''E's got some big gime on. *You've* played with 'im afore, so that oughtn't ter be no noos!'

'What's the game this time?'

'Ah, I dunno orl of it—tha's wot I'm 'ere ter waite for.'

'How much *do* you know?'

'I wasn't ter say nuffin'. "Arsk no questions," sez that bit o' paiper. But if yer was ter send me orf and the pleece watchin' this 'ouse copped me, they'd put me through it and I'd 'ave ter tell 'em wot I was 'ere for, and then they'd go on watchin' and cop Oscar, and they'd put '*im* through it, and 'e'd 'ave ter tell 'em wot '*e* was 'ere for, and orl 'e knoo abart *you*, and seein' it's a murder caise—well, 'ow do yer s'pose yer'd come aht o' that? In the witness-box, if it wasn't in the dock?'

Maudie jumped up, and then sat down again.

'You're just trying to frighten me!' she muttered.

'I'm jest tellin' yer wot's called the facks,' Ben replied.

'Well, one fact is that *I* haven't murdered anybody!'

'I ain't sayin' yer 'ave—'

'All right, then—'

'There's sich a thing as a hackersessory—'

'Damfool!'

Was he getting her on the hop? He plunged on, speaking sepulchrally:

'Or knowin' abart it withaht ackturelly doin' of it, or even bein' there when it was done, they can git yer fer that if yer was in the know like—'

'But I *don't* know!' she exclaimed.

'Do yer know Norgate Road, miss?'

Her dim figure became rigid, as it had become at his first mention of the murder, but he could not decide whether she knew it or not.

'Or Drewet Road?'

There was no mistake this time. Once more she leapt up from her chair, and it almost went over.

There was a sound in the passage, and the door opened. It was Mrs Kenton.

'What, in the dark? Has he gone?'

She switched on the light.

'What's the matter?' she asked sharply.

'He's not gone, and he's not going,' answered Maudie. 'Where's the brandy?'

10

Concerning Two Others

And so Ben stayed, and spent the night at No. 46, Jewel Street, SE, but before following his further disturbing history let us follow the course of two other characters connected with the strange network of events in which Ben had been caught up after the inconsiderate itching of his thumbs. Both these characters he had already met, though one only for a very brief moment. This was the man into whom he had bumped, and who presumably had dropped the jemmy.

After that incident, a little incident with big consequences, the man, to borrow Ben's phraseology, had bounced up as though made of rubber and vanished into the mist. His course for a while was vague and indeterminate. Like Ben he was running away; but, unlike Ben, only his own fancies were following him, and so he might have been running away from himself. Having no prescribed direction, or coordination to adhere to one had it been prescribed, he followed the natural instinct of the blind and travelled round in wide circles. His need for the time being was just movement. The fact that this was not getting him anywhere did not seem to matter, because he had no notion where he wanted to get. Indeed, in the complete chaos of his condition, such a place did not appear to exist.

Once he did stop. A seat grew into his misty vision, and breathless he sank down upon it. But only for a moment. He found its immovability nauseating. Was he going to be sick? So up he jumped again, and continued his aimless wandering.

The next time he stopped was at the top of a street. He stared, bewildered. He had been walking for twenty years, quite that, and here he was, almost back where he had started from! Was he dreaming?

Dreaming? The idea grew. When men are ill, or drunk, or worried, they hatch grotesque fancies! Even this curling mist was taking strange shapes—writhing snakes, coiling ropes, funeral wreaths. If you could see things that were not there, you might do things that were not done? For example, it seemed as if he were walking down the street, but he could not be, because that would be an act of sheer lunacy! . . .

And then he found he was. And then he found himself outside the house he had hoped to be a dream. Dim behind the wreathing mist, it looked like one! But, perhaps, *inside*! . . . He went inside. He came out again. Presently, after another twenty years, he stopped running.

A dirty old woman in a shabby black dress peered at him. 'You look done up, dearie,' she said. ''Ow about a cup o' tea?'

'No,' he muttered.

It surprised him to find he still had a voice. Even the old woman's voice sounded unnatural. Like something out of a forgotten past.

91

'Oh, I ain't got the price'—she grinned—'but I thought I could do with one, too. What 'ave you been up to?'

She laid a bony hand on his sleeve. He shook her off and fled again.

A cup of tea! It sounded good. He had not imagined that anything could ever seem good again—but that cup of tea did! He thought of it hard. Just a cup of tea. Yes, but you needed money for even that. He hadn't any money. Or—had he? It occurred to him, with a frightening shock, that he did not know. He did not know if he had any money! He might have nothing, or fifty pounds! Come, that was *funny*! Here was his hand going into his pocket, and he did not know what he would find in it. Laugh! Laugh! He tried to, but no sound came.

His groping fingers touched only fluff and crumbs. No cup of tea for him! Then he thought of the obvious. Hadn't he any other pockets? He had a feeling that something had been in one of them, something hard . . . No, it wasn't there. But now his fingers touched other things. Coins. *Coins!* He brought them out, and something else with them. A train ticket.

The coins were sixpence and three coppers. The train ticket was Euston to Penridge. Single. Third class. 58s. 6d.

For a few moments he forgot the tea, thought only of the ticket. Penridge. Where was that? It must be some distance, if it cost 58s. 6d. to get there. Devon? No, that wouldn't be Euston. Wales? The North?

'Penridge,' he muttered, and then repeated to himself, 'Penridge—Penridge—Penridge.' And here was a ticket to it. And at Euston he could find both the train and a cup of tea.

He found his way to Euston. After all, why not? He knew London. So why not? But with the mist in the streets and the greater mist in his mind, it seemed a miracle that he got there. Was something outside himself guiding him? Had he now yielded his initiative into other hands? Surely it must be so . . . Otherwise, could he be going to an unknown place called Penridge?

As he entered the sombreness of Euston station, a man—heavily built, with a crooked nose, high cheek-bones and thick eyebrows—moved towards him, then paused, as though vaguely surprised. Had he expected recognition? He received none. The new arrival faced him fully for a moment, then turned aside towards the buffet without any change of expression. The man with the heavy eyebrows blinked, rubbed his stubby chin, then smiled and followed, keeping his distance.

Unconscious of this, the new arrival entered the buffet, and ordered a cup of tea at the counter. He took it to a small table and sat down to drink it. The man with the thick eyebrows ordered a cup for himself, and carried it towards the same table. There was an unoccupied chair, and he walked up to it.

'This engaged?' he asked.

The other looked up quickly, shook his head, and then looked down again.

'Thanks,' said the man with the thick eyebrows.

But he did not sit down. With an odd smile he suddenly turned away, and walked back to the counter with his cup.

The man he had left so abruptly seemed worried by the incident, and gulping his tea down, left the table and ran out into the station. When he was well away, he turned and looked back at the door from which he had just come. The man with the thick eyebrows did not come out after him, and he breathed a sigh of relief. He did not know that the man had come out through another door, and was watching him from behind a luggage truck.

He moved to a porter.

'When's the next train to Penridge?' he asked.

'Penridge?' replied the porter, as though he had never heard of it.

'Yes. Is there one soon.'

The porter studied his interrogator, and decided after all to be informative.

'In ten minutes,' he said. 'Platform 9.'

For a moment, the man hesitated. The definiteness of the words—in ten minutes—Platform 9—seemed to percolate to his muzzy brain. Then the hesitation passed, and he walked to the barrier of Platform 9.

The inspector clipped his ticket.

'Front part of the train. Change at Applewold.'

He passed through, gripping his ticket tightly as though it were gold. To him it was, for if he lost it he only had three coppers with which to buy another. Three coppers and a railway ticket between him and—what?

He joined the stream of humanity that flowed past the waiting northbound train. It was a thin stream, and it grew thinner as he progressed and as the passengers chose their compartments, but he kept on till he came to the very front coach, next to the engine. There he found an empty carriage, and he entered it with the sense that he had achieved it with his final effort, and that what happened next had nothing to do with him.

He leaned back in a corner seat and closed his eyes. After a period in which he seemed to be neither awake nor asleep a voice caused him to open them.

'Got a match, sir?'

He was surprised to find the platform still outside the window. The train had not yet started, and he could not believe that the porter had told him the platform less than ten minutes ago. The man who had just entered, he looked a sporting type, repeated his request.

'Could you give me a match?'

The reply was a shake of the head, and after feeling in his pockets in the vain hope that he had a box himself, the newcomer grunted, allowed his unlit cigarette to dangle from his lips, and began to read an evening paper. Suddenly he gave an exclamation.

'Hallo! It says here the police are expecting to make an arrest!'

No response.

'The Penzance murder. Well, they've taken their time about it, but these fellers always get caught in the end. I wonder sometimes how they feel? I suppose it depends to some extent on what sort of chaps they are to begin with. Mistake some people make is to imagine they're all the same.' His unlit cigarette dropped from its insecure adhesion to his lips, and he just caught it before it fell to the ground. 'Well fielded, what? Yes—now take that little jockey who killed his trainer—I mean, trainer of his horse *Jersey Pants*—last year at Newmarket—incidentally, I put my shirt on those pants so you might say I had a grudge against that trainer myself, ha, ha!—mild little feller, the jockey, last sort you'd say to become a killer, and compare him with—well, this Penzance bloke? Now, then. Deed's done! Do these two chaps feel identical the moment after? You get me? How'd I feel? How'd you feel? Speaking for myself—hallo, we're off!—funny if twenty or thirty trains dashed away after the whistle and began leaping over bridges!—speaking for myself, I don't think I'd do any dashing away after a murder, I think I'd take a swig of whisky and stay put to get it over—'

For the second time his useless cigarette slipped from its mooring, and this time he wasn't so lucky and the cigarette dropped to the ground.

'Blast! If I don't get this thing lit, it'll die on me!'

He picked the cigarette up and turned to his companion for sympathy, but he got none. The man in the corner had his eyes closed. Nice journey this was going to be! No smoke, and only a sleeping man to talk to. Disgustedly the loquacious one rose, and tiptoed from the compartment. He found a light and a better companion in a compartment three down the corridor. Rather an interesting chap. Big feller, with a broken nose. Been in the boxing game? And with heavy eyebrows . . .

The train increased speed. The man in the front carriage remained in his corner with his eyes still closed. How blessed it was to be alone again! He had tried not to hear the words of the chatterbox who had just left him. He did not want to hear anything but the voice of the train, or to feel anything but the rhythm of its smooth harmonious movement, or to see anything but the blackness of his closed lids. The trouble was that it did not remain just blackness permanently. He wanted the blackness to envelop everything for ever, blotting out the compartment, and the views he was passing through, and the globe and the universe, but periodically it became a mere background for phantom figures and sinister visions. Then, when he could (sometimes his eyelids stuck) he opened his eyes to seek comfort in the temporary security of the intimate little reality around him—luggage-racks, window-straps, coloured pictures of

England's beauty spots to which this train could convey contented people, cushioned seats on which lovers had sat, and would again. He tried to visualise the compartment through the eyes of lovers. Suddenly he did so, startlingly, for one of the lovers was himself. With a groan he closed his eyes again, and wooed the darkness.

Backwards and forwards. Where was escape?

He lost all count of time. The metropolitan fog faded away and natural gloaming took its place, itself to darken into night. Little incidents occurred of which he was only half aware. Had the train stopped just then? That rather loud voice, calling words he had not heard or could not remember—had it sounded from a platform outside or been hatched within his own ears? Had someone got in? Had someone got out? What, anyhow, was the object in knowing? There was nothing for him to do about it? Or about anything, beyond holding on to the comfort of his corner, a comfort needed physically as well as mentally after his long and fatiguing wandering. If only his head would stop throbbing. Was it his head throbbing? Or was it the engine?

But some things happened of which he was completely unaware. He was unaware, for instance, of two occasions when a burly figure appeared from the corridor and stood in the compartment entrance, silently contemplating his relaxed form across the carriage's length. The relaxed form was in a corner farthest from the corridor, head drooped loosely over chest. An ugly mark on the forehead, which had been previously noticed, was now not visible in the recumbent position. 'That head may look like that again one day!' reflected the watcher ironically; and on this, the second of the two occasions, he did not return to his original compartment, but slipped instead into the compartment immediately next, no longer occupied by two chattering women.

The chattering sportsman had alighted an hour earlier at a previous station.

At last sleep came, sleep without dreams—a blessed victory for weariness. The respite could merely be temporary, however, and suddenly the sleeper was awakened by a voice calling from the corridor.

'Hey! This is Applewold! Are you changing here or going on?'

Applewold! Yes, wasn't that what the inspector had said at Euston? Change at Applewold?

Mumbling thanks to his informant, he stuck his fingers into his eyes to dissipate their heaviness and lurched out on to a grey platform. Faint light was appearing in the east, but a station lamp still flickered rather grudgingly till sunrise relieved it. The informant, withdrawing a little distance, watched him while a porter moved towards the half-awake man.

'Ticket?' said the porter.

'What? Yes. I think—'

The porter looked at the ticket, then at the passenger. Was he comin' down with 'flu or something?

'Couple of hours to wait, sir,' he announced. 'There's a seat in the waitin'-room.'

Two hours to wait. To wait for what? For another train to take him to another station which, when he got there, would mean no more to him than this one? Well, having covered the major stage of his journey, he might as well complete it. It delayed the necessity of making any further decision, and that alone had its value. Besides, he discovered a few moments later, the seat in the train would be less hard than the seat in the waiting-room.

Nevertheless, in spite of the hardness of the seat in the waiting-room of Applewold station, he went to sleep once more, watched by eyes that remained wide open beneath a pair of bushy brows.

He had to be woken up again.

'Train just coming in—if you're for Penridge?'

He rose from his seat automatically. Everything was becoming automatic now. His own initiative was defunct, burned by the fever which was smouldering inside him and making him hot at one moment and cold the next; and something else was taking charge—something or someone. A man, wasn't it? Or was that an illusion, and would the man change into a nurse? Yes, perhaps he was in hospital, and nurses were looking after him, and presently one of them would say, 'He's coming to,' and he would discover that he had had an accident—knocked down by a motor car—and had passed through delirium and nightmare. Very probably, very probably. Feeling as hot as he did, he must have a high temperature. A hundred and five or six, at least. So all he had to do was what the nurses would tell him, and not worry about decisions, and just wait for those words, 'He's coming to—'

But he wished he would come to. It was the hell of a dream! For here he was in a train again, and it wasn't half as comforting as the last. The seats weren't so soft, and the corner didn't take him as comfortably, though that might have been because his body was aching more, and there wasn't the same smooth rhythmic motion. Yes, this train was noisier than the last one. That might mean he was nearer the point of waking up, but he wished he could be sure, because the noise made his head ache and shook all his bones. It was a pretty rotten hospital! They didn't even feed a fellow! He would be sick if he didn't get some food inside him—had he had anything for a week?—but he couldn't think of any food he wanted. A desire to cry swept through him. A desire to say things through tears. Say things? Oh, no, he mustn't do that! Why not? There was a reason, if only he could remember it. He mustn't talk. Not if he was delirious. God, *had* he been talking? There was somebody else in his compartment, somebody in the far corner . . . Who? Oh, yes, that sporting man, it would be. Better pretend to be interested. What had he just said? Something about a jockey who had killed a trainer . . .

'No, I don't suppose one would,' he said, opening his eyes wide.

'Would what?' asked the man in the other corner.

'Eh? What you've just said . . . a mild little fellow like that.'

'Quite so,' agreed the man in the other corner. 'Quite so.'

Something was wrong. It hadn't gone the way it should. Something was wrong. Wake up, wake up, wake up!

The train stopped.

'I'll help you out,' said the man in the other corner. 'This is Penridge.'

11

Start of a Bad Day

Ben could sleep anywhere. The acquirement had been developed through a lifetime of necessity, and he boasted that he had slept in every possible location between, and including, the pavement and the roof. Once on a very dark night he had slept quite comfortably on a dead cow. True, he did not know at the time that it was a cow, or dead, the alarming discovery being made on waking, but in the darkness the mound had made a comfortable pillow for the head, and what you don't know doesn't trouble you.

But tonight, in the small bed lately occupied by Bushy Brows in Jewel Street, sleep took a long time in coming. He had been accepted as a necessary guest, but not a welcome one, and the information he had come here to get had still to be won. After the conversation in the parlour which had culminated in Maudie's decision that he should stay, she had shut up like a clam, and her mother had retired early, and during the hour before Maudie followed her up, the parrot, becoming nocturnally loquacious, had done most of the talking. What it had said had not helped, its remarks being somewhat embarrassingly amorous.

Why, in these circumstances, they both stayed up at all seemed pointless on the face of it. Maudie sewed, and Ben looked through a copy of the *Picturegoer* eighteen times till he knew every film smile backwards. But the truth was that each had a secret hope of learning something from the other, and each was disappointed. The reason for this double failure may have been that they were both too tired to start the ball rolling again.

Just before they parted for the night, Ben observed, 'It's bin a 'appy little hevenin', ain't it?'

'If you weren't going to talk, I didn't see why I should,' she retorted.

'P'r'aps we'll git on better termorrer,' he answered. 'I never believe in givin' up 'ope!'

'Well, if you're hoping for early morning tea, you won't get it!'

'That's orl right, miss—I always begins my day with sherry.'

'Give her a bloody kiss,' said the parrot.

That had effectively ended the conversation.

Lying in bed, and hearing snores through the wall—whether the mother's or the daughter's he did not know—he tried to work out what his next step should be on the morrow when he got up again. He was here, he recalled, not as Bushy Brows' accomplice as he had to appear, but as Mrs Wilby's private detective, and as such he had to find out things in order to return to Drewet Road to report them. All right. That much was clear amid much else that was not. Had he found out enough for a first instalment?

An intensive survey of all that had happened since his arrival at the Kentons gave small results. The only definite event had been the visit of the police and their unsuccessful attempt to discover the whereabouts of Oscar Blake. Apart from this, all he had to add to the bag were the Kentons' reactions to what he himself had let out. And what did these amount to? He went over them in his mind:

'Nummer One. They was proper upset when I lets on there's bin a murder. Well, 'oo wouldn't be? When they wants ter know 'oo done it I didn't tell 'em, 'arf ter find aht if they knoo already, and 'arf becorse I didn't know meself.

'Nummer Two. They dunno 'oo's bin murdered, but Maudie thort at fust it was a woman. Wot I gotter find aht is wot woman she thort, and why?

'Nummer Three. She knows now it's a man, and I'm bettin' a penny to a pahnd of acid drops she's got some'un in 'er mind fer the corpse. Wot I gotter find aht is 'as she got the right man, and if not, 'oo?

'Nummer Four. When I menshuns Drewet Road it 'its 'er bang in the middle of 'er stummick. Wot I gotter find aht is why?

'Nummer Five. She's worked with Blake. They've 'ad some gime on tergether. Wot I gotter find aht is wot?'

The list was richer in what he hadn't found out than in what he had, and it was certainly impossible to find out anything with that insistent snoring in one's ears. Recalling that he could pass through the cupboard between his room and that of the snorer—or were they both at it?—it was loud enough for a duet—Ben contemplated the audacious and indelicate idea of paying them a visit and demanding, if not silence, some modification of the nocturnal music.

If one had to snore, couldn't one do it under a pillow? But in the end he lay still and suffered stoically, until at last Nature took pity on him and bore him away into dreams.

Next morning when he opened his eyes he awoke to silence. He heard no sounds either inside or outside the house, and after he had rolled out of bed and picked himself off the floor, he shuffled to the window and discovered the reason. The muffling fog was thicker and yellower than ever.

Perhaps it was as well. If you do not choose a foggy day to go out, neither do others choose it to come in, and Ben wanted undisturbed hours. What time was it? He had no watch, and the fog gave no indication. Suddenly wondering whether he were late, and breakfast would be over, and Maudie would have departed for Woolworth's where he understood she worked, he performed his one-minute toilet and hurried downstairs.

How gloomy the staircase looked, and how uninviting the little passage at which it ended, with its twist back to the kitchen behind the stairs, and the parlour door needing a fresh coat of paint on the right, and the front door with its cracked fanlight ahead. Ben never liked the dark, but he could accept it when it was supposed to be and when it was its natural black colour. Heavy yellow darkness was darkness out of season.

The silence persisted below as it had above. No sounds came from the kitchen. None from the parlour. None from anywhere. Was he early, after all, instead of late, and was this a new kind of midnight, with the two women still sleeping in their bedroom? They certainly had stopped snoring, but even snores had their limit, like everything else, and ceased when they had reached their allotted span. This thick yellow light might be due to one of them ickilipses. Ickilipses could turn things topsy-turvy, couldn't they? Like sun spots.

He advanced to the parlour door and pushed it open. A nasty moment followed. Maudie and Mrs Kenton were there. They were seated at the breakfast table. They were not merely silent; they were completely motionless. They might have been two wax figures at Madame Tussaud's, in the Chamber of 'Orrers. 'Mrs Kenton and her daughter, just before their arrest.'

But they were flesh and blood, not wax, and after Ben had stood staring at them for a couple of seconds Mrs Kenton turned her head. Ben had the sensation that somebody had put a penny in her somewhere and made her move. Maudie did not move, but remained with her eyes fixed on the table before her. A newspaper was lying by her plate.

'Wot's up?' said Ben.

Life now came into Mrs Kenton's glazed eyes.

'Do *you* have to ask?' she hissed.

Ben had often read of people hissing. Not in a theatre, but conversationally. He shouted. She muttered. He rasped. She hissed. But he had never actually heard the hissing done. Mrs Kenton did it.

He decided to keep clear of it himself.

'Oh! Yer readin' abart it?' he asked innocently.

'Why didn't you tell us?' demanded Mrs Kenton shrilly.

'Wot would yer 'ave done if I 'ad?' replied Ben. 'I sed there was a murder. Is it anythink ter do with you?'

Now Maudie raised her eyes. She looked pale and ill, and Ben thought she was trying to pretend she was not frightened. To his annoyance, he began to feel a little sorry for her. See, when it's a woman . . .

'Don't make things worse, Ma,' she said.

'How could I do that?' cried Mrs Kenton. 'Didn't I tell you from the start? Didn't I warn you? But young people don't listen these days, dear me, no, they know better! You might as well talk to a statue as to—'

'Be quiet!' exclaimed Maudie angrily. 'You soon stopped your warnings, as you call them, when you found the money there was in it!'

'That's a lie!' screamed Mrs Kenton.

'That's right—yell the house down and bring the police!'

Mrs Kenton, pulled up by this reminder, spluttered incoherently, then rose from her chair and, pushing by Ben, ran out of the room and into the kitchen.

'She drinks,' said Maudie bluntly.

'Oh,' blinked Ben.

'She was at it last night when I went up to bed, and she started again this morning. And then, when I read her out—this—' She thrust a hand on the newspaper, and gave it a little shove. 'Well, that finished her.'

'I didn't 'ear nothink as I come dahn—'

'No. You slept late. And you came in here during the calm before the storm!'

She looked at him with grim desperation. It was a different Maudie from the Maudie of the night before.

'Yer know, I ain't got orl this, miss,' said Ben, after a pause. 'As I sed just now, I told yer there'd bin a murder larst night—'

'You didn't say who it was!'

'No, I kep' that fer a bit. But—when yer fahnd aht it wasn't a woman, I thort yer might be on ter it?'

'Did you?'

'Wasn't yer?'

'I hadn't seen it in print.'

Ben nodded. Then he moved nearer the newspaper, and lowering his nose over the teapot, read the paragraph which had destroyed the final peace of No. 46, Jewel Street.

It did not give many details. It was headed 'Gruesome Find in Cellar', and it gave the name and address of the body that had been found there—George Wilby, of 18, Drewet Road, SW3, identified by his wife—and it mentioned the 'phone call that had taken the police to the spot. Then the usual little build-up. The police were following up important clues. There was a man they wished to interview . . . arrest expected shortly . . .

'How did *you* know!'

Ben looked up.

'I didn't do it,' he replied solemnly.

'Was it you who phoned up the police?'

'Eh?'

'Was it?'

'Why should I?'

'You wouldn't—if you'd done it!'

'Tha's right.'

'And I'm believing you.'

'Well, there yer are—'

'So you *could* have phoned the police! And suppose I go off and tell them.'

She was looking at him hard. He wondered whether she meant it, or whether she were bluffing—and, if so, what was the game behind it.

'Wotcher mean, I s'pose,' answered Ben slowly, 'is that,

if I could git you inter trouble, you think you could git me inter trouble—'

'Don't act the fool!' she interrupted. 'Though I'm beginning to wonder which is the biggest! Of course we can get each other into trouble, but what we've got to decide—isn't it?—'a moment of wavering—'is whether we're going to? You're not getting any mad idea into your head, are you, that because—because we're upset, I've had anything to do with this business? I mean—you know—*that*!'

She pointed to the paper, and Ben shook his head.

'Corse I knows yer ain't done it,' he said. 'You ain't goin' ter swing no more'n me. But yer done somethink, ain't yer?'

'Pumping me, Eric?'

'Oh! Yer ain't fergot me nime?'

'I haven't forgotten the name Oscar—Mr Blake—gave you in his note. Tell me, if you're such a friend of his, doesn't he take you into his confidence?'

'Meanin' that if 'e did, I wouldn't 'ave ter arsk yer nothink?'

'You've said it exactly.'

'P'r'aps,' said Ben darkly, 'I knows a lot, but not quite orl?'

'How much do you know?'

'Enuff ter mike me think it'd be best ter tell me the lot!'

'Best for who? You or me?'

'I'll leave you ter work aht that one!'

She frowned. 'Yes, and I've got to work it out before we go any farther.' Suddenly she jumped up and ran to a small desk in a corner. Opening a drawer, she took something out, then returned and handed it to him. It was a page torn from a picture paper. 'Bottom picture. Have a look at it! See anything that interests you?'

Ben examined the photograph. Above it were the words,

'London Greets Film Star', and the film star was waving from an open car.

'Yer wouldn't git me standin' in the street fer that,' he commented.

'No? See if you can find yourself in the crowd,' suggested Maudie.

Ben's eyes left the film star and began searching among the star's admirers. All at once he lowered his nose to look closer. Maudie was watching him intently.

'Found yourself?' she inquired.

'I've fahnd you,' replied Ben.

'Only me?'

Ben stared at the picture for a few more seconds, then laid it down.

'The bloke with yer,' he said.

'With his arm round my shoulder,' nodded Maudie.

'Yus!'

'Know him?'

'Looks like we both knows 'im, miss.'

'That's when I last saw him. When did you last see him? Was he alive—or not?'

Ben did not answer.

'And when did you last see Oscar Blake? . . . God!' All at once she burst out. 'Have you lost your tongue? Did Oscar kill Mr Wilby? Tell me, tell me, tell me!'

'Wot I needs,' thought Ben, 'is ter be a bit more clever like! This is gittin' me beat!'

And then, more by instinct than by reason, he took a chance and gave up bluffing.

'Lummy, let's 'ave a spot o' truth!' he exclaimed. 'No, I don't think 'e done it, but I think 'e knows 'oo done it, 'e sed so, and that's wot I'm 'ere ter find aht a bit more of!'

She stared at him, trying to take it in.

'He—said he knew?'

'Yus.'

'But it was Oscar who sent you here.'

'That's right.'

'But if he knows—'

'Ah 'e didn't send me 'ere fer that, 'e's got some gime on, like I told yer, and I'm s'posed ter wait 'ere fer the next move like.'

'Was it Oscar who telephoned to the police?'

''Im? Lummy, no!'

'It *was* you, then?'

'Yus.'

Things were moving a bit fast, but there seemed no stopping them now.

'Did Oscar tell you to?'

'To telerphone?'

'Yes! Was that part of his game?' Her eyes narrowed. 'I see it wasn't—you did it on your own!'

'That's right.'

'Why?'

Ben replied to the challenge with another dose of truth. The reply, to him, was obvious.

'Nah, listen, miss,' he answered. 'I come acrost the body haxerdental jest afore Bushy Brows—that's Blake—turns up. When 'e goes orf agine, can I leave it there and say nuffin'? Would *you* of? You ain't got no wings, that's heasy ter see, don't git 'uffy, nor've I, but wotever we are we ain't murderers, we bar that, don't we? And if yer ain't no murderer yer carn't leave corpses lyin' abart. That's right, ain't it? So I 'phones up the pleece, and—' He stopped short. No, in this spate of veracity there was one thing he would leave out. Perhaps he had said too much already, but there was to be no mention to Maudie of his visit to Mrs Wilby until he knew a little more about that picture of Maudie and Mrs Wilby's husband. 'And—well, 'ere I am,' he concluded.

'Yes, here you are,' muttered Maudie. 'So what?'

Clearly undecided, she removed her eyes from Ben's and lowered them to the picture. Then she took the picture up and returned with it to the drawer. 'Fillin' in time while she's thinkin',' reflected Ben. Aloud he said, to her back:

'I could tell yer wot, if yer'd listen.'

'Well?'

'Yer ain't killed nobody, 'ave yer?'

'If you say that again, I'll scream!'

'Don't do that or we'll 'ave yer muvver back. I like the sahnd of it—wot I sed—but the next ain't so good, miss. Yer in a mess.'

'Thanks for the news!'

'And if I don't know the 'ole of it, I know a part of it.'

'What part?'

'The part yer've showed me. That pickcher yer've jest put back in the drawer. Yer've been seen abart with the corpse's arm rahnd yer neck—afore 'e was a corpse, o' corse—and yer pally with this bloke Blake the pleece wanter see, so if yer don't watch yer step yer'll hend up like I sed when I fust come 'ere larst night—in the witness-box or in the dock. P'r'aps yer can see yer way clear? Can yer? 'Ow much longer 'ave I got ter tork to yer back?'

She turned round from the desk.

'Go on,' she said. 'Let's suppose I can't see my way clear? Well?'

'In that caise, yer want somebody ter 'elp yer to work it aht.'

'I see. And you're telling me you're that person?'

'So long as yer ain't done nothink ter put me orf yer proper—yer know wot I mean, 'urtin' children or anythink like that—wozzer matter?'

For she had leapt towards the door as a clock with a cracked face on the mantelpiece began striking.

'I'm late!' she gasped. 'I can't stop! But I come back here for lunch—I'll tell you everything then!'

The next moment she was out of the room.

12

Waiting for Maudie

During that trying morning, while waiting for the information which Maudie had promised him on her return to
lunch, Ben found the parrot a better companion than Mrs
Kenton. Indeed, until just before lunch time Mrs Kenton
kept studiously away from him, giving him none of her
companionship at all. This had its points. The parrot, on
the contrary, provided him with some entertainment after
he had eaten a cold kipper which he assumed had been
intended for his breakfast, together with three pieces of
equally cold, hard, unadorned toast and the remains of
two other kippers to which, in their preoccupation with
larger matters, Mrs Kenton and Maudie had done scant
justice.

He hoped that his spell with the parrot might prove
profitable as well as entertaining, and it was not merely
through lack of other company that he drew his chair up
to the cage and sat down to study the bird. 'Parrots repeat
things they've 'eard,' ran his thought, 'so let's see if we can
git this 'un ter repeat somethink worth 'earin'.'

For twenty minutes the parrot paid no attention to him. He might not have been there, and he felt a little hurt. He wondered what parrots thought about when staying so still that they might be stuffed or dead. Other parrots? That seemed most likely till you worked out that it couldn't be. Parrots who lived all their lives in a cage by themselves didn't know any other parrots, so they couldn't think about them. What else, then? There didn't seem much else beyond counting their bars. Must be dull like, being a parrot. Though, mind you, restful.

Then Ben recalled Conversation, in which the present parrot was proving so lacking. Yes, when they talked, that must liven 'em up a bit. They probably did it out of sheer boredom, because there was nothing else to do. So why didn't they all talk? He recalled a parrot on a ship that had never stopped talking till a stoker had thrown it overboard, but this one—was it dumb? No, it had made a few remarks on the previous night, Ben remembered. Perhaps it just needed encouragement?

'Come on, Polly, let's 'ave a jaw,' he said. 'Jest you and me. Owjer like this fog?'

For a while it proved a one-sided jaw, and Ben's voice evidently had a soporific effect, for the parrot gave up staring at nothing, and closing its eyes, sank into deep sleep. But when it suddenly opened one eye and told Ben to lock it up, hope revived.

'Lock what up?' asked Ben.

'Lock it up, lock it up, lock it up,' replied the parrot.

The remark gave Ben an idea. He went to the drawer from which Maudie had taken the picture of herself and Mr Wilby looking at a film star, and in which she had replaced it. Perhaps he would find something else worth looking at in the drawer? But Maudie had locked it up. Which, after all, was only to be expected.

Returning to the parrot, Ben continued to address it, and after hearing Mrs Kenton's footsteps ascending the stairs and moving overhead, he risked some direct questions.

'Does the old lidy hupstairs know orl Maudie's goin' tell me?'

No answer.

'Does Mrs Wilby know abart 'er 'usband's goin's hon?'

A look of contempt.

'I see wot yer mean. If she'd knowd, she'd ave knowd where I was comin', 'stead o' not knowin' 'oo lived 'ere no more'n me?'

The open eye began to close.

''Old it, 'old it! She might know abart the gall withaht knowin' the address? The gall knows *'er* address!'

'Duck him dry!'

'Wozzat?'

'Duck him dry!'

''E'd be wet arter yer ducked 'im, wouldn't 'e?'

No answer.

'Duck 'oo dry?'

'Dilly fool, dilly fool, dilly fool!'

'Silly fool yerself! Carn't yer pernounce yer s's?'

Insulted, the parrot refused to talk any more, and went to sleep for the morning.

When at last Ben gave up, and wondered whether to follow the bird's example, he asked himself what he'd got out of it. Lock it up—that made sense. Probably the bird had heard that said many times in this room. Duck him dry—that didn't make sense. Dilly fool! That was easy. Another remark the parrot often heard, but it couldn't say its s's. Not at the beginning of a word, anyhow—it had spat one out clear enough last night when it had told Ben to kiss Maudie! Dilly fool—silly fool! Duck him dry—suck him . . .

'Suck 'im dry!' muttered Ben. 'Lummy—*that* was it! Suck 'im dry! Where does that tike us?'

He was about to try and discover where it took him when he changed his mind. Wasn't Maudie coming back in two or three hours for a heart-to-heart? Why worry his head when she'd save him the trouble? What Maudie told him would cover more than could be deduced from a parrot, and those kippers were sitting sort of heavy like on his stummick. The parrot was asleep again. He'd join it. Rest up for the trouble that was coming!

So he made himself comfortable, and was soon as oblivious to the fog as the large green bird beside him.

When he woke up he noticed a slight difference in the room. What was it? It disturbed him. Fog just the same. Parrot just the same. Table—oh, it had been cleared. Mrs Kenton must have been in and took the things away. Wunner what she'd thort, findin' 'im asleep? The idea of her hovering around him while he was unconscious—why, she might feel in 'is pockets and steal some of 'is 'oles!—decided him not to go to sleep any more. A minute later he was snoring.

He woke up again. This time someone was at the front door and he guessed that must have woken him. 'Oo? Copper? Sahnded like one. And the other voice was Mrs Kenton's . . .

'What do you want to see her for?'

'Oh, we'd just like a word with her.'

'What about?'

'We'll tell her that.'

'I see. I'm only her mother, so I needn't know! Well, she's not here!'

'You're quite certain of that?'

'Certain? Wouldn't I know? She's at her work, but if you don't believe me you'd better come in and look!'

Ben's heart gave a bound. So did his body. He heard the rest from under the table.

'She works at Woolworth's, doesn't she?'

'She works there, yes.'

'And—you believe—that's where I'll find her?'

'Believe? Why not? But if you think it's the right thing to go disturbing a girl at her work—'

'When will she be back here?'

'After her work, wouldn't she?'

'I had an idea she returned here for her lunch?'

'Well—yes, that's so.'

'Then I can find her here if I call again between one and two?'

'Why not?'

'Thank you. Oh, by the way, have you heard anything more of your lodger? Oscar Blake? Has he been back, by any chance?'

'No.'

'And you've heard nothing from him? Or of him?'

'No.'

'Nothing at all?'

The control Mrs Kenton had just managed to keep gave way, and now nervous anger quivered through her voice.

'What are you asking for? Wouldn't you know? We've no telephone here, and I expect you're watching the postman! A nice thing that is, isn't it, for a respectable woman's house? Mr Blake's gone, you've been told that, and I don't know anything about him, or want to know anything about him, or to have any more to do with him. Do I have to stand here all the morning answering your questions? Is this my house or isn't it? I've got my work to do!'

Sternly came the response to this outburst:

'And I am doing mine, Mrs Kenton. I'll be back here at half-past one. If your daughter returns, see she stays here till I call. Good morning.'

The front door closed. Ben leapt from under the table, and stood facing the parlour door, ready to tell Mrs Kenton what he thought of her for asking the policeman in, but she went by the door and he heard her entering the kitchen. He swallowed, and wiped his brow.

'Dilly fool!' muttered the parrot, in its sleep.

'Ah, shurrup!' retorted Ben.

He did not sleep any more. The clock on the mantelpiece informed him through its cracked glass that it would soon be one o'clock, and that it was getting too near the time for action. Precisely what the action would be was less certain, but shortly after the clock struck Maudie would return from Woolworth's, which presumably was not far off, and shortly after that the policeman would also return. Maudie looked in for a busy time—and so, with little doubt, did Ben.

Sitting now with his eyes wide open, he tried to work out what the busy time would involve. Zero hour was one o'clock, and it was in the thirty minutes after this that so much would have to be crammed. As far as Ben was concerned, the events would begin with the arrival of Maudie and end with the departure of himself, for he did not mean to be present when the policeman paid his next call. His luck might not last, and he was by no means sure that, in an attempt to white-wash herself with the police, Mrs Kenton might not hand him over. But could he learn what Maudie had to tell him and make his escape in thirty minutes, with Mrs Kenton hovering around and the business of lunch to be attended to? He could imagine Mrs Kenton's voice rasping, while he and Maudie were trying to manoeuvre their *tête-à-tête*, 'What are you two up to? Have your lunch, or that policeman will be back in the middle of it!'

And would they have thirty minutes? He tried to work out the time-table. Say Maudie left Woolworth's at one sharp, though it was more likely to be a couple of minutes past, and say the shop was five minutes away, or say seven, better allow a bit more in case you'd allowed a bit less, all right, that made it she'd arrive back here at when? Well, say ten past, and say the policeman turned up at twenty-eight past, because when you wanted people to be punctual they were late and when you wanted them to be late they were early, that was life, this would leave what? Twenty minutes, no, eighteen, weren't it, ten off twenty-eight was eighteen. Okay, so you'd only have eighteen minutes for the lot, with bobbies watching back and front, that was, if they were . . .

The door opened, and Mrs Kenton came in.

'Oh! You're here?' she said ungraciously.

'You're good at guessin',' answered Ben.

'And I'm supposed to provide your lunch for you, as well as your breakfast and your supper?'

'Tell us wot a cold kipper corsts, and yer shall 'ave it.'

He did not mention his intended departure. For one thing he thought it would please her too much, and for another, he could not say yet whether the departure would be temporary or permanent. That depended on circumstances still to be resolved.

'I don't want any more of your backchat,' answered

Mrs Kenton. 'You don't seem to realise anything! Did you hear that policeman at the front door just now, or were you still asleep?'

'I 'eard 'im,' replied Ben, 'and I 'eard you, too, arskin' 'im in ter search the plice!'

'Oh, you did!'

'I did! And s'pose 'e *'ad?*'

'He wasn't looking for you,' she snapped.

'No, but 'e might 'ave fahnd somethink 'e wasn't lookin' for, sime as 'e might lars' night,' retorted Ben, 'and then wot would 'ave 'appened?'

She scowled at him in desperate anger.

'How do I know?' she exclaimed. 'How do I know? Why don't you *go?* How long have I got to add hiding you to the rest of my troubles? If you heard all that then you heard me say I didn't want any more to do with your friend Mr Blake, and the same applies to you! I'm not going on for ever like this.' He watched her apprehensively as she worked up again. 'I won't stand for it—no, and that's what I'm going to tell Maudie when she comes back! I won't stand for it! Do you want to bring the lot of us to the gallows?'

The terror which had been behind her outburst over breakfast and which she had struggled to suppress since now re-entered her eyes. Ben hardly recognised her as the slow-moving, superficially cowlike woman who had greeted him on arrival as she spun round after this fresh outburst and abruptly left him.

'It may be dull fer yer,' said Ben to the parrot, 'but I'd chinge plices!'

Mrs Kenton did not return. Even when one o'clock struck, the hour for which he had so anxiously waited, she did not come to lay the cloth. What did that mean?

Lunch in the kitchen? Well, that would not affect him if he was not going to be there to eat it. All he hoped was that it would be a lunch he could miss without tears, and would not include, say, Welsh Rabbit that tickled yer nostrils or Termerter Soup that was good all the way down. He dreaded succulent smells from the kitchen that might weaken him into taking risks!

Fortunately, none came while he fixed his eyes on the clock and watched the slow movement of the minute hand. He watched it move to one-past and two-past—was Maudie now leaving Woolworth's?—and after another couple of minutes he began to listen for her rapid clicking steps. Maudie's steps clicked, he'd noticed that.

The minute hand continued its slow but insistent progress, but Maudie's steps from the street were as non-existent as the succulent smells from the kitchen. Oi, Maudie, wot's keepin' yer? The large black hand—rather a rusty black, and slightly bent, like a patient old man carrying on with his job of recording the very time that was destroying him—moved to five-past and ten-past. Lummy! Eleven—twelve—thirteen—git a move on, Maudie! There's a copper comin' ter see yer, and I gotter see yer fust . . .

Sounds at last! But not the sounds Ben was listening for. The kitchen door opened, and Mrs Kenton came along the passage. She was getting restive, too? Her steps did not click like her daughter's. More of a shuffle, like. They shuffled past the parlour door to the front door, and then stopped. What was she doing? Jest standin' there, waitin'? Meanin' ter git 'er word in fust?

Hallo! The bell! Maudie wouldn't ring! Not unless she'd fergot 'er key? But Ben had not heard that informative clicking along the pavement. Of course, the fog might have something to do with that. He listened to the front door opening.

'Is Miss Kenton back yet?'

Ben's heart descended into his boots with a thump at the unwelcome, familiar voice!

'You're early!' came Mrs Kenton's retort.

'She's not back, then?'

'When you say a time, I should think you'd stick to it!'

'Isn't she usually back by now?'

The sergeant was walking right through her, and she gave up evasion.

'Yes, she is. I expect she's been delayed.'

'You've had no message?'

'Message? What do you mean? What would a message be about?'

In the little pause that followed the parrot opened an eye, failed to sense drama, and reclosed it. The sergeant spoke again.

'I'll come in, if you don't mind.'

'I do mind! I'm busy getting lunch!'

'Just the same, as your daughter isn't here, I'd like a few words with you instead.'

'I've got nothing to tell you!'

'No? Well, ma'am, perhaps not, but you see I've got something to tell *you*!'

'Oh, what?'

'Your daughter isn't at Woolworth's.'

'That's nonsense! She must be, if she isn't here—'

'I'm telling you that she isn't. She hasn't been there all the morning, and we're needing to get into touch with her. So with your permission, ma'am, I'll step in and we'll continue our conversation inside.'

13

Parlour Tricks

Ben never knew whether Mrs Kenton brought the policemen—there were two of them—into the parlour, or whether the sergeant came in on his own initiative while his unwilling hostess was intending to lead him into the kitchen. Subsequent events gave some indication of the former theory. But by whatever process, here they all were in the parlour—the sergeant, the constable, Mrs Kenton and Ben. With one notable difference, however. Whereas the first three were visible, the last was not.

In sudden emergencies, his life-score of which ran well into four figures, Ben was never without a temporary solution. 'Yer not done till yer dead' was his motto, and aided by this optimistic philosophy he never gave up hope. Another man might have stood frozen while the parlour door opened to admit his doom. When the police entered now, however, the only living thing they saw besides themselves and Mrs Kenton was the parrot.

Ben had not sought sanctuary this time beneath the table. He was behind a long, heavy, maroon window-curtain, which he had pulled right across the window as he had slid behind it. On a sunny day this would have been immediately notice-able, but the yellow fog was itself a curtain which had already necessitated the switching on of the electric light for the room's illumination. So the dreaded comment was not made—perhaps Mrs Kenton assumed Ben had pulled the curtain across to shut out the ugly pea-soup prospect?—and the conversation begun on the front doorstep was now resumed. It was the sergeant who resumed it.

'I don't suppose your daughter mentioned to you that she was not going to Woolworth's this morning?' he began.

'Wouldn't I have known about it if she had?' interrupted Mrs Kenton.

'Quite so—'

'How do *you* know she didn't do so?'

'Please let me ask the questions. We know because we called there.'

'That was a nice thing to do!'

'You must agree it was necessary. I want you to tell me whether she said anything to you before she left this morning that may help us to trace her movements?'

'If she did, of course I have to repeat it?'

'I should like to get this clear, ma'am. Your daughter is missing. You don't know where she is—is that correct?'

'Haven't I told you?'

'But you're not anxious? You've no interest in trying to find out what has happened to her?'

'That's right, try to get me all tied up!' exclaimed Mrs Kenton. 'I see what you're getting at, but why should I be anxious? My daughter is a grown woman, and she can look after herself, and she goes her own way. I've nothing to do with whatever you're calling here about—'

'You mentioned that you were getting lunch. Were you getting it for her, as well as for yourself?'

'What?'

'Just the two of you? If we went in the kitchen I suppose we'd find—'

'Yes, yes, of course I was getting hers, too!'

'Then, when she did not return, and you are told she did not go to Woolworth's, you would naturally want to know the reason, I take it, and would ask yourself whether she had said anything to you in the morning to explain her absence. Not,' the sergeant added, somewhat ironically, 'because you were anxious, but because of the inconvenience she had caused you by making you prepare for a meal she had not come home to eat.'

'She certainly didn't say anything to *me* in the morning before she left, whatever she may have said to anybody else!'

'Anybody else?'

'What?'

'Who else?' A short, pregnant silence occurred before the sergeant continued: 'If you have your lunch in the kitchen, would we find places laid there for only two?'

Behind the window curtain Ben's forehead grew damper. Now for it! How was Mrs Kenton going to get past that one? He learned a moment later. Answering shrilly, Mrs Kenton cried:

'All right, all right, all right! If you want the truth, you shall have it, and but for others whose doings are nothing to do with me, and don't you forget *that,* you should have had it from the start! Mothers are supposed to look after their daughters, I suppose, if you're married ask your wife, only I hope your daughter's less trouble than mine is! It was her made me take that lodger you're inquiring about who's gone, he was her friend, not mine, though I'm not saying she ever knew he was as bad as he was, and when he sends another man here what am I to do? I said only an hour ago I'd wash my hands of the whole affair, "Have it out with Maudie the moment she comes back," I said, and that's what I would have done if you hadn't come back first! And just because she isn't here to talk to you, and as if I haven't got enough on my mind, you try to put all the blame on to me—' Her voice rose, hysterically. 'On me, when I've done nothing at all, nothing whatever—'

'Stop! That's enough!' interrupted the sergeant, sharply. 'Where's this other man? Is he here?'

'What?'

'Answer quick, please!'

'You can see he's not—'

'In the house? Try the kitchen, Jones—'

'He's not there!'

'We'll look for ourselves, if you've no objection!'

'Look where you like, you won't find him down here. Upstairs most likely—yes, and I hope you do find him!'

The policemen were out of the room as she spoke, and in a confusion of sounds Ben heard their hurrying feet, and Mrs Kenton's heavy breathing, and the tattoo of his own heart. Well, it was now or never, wasn't it? They would soon have searched the kitchen and the bedrooms, and then they would be back in the parlour for a more intensive search here. But in spite of the urgency of the

126

moment Ben waited for a second or two in the hope of hearing Mrs Kenton's steps following the policemen out. He listened for them in vain. All he heard was her breathing.

All right! She'd have to have it. The heavy maroon curtain moved convulsively, the movement followed by the protesting squeak of a window suddenly thrust up. Mrs Kenton shrieked. She went on shrieking, and while she shrieked Ben hurled himself out into the fog, tripping over indecipherable objects, jumping into others, hitting walls, bouncing off on to railings, and generally disturbing everything in the immediate universe. And when at last it seemed that he had found a region free of entanglements and Mrs Kenton's shrieks were mere faint echoes, a hand descended heavily on his shoulder.

'Now, then, what's all this?' cried a voice at the other end of the law's long arm.

There were rare moments when Ben revealed a capacity that made him wonder whether he had not really been born for better things. Such a moment came now. Expert wriggler though he was, the grip on his shoulder was too firm to squirm out of in his breathless condition, and he had to depend on strategy. The strategy took the form of assumed delight.

'A copper! Thank Gawd,' he gasped. 'Did yer 'ear that screamin'?'

'Yes, and I was just—'

'Don't stop ter tork! The sergeant and the constable—they're arter Blake in there, and there's hothers, too, and they're murderin' the old lady. I was sent aht fer hextra 'elp—yer wanted inside, quick!'

'Blake? Did you say Blake—'

127

'Gawd, this is when yer want ter 'ear the fust time! 'E's got a gun—lummy, there's a shot! 'E's used it!'

For an instant the heavy hand on Ben's shoulder relaxed. It was all he needed. Before the constable had realised his Waterloo, ten yards of London fog separated them, and he had lost both Ben and his chance of promotion.

14

Back in Drewet Road

The fog was not as thick in Drewet Road as it was in Jewel Street, but it was a cheerless prospect at which Ada Wilby gazed as she sat at one of her drawing-room windows after a solitary lunch. She hardly saw the depressing yellowed view, however, for her mind was far beyond it, dwelling on other times and places. It was a very tired mind, and a very confused one. She found it difficult to know what she thought, and what she felt. Anger mingled with reproach, grief with fear, and she seemed to have lost herself as well as her husband. Dismayed by a sense of loneliness, she needed to talk. But there was no one to talk to.

She was in this mood when she became conscious of a movement in the yellowed back garden, and she shortened her focus to discover what it was. Bending forward she watched the movement, till a blur became a vague, approaching figure, which as it drew cautiously closer materialised into that of a man. Alarm was followed by recognition. This was the strange little fellow who on the previous day had brought her the first news of her husband's death, and whom she had engaged to try and solve its mystery. In spite of the queer appeal he had made to her, she had wondered whether she would ever see him again. Now here he was, to dispel her doubts, returning in a way which, although unusual, probably suited the necessity of the role she had allotted him. For, after all, it was hardly likely he would come to the front door, and he might consider it in their mutual interest to avoid being seen by a maid at the back.

This, precisely, had been Ben's reasoning when, after a trying and groping journey, he had found himself back in Drewet Road.

There was a narrow balcony outside the drawing-room window, with a narrow iron stairway running down to the garden beside the high dividing wall. Leaving her chair, she opened the window and beckoned. The figure below did not immediately respond. He slithered against the wall and waited while a faint streak of light came from below the balcony. 'Daisy in the pantry!' thought Mrs Wilby. In a few moments the streak vanished, and the unorthodox visitor leapt catlike up the stairway. Reaching the open window, he breathed conspiratorially, 'Orl right ter come in, mum?' Mrs Wilby nodded, and he slid into the room.

They made an odd, ill-assorted couple, Mrs Wilby in her smart costume—only complete incapacity could cause her to neglect her appearance—and Ben in his patched and shiny suit, but the contrast was softened by the dimness of the drawing-room, for Mrs Wilby had not switched on the light, and as she softly closed the window behind her guest she made a shadowy silhouette against the panes.

'The reason I come this way, mum,' began Ben, in a whisper, 'was 'cos I thort it best not ter be seen like.'

'Yes, I guessed that was the reason,' Mrs Wilby whispered back.

'Wot abart bein' 'eard? This is over the kitching, ain't it?'

'It is. Wait a moment!' She reflected. 'You've come to tell me something?'

'Yus.'

'Will it take more than a minute?'

'Lummy, yus! See, we gotter work it aht!'

'Is it very urgent—'

'Hurgent?'

'I mean, must it be this instant? Is it something I ought to know at once?'

'Oh, I see! Yer got some'un comin', and yer want me ter slip ahtside fer a bit—'

'No, no,' she interrupted, 'but I was remembering that in about half an hour my maid will be out, and then we'd have the house to ourselves and wouldn't have to be so quiet.'

'I git yer,' answered Ben. 'But won't the fog keep 'er 'ome?'

'She's got a boyfriend.'

'Oh! Well, mum, wot I gotter tell yer ain't immejit hurgent, if that's wot yer call it, and p'r'aps now I've got 'ere it won't mike no bones waitin' a bit longer. Where shall I go, mum?'

'You can stay here,' she replied. 'There's a comfortable chair over there. If I hear the maid outside I'll go to the door and see she doesn't come in.'

It was a very comfortable chair. Almost too comfortable, for it invited slumber, and even after a decision not to talk it is not socially correct to go to sleep when you are paying a lady a call. But perhaps, thought Ben, when he had

131

tiptoed to this comfort, he might just close his eyes? After all, he wouldn't be expected to sit and look at Mrs Wilby if he wasn't talking to her, and she certainly wouldn't want to sit and look at him! A couple of seconds of Ben was an eyeful. So he allowed his lids to drop, and the oppressive fog he had groped through melted into a rosy region inhabited by little white horses. You never knew what would come when you closed your lids. Sometimes it was nothing. Sometimes it was cheese. You never knew. But quite often it was white horses, and when he got white horses he liked watching them go round and round. They were pretty, you couldn't get away from it.

He thought he was still watching them, although in fact they had long departed, when Mrs Wilby's voice opened his eyes and brought back the dimness of the drawing-room. He found her standing before his chair.

'She's gone,' she said.

'Eh?' blinked Ben. ''Ave I bin asleep?'

'Sound.'

'Lummy—I 'ope I didn't snore!'

'I'd have woken you if you had! Come over to the fire. Now we'll talk.'

There was something comfortable and secure in the firelit gloom. Outside was trouble, but here—for the time being—there seemed none. No policemen. No hysterical women. Not even an unpredictable parrot. Of course, it wasn't going to be no picnic giving Mrs Wilby his news if he told her about that picture of her husband and Maudie, but she had already proved she was not the sort of woman to go off the handle, whatever she was feeling like inside, and there was a friendliness about her that was as reassuring as surprising. Same as she had shown on the day before. Wunner why?

'Well? Did you go to that address?'

Ben nodded.

'And who did you find there?'

'The gall and 'er mother, like Blake said—'

'Blake?'

'Yus, that's the feller 'oo was stayin' there and 'oo give me the note—the feller I met—well, you know where. The note was signed O.B., and I found that meant Oscar Blake. Do you know anythink abart 'im?'

She shook her head.

'But *you* must have heard something about him,' she said. 'Tell me! And about the Kentons—wasn't that the name?'

'Tha's right. Mrs and Maudie—and a nice couple *they* are! Maudie works at Woolworth's, and she's been on some gime with Blake, but she didn't know nothink abart the—abart wot 'appened yesterday, no more'n 'er mother did, and they was fair hupset when they read abart it this mornin' in the paiper.'

Mrs Wilby looked a little puzzled.

'Didn't you tell them, then?' she asked.

'No,' responded Ben. 'See, if they wasn't tellin' me wot they knoo, I wasn't tellin' them nothink fer nothink. But I did drop a sorter 'int larst night, ter put the wind up 'em, arter the pleece 'ad called lookin' fer Blake.'

'What! Did the police call at Jewel Street?' exclaimed Mrs Wilby.

'Tha's right, mum.'

'Did they find you there?'

'It was a narrer squeak, but I was jest too quick fer 'em.'

'And I suppose they didn't find Blake, either?'

'No, mum.'

'What did the Kentons say about him? To the police? Or don't you know?'

'Oh, I 'eard it. Corse, the sergeant pumps 'em proper, but orl 'e got was that Blake 'ad gorn, and that they didn't know nothink abart 'im, and that 'e wasn't comin' back.'

'What did they say about you?'

'Nothink—not then. Well, arter they'd left and I'd come aht of 'idin', we 'ad a lovin' hevenin', I don't think! I couldn't git no more aht of 'em than the pleece 'ad, and the on'y way I got 'em ter let me stay the night was by pertendin' ter know more'n I did abart 'em and sayin' that if I left it'd be fer the pleece staishun. Oh, yus, I fergot. There was somethink I got aht o' Maudie afore we went ter bed. I arsked 'er—yer know, sort o' cashel like—if she'd ever 'eard o' Drewet Road. 'Ad she! You orter've seen 'er fice!'

'She knew it?'

'I'll say she did!'

'Yes? Go on!'

Mrs Wilby looked at Ben eagerly, and he returned her gaze uncomfortably. He was coming to the part of his story he liked least.

'I didn't git no more aht of 'er that night.'

'I don't mind when you got it out of her,' retorted Mrs Wilby, 'so long as you tell me what it was!'

'Yus—well, see, I'm jest goin' ter. It was nex' mornin'. Well, that's this mornin', ain't it? They'd read abart—abart it in the paiper, and Mrs Kenton 'ad gorn orf inter the kitchen in a fit of wot yer might call proper hysterieryonics, leavin' me and Maudie ter git on with it, as yer might say, and orl of a suddin Maudie tikes a pickcher aht of a drawer, one o' them noospaiper ones, and puts it unner me nose, and—well, wotcher think it was?'

'I've no idea.'

'Aven't yer?' muttered Ben. He hoped she would. 'Well, see, mum, I dunno jest 'ow ter tell yer—corse, there mightn't be nothink in it, on'y if there wasn't, why did she show it ter me? See wot I mean?'

A sudden change of expression shot into Mrs Wilby's face, revealed clearly in the firelight. Ben gathered that she not only saw what he meant, but saw even more, and he watched her with astonishment as she went to a drawer, as Maudie herself had done, and, history repeating itself, brought out another copy of the same picture.

'Was that it?' she demanded.

'That was the one,' answered Ben. 'So now I ain't got ter tell yer.'

'And you mean that—that Maudie, at Jewel Street, is the girl in this photograph?'

'Tha's right.'

There was a long silence. Ben wondered whether to continue or to leave the next step to her, but the next step seemed so long in coming that it was he who broke the silence.

'I'm glad yer know,' he said; 'but I'm fair sorry abart it.'

She looked at him, as though surprised at his expression of sympathy.

'That's nice of you,' she replied, and then added lightly, 'But these things happen, you know.'

'That don't mike 'em no better,' answered Ben. 'Wars 'appen.'

'Are you a philosopher, by any chance?'

'Wot, me, mum? Lummy, no! Yer need learnin' fer that, but we orl does a bit o'thinkin', don't we?'

'Tell me something else you think?'

135

''Owjer mean?'

'I'm not sure that I know. Perhaps I just meant that I find you interesting to talk to.'

'Go on!' murmured Ben, slightly embarrassed. He had never regarded himself as a drawing-room conversationalist.

After a moment, she reverted to the picture.

'You know, of course, who the man with Maudie is?'

'Well, mum, I thort I reckernized 'im,' he answered.

'Particularly as you'd found she knew of this address.'

'That's right. Two and two's four, ain't it? 'As she—bin 'ere?'

'Hardly!' She added, dryly: 'At least, not to my knowledge.'

She returned to the drawer with the picture, dropped it in, hesitated, then took out another and brought it to him. Ben blinked at it.

'The tart!' he muttered.

'Yes, and you've seen the tart—I haven't,' replied Mrs Wilby, as she put the compromising photograph back. 'Have you anything more you can tell me about her?'

'There'd 'ave bin a lot more if things 'ad gorn right.'

'Oh!'

'See, she works at Woolworth's—oh, I've told yer that— well, any'ow, she does, and afore she goes orf this mornin' she begins ter git confidenshal like—people does ter me sometimes.'

'I can understand it.'

'Eh?'

'Go on.'

'Wot I mean is—yer'll think this funny arter them pick-chers—but wot I mean is, p'r'aps there might be somethink not so bad in 'er once yer got ter know 'er proper.'

'Only the way one generally gets to know her is improper.'

'Wot? Lummy, that's a good 'un! Yer've sed it! Any'ow jest as we're torkin' she finds aht she's laite fer the shop, so orf she goes, sayin' she'll tell me the lot when she comes back fer lunch. But she don't come back. No, the pleece comes back. They comes back twice, ter try and see 'er like they wanted ter see Blake, but it's a wash-aht with them, sime as it was with me, 'cos she never come back at all.'

'Did the police know she worked at Woolworth's?'

'Yes, but she never turned up at Woolworth's.'

'Do you mean—she's disappeared?'

'Seems like it! And when the pleece is gettin' on ter me, I thort it was time I disappeared, too, so I did, and 'ere I am, and I've only got one more thing ter tell yer, see, it was wot the parrot sed.'

'What parrot?'

'The one they got. See, they got one.'

'What did it say?'

'Well, that's goin' ter tike a bit of hexplinin'. Parrots pick up wot they 'ears, don't they?'

'Yes.'

'So when you 'ear 'em say anythink, it means they've 'eard it.'

'You've just said that.'

'When?'

'Go on.'

'Okay. So when this bird sez "Lock it up," yer'd tike it ter mean there was plenty ter lock up in that 'ouse, wouldn't yer? But it carn't pernounce its s's.'

'This parrot can't?'

'There wasn't no hother. But it's funny abart that, 'cos

though it carn't pernounce 'em at the berginnin' it can at the hend, like when it sez "Kiss 'er"—well, we won't go on abart that, see it come in a bit orkward like, but any'ow when it sed "Duck 'im dry"—well, at fust yer thort it was orf its rocker, but arter yer'd got on ter the way it torked and 'ad done a bit of a think like—well, mum, do yer see wot I mean, or doncher?'

It was just as necessary to get on to the way Ben talked as the parrot, but by this time Mrs Wilby was becoming educated, and she nodded.

'And what did you take that to mean?' she asked.

'Suck 'im dry,' answered Ben, obviously.

'Yes, I got that. I was referring to the remark itself. What do you suppose that meant?'

'It mightn't 'ave meant nothink.'

'In that case, why mention it to me?'

'Gime ter you, mum. I thort the 'im might be Mr Wilby, and that 'e was the bloke—the one, I mean—wot some'un was suckin' dry.' He paused uncomfortably. Mrs Wilby's eyes were fixed on the carpet. 'I was goin' ter leave that one ter you,' he went on, 'but yer did arsk me, didn't yer, and p'r'aps I thort wrong.'

Mrs Wilby continued to gaze at the carpet. 'If she goes on much longer,' thought Ben, 'she'll mike a 'ole in it!' Then she got up and walked to the window. Out of the corner of his eye Ben watched her back, wondering what was passing through her mind. Queer, this 'usband and wife business! He couldn't never get the 'ang of it. When there was all this trouble what did people get married for? Seemed sorter senseless, didn't it? Besides, if people'd stop marryin' then there'd be no more people, would there—just trees and fields and birds and things—and trouble would be over. Nice, the world would be then. Nice and restful. Just trees and fields and birds—

Mrs Wilby turned from the window.

'Did you say the police were after you?' she asked.

'I shook 'em orf,' replied Ben.

'What are they after you for?'

'They never worry abart that till they git yer—then they see if there's a reason.'

'How did they learn you were at the house?'

'They didn't, not till Mrs Kenton told 'em.'

'I see. And are you quite sure you shook them off?'

'Where are they? Sure as cheese!'

'Then nobody, nobody at all, knows you're here, apart from myself?'

'"Ow could they, seein' they don't?'

Mrs Wilby smiled faintly. It sounded conclusive.

'So what do we do now?'

'Ah, now we're comin' to it,' replied Ben. 'That's wot we gotter tork abart. I'm s'posed ter be with the Kentons till Blake gits in touch with me, but 'ow is 'e goin' ter git in touch with me if I ain't there? So I've missed wot 'e was goin' ter tell me, and I've missed wot Maudie was goin' ter tell me, and if nobody tells me nothink I carn't do nothink and might as well drop aht. Do yer see wot I mean?'

'Nearly, but not quite,' answered Mrs Wilby.

'Wot doncher see?'

'Do you *want* to drop out?'

'No.'

'Why not?'

'Well—I was tryin' ter 'elp yer like, wasn't I? But I've mide a fair muck of it!'

She regarded him curiously.

'You haven't answered me completely yet. What I want to know is why you want to help me? Wouldn't it be safer for you if you did drop out of it?'

'Eh? Oh—yes, I dessay.'

'So I'm still waiting to know your motive.'

''Oo's that?'

'Your reason?'

'Oh! Well . . .' Suddenly he frowned. 'No, mum. It ain't that.'

'Isn't what?'

'Wot yer was thinkin'.'

'What was I thinking?'

'That's easy! Yer thort I thort that by stayin' in I might mike a bit aht of it.'

'You're wrong,' she replied. 'This may surprise you—perhaps it surprises me, too—but that reason never entered my mind. Yes, if I'd thought that, it would have seemed too obvious to have questioned you about it. Never mind whether you've understood what I've just said or not,' she added, noting Ben's rather puzzled expression; 'but just tell me what your real reason is, because you know I'm still waiting to hear it. I can't see why you should want to run into danger for somebody you never met till yesterday. And I'm not asking you just out of curiosity. I really and truly need to know.'

Impressed by her seriousness, Ben tried to give her the right reply. But he began by asking a question himself.

'Would that be, mum,' he inquired, 'becorse yer wanter know 'ow fur yer can trust me like?'

'Well, if you put it that way, you mayn't be far wrong,' she responded.

140

'Okay. I git yer. Well, if yer want the truth, I hexpeck this is the reason, though I 'adn't thort of it meself not till yer arsked me. Fust, o'corse, I was sorter—well, plumped inter the bizziness, weren't I? I mean, I walks inter a cellar, and there's this corpse, and then in comes some'un helse wot don't look too good, if yer follers me, mum, and—well, there yer are, aren't yer? Corse, yer'll say I could of jest telerphoned the pleece and then 'opped it and lef' it at that. Yus, I could of. But—this is a bit orkerd, but yer askin' me, so 'ere I am, tellin' yer—when I see that photo of yer aht of 'is pocket—and don't fergit, mum, 'e kep' it on 'im, that was somethink, wasn't it? Where've I got ter?'

'The photograph in Mr Wilby's pocket,' Mrs Wilby reminded him, rather unsteadily.

'Yus, that's right. Well, see—I dunno, but it seemed a sorter shime like, and I reckon I saw a bit o' red, and so I come along and looked yer up, and the reason I kep' up arter that was—well, yer was decent ter me, wasn't yer?—so I hexpeck I sort o' took to yer. If yer git me.'

He took a handkerchief from his pocket, and was about to wipe a perspiring forehead when he changed his mind and put it back. Even a perspiring forehead was better in a lady's drawing-room than his pocket handkerchief.

But Mrs Wilby's handkerchief, more suited to the environment, came out as she turned away from him for a moment and pretended to blow her nose.

15

Mrs Wilby Talks

Ada Wilby had found someone to talk to, and since she was assured of his sympathy, if not of his understanding—for how could a queer, simple, uneducated fellow like this comprehend all the subtle undercurrents of uneasy married life?—she felt that the very difference between them would make him easier to confide in than somebody of her own class. It would be something like thinking aloud to a faithful pet.

But before she spoke of the things that had lived for so long only in her thoughts she left the room, returning after a few minutes with a loaded tea-tray. Ben's eyes grew big with surprise and appreciation. He hadn't eaten since breakfast, and those generously-filled plates of bread-and-butter and cake were sights for the gods!

'Lummy, mum, this is nice of yer, but yer didn't 'ave ter do it,' he said.

'You don't look as though you mind,' she replied, 'and I didn't do it because I had to.' She glanced at the clock. 'I'm ready for a cup myself, although it's rather soon after lunch.'

'Lunch? That don't affeck me, mum.'

'Didn't you have any?'

'Well, see, I orlways gives lunch a miss when I'm slimmin'.'

She shook her head, as at something beyond her. 'Please don't slim this afternoon, or all that bread-and-butter will be wasted.'

'No charnce o' that, mum,' murmured Ben, and began the attack.

When the tea was poured out and Ben well under way, she suddenly put a question which caused his second slice to halt two inches from his waiting mouth.

'Are you married?' she asked.

'Wot, me?' he answered. 'No. Not now I ain't.'

'But you have been?'

'As a matter of fack, I was once, but 'oo'd berlieve it?'

'Why not?'

'Eh? Well, tha's right. See, it wer' a long time ago, afore I'd got fixed like wot I am nah.' As she did not respond at once, memory matured in the little pause, and he added reminiscently: 'She was a bit of orl right. So was the kid. But, see, they both went.'

Sympathy entered Mrs Wilby's eyes as she watched the suspended piece of bread-and-butter complete its interrupted journey to the speaker's mouth.

'I'm sorry,' she said.

'Oh, it don't matter nah, mum,' replied Ben, stretching automatically for the third slice. 'And, arter orl, sometimes I thinks that p'r'aps they didn't miss so much. Once yer aht of it, yer aht of it.'

She nodded gravely. 'Well, that's one view to take. And— of course—nothing came along to spoil the memory.'

'Tha's right.'

A question shot into his mind, and while he was deciding not to put it, she guessed it.

'Ask what you were going to,' she said.

'It weren't nothink,' he answered.

'Then must I ask it for you? You were wondering whether anything had come along to spoil *my* memory?'

Ben took a bite, to give himself a little more time to find the right reply. Corse, he'd seen that there photograph, and in this rummy job of being her private detective like, he'd had to come across a bit. Jest the same . . .

'Was that it?'

'That was it,' he admitted, since there was no way out. 'But wot I can't mike aht, mum, is 'ow you and me comes ter be torkin' like this.'

'Perhaps I can't make that out, either, but since we are let's leave it at that. Oh, yes—plenty came along to spoil my memories—and here is something else I can't make out. How it all happened! You see—' She paused for an instant, to contend against her last hesitation. She found that, having started, she did not want to stop. 'You see—Mr Wilby and I began as happily as I gather you did.'

'I got it,' nodded Ben. 'And then things went wrong like.'

'But not for a long while. In fact, only recently. A few months ago. Yes, until then I am sure we were much happier than most—and one rather odd thing about our happiness was that nearly everybody thought we weren't going to be. Including my own family. But—after all—there's no need to go into that.'

There was no need. It was only recent events that required to be talked of here. But with her eyes on the fire, her mind reverted to those early days which, although centred in universal experience, always seem to possess their special, personal magic which can never be conveyed to anyone else. How, for instance, could one convey the magic of that May morning when George Wilby had plucked up courage to propose to her on a Hyde Park seat? She had not believed he would, for courage had never been his strong point, and she had not been sure that she wanted him to. She moved in a circle that rotated above his own, and she knew that her parents were not too happy about her sudden and rather surprising friendship with this assistant bank manager who had been removed from a Midlands branch to London. Ada Hughes, as she then was, was an only child, and had been designed for a better match. But once the proposal was made, its very simplicity and humility touched her. She discovered an elation which could not have been entirely due to the soft spring sunshine and the song of a robin. She had money, if George had little, and a man who had begun life in a bank need not necessarily end there. Indeed, in a swift and intoxicating survey of all the years that lay ahead of them, she decided that George should not. She would infuse him with her ambition, and instead of dropping to his level, he should rise to hers. So she had accepted him, and in the golden glamour of their confessed affection and the exciting mystery of new horizons, they had walked through their difficulties until they had walked along the aisle to be made man and wife.

The magic had continued through the honeymoon and the first year. The modest assistant manager's mind soared into the sky with that of his wife, and he rose in their visions to a high place in the world of finance. Now, twenty years later, Ada saw those visions again in the firelight, and while her queer visitor profited by the silence to pass from his third slice to his fourth, she listened to a voice—her own—saying, 'Why not, George? If a miner can become an MP, there's no reason why you shouldn't aim at it, and with your knowledge of finance—who knows? One day you may become Chancellor of the Exchequer!'

But after that first year, the ambitious plans gradually died of apathy. They were beyond George's capacity, and she realised with disappointment that they frightened him. He did not become Chancellor of the Exchequer. He did not even become an MP. He became, by conscientious work and the patient, full exercise of his limited talent, a bank manager minus the prefix 'assistant', and a bank manager he had remained; and it was to the credit of both of them that, after her period of disappointment, Ada was able to accept life on the modest pattern it offered, and they continued to be good companions, living in material comfort on their affection and in the hope of the child they never had . . .

'Yes—recently—until only a few months ago.'

She jerked herself out of her reverie, though her eyes remained on the fire. She had no idea how long she had been silent. Ben could have told her. Two slices and the top half of a small cake crowned with pink icing. You ate the top half by itself, because you got a fuller sweetness if it was not handicapped by the bottom half, and you ate it first because if you suddenly died, and one never knew, that was the best way to make sure of it.

'Eh?' blinked Ben. 'Tha's right. Er—wot 'appened then?'

'That girl happened,' answered Mrs Wilby.

'Yer mean Maudie?'

'Yes, though I didn't know it was Maudie at the start.

In fact, I don't think I can tell you just when the start was. I think it was a letter. I think it had an Australian stamp on it, though I've never been sure of that. Anyhow, I remember my husband seizing it, and when I asked him who it was from he said it was an advertisement, and changed the subject. I dare say I could have pressed him, but I felt a little annoyed and I wasn't going to be curious. It just seemed to me a silly unnecessary incident. An advertisement from Australia! Well, I let it drop.'

'But yer wasn't sure it was from Orstralyer,' Ben reminded her.

'No, I wasn't sure it was from Australia.'

'And even if it 'ad bin, couldn't it of bin abart one o' them Lotteries?'

'It might. You're doing very well. But the rest won't be so easy. Some weeks later the same thing happened again. Another letter came that he didn't want me to see. I wondered how many other letters there might have been in between! I tried very hard not to be suspicious.'

'Was this 'un from Orstralyer, too, mum?'

'No.'

'Oh!'

'I noticed the stamp this time—and the postmark. It was Southampton. And—as I say—again he wouldn't let me see it. Or, rather, tried to hide it, and then when he couldn't mumbled something about it being only a business letter, and was so palpably lying that it was humiliating to pretend to believe him. So I didn't pretend. I just let the matter drop, as before. But—naturally—I felt worried, and my husband's nerviness only made things worse. I found him not only watching for the postman, but also hurrying to the telephone every time the bell rang, as though anxious to get there first, and as most of the calls were for me—he got his business ones at the bank—well, it became clear that he was only answering the 'phone like this because he expected one—and one morning, just before he left for the bank, it came. I was upstairs when the bell sounded and I let him answer it as usual, and when he didn't call me I knew of course it was for him. I could hear by his quick voice that he wanted to end the conversation before I came down, so I didn't hurry, and I didn't come down till he'd rung off and called up good-bye to me.' She gave a short hard laugh. 'It wasn't till the front door slammed that I remembered I hadn't replied.'

Ben asked: 'But yer 'adn't 'eard nothink o' the conversashun, 'ad yer?'

'Only the end of it,' she answered.

'And wot yer 'eard hupset yer like?'

'He said—to whoever it was: "Yes, yes, I'll meet you there, three o'clock, but you must promise never to 'phone me up here again."'

'I git yer.'

'Yes, if you'd heard that, what would you have thought?'

'Same as you, mum. But it mightn't of bin nothink.'

'It mightn't, and when he came back that evening you'd have thought it had been nothing. Until that day he'd been terribly nervy, as I've told you, but now his nerviness seemed to have gone, and he was all smiles. I'd almost decided during the day to have it out with him—I can hardly believe I'm telling you all this, but I've got to finish now—yes, when I heard his latch-key in the lock I was primed for a row. But the moment I saw him I realised the change, and when I asked him if he'd had any good news he replied yes, he had, and that we were going to a theatre on the strength of it. He said some of our shares had soared. I think—I think that was the last time I believed him.'

Still defending the dead man, Ben remarked that it could have been true. 'And that there telerphone in the mornin', mum, might 'ave bin jest abart them shares doin' wot yer sed 'e sed, on'y p'r'aps 'e didn't want the bloke ter go on telerphonin' 'ere bercorse 'e wanted ter surprise yer like.'

With a faint smile, Mrs Wilby nodded.

'I was ready to think something like that. Yes, even up to then, and during the next two days.' Her eyes narrowed. 'Then came another call. On a Sunday afternoon. You don't do business on Sundays. We were chatting together in this room, and the 'phone was here—we'd moved it in from the dining-room. He lifted the receiver, and it might have been red-hot he dropped it again so quickly. "What's the matter?" I asked. "Wrong number," he answered . . . The world just turned black!' She pulled herself up. 'Sorry—I didn't mean to get emotional.'

'That's orl right, mum,' replied Ben solemnly. 'I seen it go like that, on'y mine 'as red spots in it.'

A quick frown faded as she studied him and realised he was not trying to be funny but was responding to her with a simple, sober fact. There was no middle course with this quaint fellow. You had to take him or leave him.

'And, corse, mum, that put the lid on?'

'It did.'

'And then you 'ad the row?'

She shook her head.

'No. I couldn't have borne it. I just left the room, and we didn't speak to each other for the rest of the day . . . Well, I'm not going into all the details. It isn't necessary.

I knew after that he was meeting somebody secretly, and presently stories began to come to my ears. I expect you can guess the kind?'

'Easy. People loves 'em!'

'Unless they are the subjects of them.'

'Eh?'

'Unless the stories are about themselves.'

'Oh, I git yer. I s'pose these was abart Mr Wilby?'

'And a girl.'

'Maudie.'

'We know that now, but I didn't know it then. It was just "a girl" Mr Wilby had been seen with at various places—at a race meeting, at a night club, in the park. There was no doubt about it. One weekend when I was away there was a bad scene in the West End where they both figured. Even if all the stories weren't true, some were, and on the only two occasions I spoke to him he wasn't able to give me an alibi, though he swore the tales weren't true.'

'Wot was that 'e couldn't give yer? Lullerby?' asked Ben.

'Oh, my God!'

'Eh? 'Ave I sed somethink?'

'No! Never mind! An alibi is proof that you were somewhere else when—'

'When yer wasn't where yer was,' Ben finished for her. 'Hallerby. Corse, that's it, on'y I fergot. Hallerby. Jes the sime, mum,' he went on, seriously, 'yer carn't orlways berlieve them hallerbies, becorse—well, s'pose yer spends orl day in a room by yerself, 'oo's there ter prove it for yer, but that don't mean it was you chucked the body in front o' the trine! P'r'aps Mr Wilby was by 'iself?'

'You're certainly working hard for him,' answered Mrs Wilby, with an appreciative smile, 'and I wish I could believe you were right, but he wasn't by himself when those photos you and I have both seen were taken!'

'Yer carn't git away from it,' Ben admitted gloomily.

'And—if further proof were needed—I found out myself, never mind how, that he'd used up nearly all his savings. He'd been spending heavily, and there was no clue to what he was spending it all on.'

'Yer mean 'e was spendin' it on Maudie?'

'Doesn't that seem clear?'

'Yer'd think so, yus, but mind yer, there's often a ketch in these things, and 'ere's one thing I've thort of wot—well, don't seem ter fit like.'

'What is it?'

'Well, mum—them letters wot seems ter 'ave started it orl off. The fust was from Orstraylyer, didn't yer say?'

'I said I thought so.'

'Well, Maudie ain't bin in Orstraylyer. Leastwise, it don't seem likely like. She lives at 'ome with 'er ma, and she works at Woolworth's, so where does Orstraylyer come in?'

'That's true,' agreed Mrs Wilby, 'now we've identified the girl as Maudie.'

'So 'oo's Orstraylyer?'

'The second letter came from Southampton.'

'Yus, she might of bin there, and then agine she might of done the telerphonin',' conceded Ben, 'and that fust letter from Orstraylyer mightn't of 'ad nothink ter do with it, but wot I carn't mike aht, mum, is—'

'Yes, but let me finish,' interrupted Mrs Wilby. 'I want to tell you something more about—yesterday. Something you don't know yet.' She paused. 'This is going to be difficult, but—yes? What is it?'

For Ben had begun to mumble.

'Well—it was jest this,' he answered. 'Yer've told me a lot, and o' corse I knows why yer done it—I mean, not becorse I orter know it but becorse we're sorter tryin' ter work it aht tergether like, ain't we, but I don't want ter 'ear nothink more wot yer doesn't want ter tell me—'

She interrupted him again, exclaiming nervily: 'You know so much that what does the rest matter? Listen, and let me get it over! Yesterday afternoon we went to a film—yes, Mr Wilby and I together. If that surprises you, it surprised me, because we hadn't done anything together for weeks. This is how it happened. I'd mentioned that I was going to this film if I could book a ticket—that was the day before yesterday—and in the evening he returned with two tickets. I expect he meant it as a sort of peace offering—you see, quite often he tried to make it up, but I wouldn't play—that seems rotten now when I think of it, as you may perhaps understand—so this time he took the matter in his own hands and bought the tickets.' She turned her head away, and her voice became a little unsteady, and as she went on Ben suddenly recalled the counterfoil he and Blake had found in the dead man's pocket. 'He had managed the afternoon off from the bank, and we were going to leave together, but about an hour before the time to start he suddenly came to me and told me he'd forgotten a business appointment, and would have to join me at the cinema, and might be a little late. He looked terribly worried—but that was nothing new—and of course I didn't believe him. How could I? But I didn't say anything, because what was there left to say? So I went alone—he had left the house at once—and—he *was* late. The feature film had begun before he slipped into his seat beside me in the dark. I paid no attention to him. We didn't exchange a word.

But I knew he had been drinking—I could smell his breath—and once he gave a—a kind of chuckle, as though he thought it funny. That finished me. I left my seat quickly and came home. I don't know whether he tried to stop me, or whether he followed me. I was too angry to notice. But he didn't follow me home, and when I got back here I was in such a state that I just wanted to end it. I—was ready to do anything.'

She stopped, and caught her breath.

'Yer—yer don't mean—' murmured Ben.

'No, not that!' she exclaimed, quickly and bitterly. 'I left that solution to George! You remember when you came along? You remember the moment?'

'Eh? Yus, o' corse.'

'I was just leaving the house, and I had a suitcase.'

'And yer wanted a taxi.'

'Yes, and if it hadn't been for you I'd have got one. You came along just in time to prevent me. You couldn't possibly guess where I was going!'

But the next moment, as Ben's head twisted involuntarily towards the mantelpiece, she wondered. Ben's mind had flashed back twenty-four hours, and in the light of his new knowledge small details that had previously passed almost unnoticed now impressed themselves. Foremost among them was the photograph of a good-looking man with a small dark moustache at which Mrs Wilby had glanced during that previous interview. The photograph was no longer on the mantelpiece.

'Well?' she said.

'I'm waitin' ter 'ear,' answered Ben.

'Do I have to tell you?' Ben looked uncomfortable. 'Was I wrong when I said you couldn't possibly guess?'

'Well—I just 'ad a thort, but I'd sooner not say it, in caise I was mistook.'

She replied evenly: 'If it was that I was about to leave my husband for a friend, you weren't mistaken. Are you shocked?'

Ben shook his head. 'Fair's fair,' he muttered.

'That was how it seemed to me. For a long while this man had been—interested in me, but it never occurred to me to take him seriously until this unhappiness began with my husband, and two days ago when he called—my husband was out—I very foolishly told him about it and he—just as foolishly—asked me to go away with him. And then yesterday, after that awful time at the cinema and after I'd got home, everything seemed to get on top of me and I acted like a lunatic . . . Am I acting like a lunatic again in telling *you* all this?' She did not give him time to reply, for she went on rapidly: 'But there's a reason, and now I'm coming to it. Do you remember when I left this room to telephone? It was after the police had gone. Do you remember?'

'Yus,' replied Ben. 'Was it to 'im?'

'You're good at the guessing game! It was, and I found that if I'd gone to his house he wouldn't have been there. He'd left suddenly two or three hours before. I telephoned again after I'd been to identify my husband—horrible!—but the contents of his pockets were recognisable!—and he hadn't returned. I 'phoned again today. He's not back yet, and no one seems to know where he is.' She paused, and fixed her eyes upon Ben quizzically. 'Well—does that suggest anything to you? Or not?'

But this time Ben refused the fence.

'I ain't doin' no more guessin', mum,' he answered. 'Wot did it serjest ter you?'

'I wondered whether his absence had anything to do

154

with my husband's death,' replied Mrs Wilby, 'and, if so, whether he was the man Blake—rightly or wrongly—had in mind?'

'I git yer,' murmured Ben. 'Yus, I git yer. Corse, yer ain't told the pleece abart 'im?'

'Hardly!'

'Corse not. That wouldn't be no good ter nobody.'

'At present, it certainly wouldn't! But if I found he *had* had anything to do with it I'd tell the police then. Whatever my husband may have done, I wouldn't shield his murderer.'

'I'm with yer, mum. I don't 'old with killin' barrin' it's fer yer country, and then I'd sooner some'un else did it. Do the pleece think it's murder?'

'I don't know. There's to be an inquest, of course, and but for what you've told me about this man Blake I'd believe they thought it was suicide. I might have thought so myself.'

'But no one fahnd no gun,' said Ben, 'and if yer shoots yerself the gun wot yer did it with don't run away!'

'Exactly, so they could hardly think it suicide. And then as they're trying to find Blake, doesn't that suggest they've got some clue?'

'That's right. *You* didn't put 'em on ter 'im, mum?'

'I? No! If I'd done that I'd have had to put them on to you, too. I told you, remember, that I hadn't mentioned you at all.'

'Yus, and I ain't fergot it. It was nice of yer, though if I gotter come inter it, I gotter. But wot I carn't mike aht is 'ow they got onter Blake if you and me ain't told 'em nothink.' All at once, forgetting such manners as he possessed, he gave a low whistle. 'I wunner?' he murmured. 'I wunner?'

'Wonder what?' she asked.

'Fingerprints! Yus, now, 'ow abart fingerprints?' He considered the notion intently. 'Corse, mine was there, too, but then I ain't never bin in quod, it's a fack, so mine ain't bin took, but if Blake's bin in quod, and 'e was the sorter chap wot mide yer think a cell wouldn't look nacherel withaht 'im, then they'd 'ave 'is fingerprints at the Yard, and that'd 'elp 'em ter trice 'im and foller 'im up. See, they got ways we don't know abart.'

'Do you mean that once people go to prison they are watched when they come out again?'

'Well, corse I dunno orl abart it, mum, 'cos I never bin inside, like I sed, but I was torkin' once to a bobby, yer can once yer know they don't want yer, and I arsked 'im if I was ever clapped in gaol if they'd foller me arterwards till I was in the 'erse, and 'e sed no, not if it was me fust offence and on'y a little 'un and they thort I wouldn't do it agine, but if I was one o' them 'ardened sort wot's got a long write-hup in the dosser, then they might keep an eye on where I was, sayin' they could, so if Blake was that sort and they spotted 'im by 'is fingerprints—well, they might 'ave knowed 'e was stayin' at Nummer 46, Jewel Street, mightn't they? If yer git me?'

After a few moments of silence Mrs Wilby got him, but before she could make any comment a bell sounded below. Ben glanced at his hostess with apprehensive inquiry.

'Back door,' murmured Mrs Wilby, with a frown. 'As the maid's out, I'll have to answer it.'

16

Face to Face

''Arf a mo, mum!' muttered Ben as Mrs Wilby moved towards the door.

She stopped and looked at him sharply.

'Do you mean you know who it is?' she asked.

'No, it's 'cos I don't know we gotter be careful—unless o' corse yer know yerself?' She shook her head. 'It wouldn't be the fish?'

'What fish?'

'Well, if yer'd ordered it, it'd 'ave ter come.'

'I'm not expecting anything, but don't worry. Stay here and I'll deal with whoever it is.'

'Beggin' yer pardon, mum,' replied Ben; 'but I think I better come with yer.'

'Why?'

'Jest in caise.'

'In case of what?'

'That's wot I mean. We dunno. That's when yer does things in caise, ain't it?'

The bell rang again. Mrs Wilby looked perplexed.

'It may be a policeman,' she said.

'If it is 'e won't see me,' promised Ben. 'Wot I thort was I'd stay on the bisement stairs be'ind yer, and on'y pop aht if yer wanted any 'elp.'

'I won't need any help!'

'Then I won't pop aht.'

Having learned by now the moments when Ben won, she gave him best and left the room, followed guardedly by her visitor. Half-way down the basement staircase she felt, rather than heard, him breathe into her ear:

'Better 'urry!'

'I thought you believed in caution!' she retorted nervily.

'Yus, at fust,' answered Ben; 'but once yer've decided ter open a door yer wanter open it quick in caise 'ooever it is goes away afore yer finds aht 'oo, see, tht's why yer doos it, and if yer laite yer've gotter go back and guess.'

'You seem to have worked it out!'

'There ain't much I don't know abart stairs and doors.'

'Do you spend all your life at this sort of thing?'

'Yer've sed it.'

He proved his knowlege by stopping at a bend eight stairs from the bottom while Mrs Wilby completed her descent. The back door was just in view from where Ben stood, and if it was a bobby behind it he could shinny back round the bend and listen, while if it was anyone dangerous, not to himself but to Mrs Wilby, he could leap the eight stairs and do his windmill act at the menace. This was to hit with all four limbs in rapid succession until they either won or lost.

He had told Mrs Wilby that he did not know who had rung the back door bell, and this was obviously true, but he had not told her that a very nasty possibility had entered

his mind—namely, that the back door visitor might be
Blake. If it were he certainly wanted to be by, whatever
the subsequent consequences to himself. He always had a
soft spot for people in trouble—a cynic or a psycho-analyst
might have described this as a subconscious form of self-
love—and for some reason which was quite beyond his
comprehension he had developed a particularly soft spot
for Mrs George Wilby. And in spite of the late Mr George
Wilby's naughtiness, it was rough luck on him losing her
like this. Ben felt sure that, given time, they'd of made it
up like.

For all of which reasons, the person outside the back
door as Mrs Wilby opened it looked like having a warm
reception should it turn out to be Oscar Blake.

But it was not Oscar Blake. Instead, a young woman
with very light hair and very red lips stared at Mrs Wilby,
while Mrs Wilby stared back. Ben, from his observation
post, stared also, and with an interest just as intense. The
eyes beneath the very light hair were not as hard as when
he had first seen them at another door—a front door in
Jewel Street. They were now uncertain and alarmed. But
there was no mistaking that they were the eyes through
which Maudie Kenton viewed her own particular and
peculiar world.

The mutual gazing match only lasted two or three
seconds. Whatever lay ahead of Maudie, and that was
clearly unpredictable, she chose it to what lay behind her,
and slipping suddenly inside she came to a second halt to
consider the next step.

Ben's admiration for Mrs Wilby increased as the tense
moments ticked by. You could hear them ticking from an
unseen clock in the unseen kitchen. You'd have thought

she'd have started storming at the girl, wouldn't you? Or ordered her out. Or fainted. Something, anyhow. But instead, what did she do? She moved to the open back door, now behind Maudie instead of in front of her, and quietly closed it, shutting out a fog-yellowed wall from view. Then she turned the key in the door and locked it. Then she spoke, and her voice was as quiet and controlled as her movements.

'You're Maud Kenton?' she asked.

'Yes—ma'am,' answered Maudie.

The 'ma'am' came as an afterthought.

'And have you something to tell me?'

Maudie did not answer at once. Her eyes travelled beyond the questioner to the stairs on which Ben stood. With her eyes still on Ben, she nodded, and Ben received an impression that what she had come here to tell was really for *him*.

'Come upstairs,' said Mrs Wilby, with sudden decision. 'We'll talk in the drawing-room.'

Up again! If any biographer of the future performed the surprising feat of writing Ben's life-story, the item 'Stairs' in the index would occupy a considerable number of pages.

It was a silent procession that trooped up to the drawing-room. Mrs Wilby broke the journey in the hall by going to the front door to ensure that it was secure against any surprise visitation, as was the door below. When they were all in the drawing-room she motioned Maudie to a chair, and said: 'Well?'

She had to repeat the word before Maudie answered, 'I don't know how I ought to begin.' And again the girl's eyes sought Ben's.

('It's me she wants,' thought Ben.)

'Why not begin by saying why you've come? Is anyone following you?'

'I—don't know.'

'Try and know something presently, please,' begged Mrs Wilby calmly. Ben was impressed by her calmness, but not deceived by it; he guessed what she must be controlling. 'If anyone *is* following you, who would it be? A policeman?'

'I—yes, it might be.'

'Or, if not, a man named Blake?'

Maudie looked startled. Then she shot out a question of her own.

'You know about Blake, then?'

'I know what I have been told by . . .' Mrs Wilby paused, and turned to Ben. 'What am I supposed to call you? So far I know you as Ben and Eric Burns. Please tell me which I am to use?'

'I'd like to know that, too,' interposed Maudie, with a little more courage.

'Well, it ain't Eric Burns, that's wot Blake mide up,' replied Ben, 'so yer can tike yer choice o' wot's left.'

Her normal reactions completely at sea, Mrs Wilby smiled, though only for an instant. Now turning back to Maudie, she went on:

'I know what Ben has told me—'

But Maudie interposed again.

'It's him I've come to see. I guessed he might be here—it's him I've got to tell something to.'

'Yes, I have been gathering that,' answered Mrs Wilby; 'but as you are seeing him in my house you will hardly expect me to go out of the room while you and he have a heart-to-heart. Especially as I am quite sure that what you may have to tell him concerns me as well. And there is one other thing, Miss Kenton, which so far you and I have not mentioned, though I am not sure yet if this is the precise moment for it. Do I have to tell you what that is?'

Maudie flushed, and was silent.

'Evidently not. I think what you have to tell Ben must be exceedingly important for you to have risked coming to my house. Don't you agree?'

Still flushing, Maudie now responded: 'It is important—and you're behaving nicer than I thought.'

'Thank you. Though I dare say you thought you might manage not to see me at all?'

'That's right, I hoped I wouldn't. I meant to just inquire below if he was here.'

'But my maid is out. That was unfortunate.'

All at once Maudie looked at Mrs Wilby directly.

'I'm not so sure,' she said. 'Not now.'

'Oh? Why not?' queried Mrs Wilby, surprised.

'Because p'r'aps I've got something to tell you, too,' Maudie responded. 'Yes, I expect I'd better. I expect it'd come out anyhow. If you want the truth, I'm all dizzy. Could I have a drink of water, do you think?'

'Nothing stronger?'

'Not on your life. I mean, no. I've had that!'

Mrs Wilby hesitated, then rose from her chair and left the room. Ben wondered what Mrs Wilby herself had been wondering. Was this a little ruse of Maudie's to have a few moments with him alone? But, if so, she did not follow it up. When she spoke she said:

'She seems okay.'

'She is okay,' answered Ben. ''Ow abart you?'

162

'When I die, they'll put me in an express to heaven,' retorted Maudie. 'You see!'

Mrs Wilby returned with the glass of water. Maudie gulped it down, and while she was doing so Ben remarked:

'She wanted that, mum, it weren't no trick. She didn't tell me nothink!'

'I wasn't really worrying,' returned Mrs Wilby. 'I knew that if you had been told anything I needed to know while I was out of the room, you would have repeated it. There is a truthfulness about our friend Ben, Miss Kenton, which you and I might do well to copy—even though it's a little embarrassing at times. Will it help you if I tell you that he has told me everything that happened during his visit to your house? At least, I think everything.'

'I on'y left aht wot I fergot,' corroborated Ben.

'So let us save repetition. I know it is you who have been about with my late husband. Well, now I have met you, I should know that, anyhow. I know that a man called Oscar Blake has been staying at your house, and that he is not staying there any longer. He seems to have disappeared since—yesterday afternoon. I know that you yourself disappeared this morning after breakfast, and that you did not turn up at Woolworth's, where you work. I know that a policeman called to see Blake yesterday after he had gone, and that he called again to see you today, after *you* had gone. Is that enough to go on with?'

Maudie nodded.

'Yes,' she replied; 'but one of the things you don't know is that it wasn't *my* idea to go about with your husband.'

'You mean, it was his idea?' asked Mrs Wilby. 'You mean he started it?'

'Well—yes—I suppose you'd say so.'

'But you must know!'

'What I mean is, he must have wanted it, but it was Oscar—it was Blake—who fixed it all up.'

Mrs Wilby shook her head.

'I don't think I understand that.'

'Of course you don't, not till I tell you,' answered Maudie, growing red. 'You see—well, I did it for money. All right, all right, I'm not white-washing myself, I'm telling you. I wasn't interested in your husband. If you want the truth—and you said you wanted it—I didn't care for him very much. In fact, not at all!'

'I see.' Mrs Wilby took a deep breath to steady herself. 'He just paid you.'

'No, Blake paid me. It was like this. Blake came to me one day and said he knew somebody who wanted a friend—that's all, just a friend—and if I'd play it would be worth my while. So I played, and every time I went out with him—Mr Wilby—I got a nice little packet.'

'Let me try and get this quite straight,' interposed Mrs Wilby. 'This man Blake introduced you to my husband, and then dropped out—so why did he go on paying you?'

'Because he didn't drop out. It was always Blake who fixed things up. If he was at the house he'd let me know there, and if he wasn't, and he often wasn't, then he'd—he'd leave a message at a shop we'd agreed on, or even write to me there saying he was away. One thing I had to do when he was away was to call at the shop twice a day to see if there was a letter.' She paused. 'And today—well, I'll come to that in a moment. What I want to say first, though, is that Mr Wilby and I only went about together. I expect you know what I mean when I tell you that. I never brought him home—in fact, Mother never saw him—Blake said I

164

wasn't to let him know where I lived—and we never went to any hotel or anything.' Suddenly a rather belated spark of independence kindled within her. 'I'd have needed a damn sight more than I was getting for that! In fact, he could have sung for it!'

'Thank you,' responded Mrs Wilby, 'for relieving my mind on that score so gracefully. The situation, then, was that the man Blake engaged you to give Mr Wilby a good time, but that you were strictly instructed not to go beyond getting drunk.'

'We only did that once!' flared Maudie. 'And then I didn't want to.'

'We won't go into it.'

'No! But how did you know? That wasn't in the papers! Or was it?'

'I got to know quite a good deal, Miss Kenton. More than once I was 'phoned by a kind well-wisher who never gave his name. I am wondering whether that was your friend Mr Blake.'

'No friend of mine, thank you! I've finished with him! I was a respectable girl before he got me into this, though I'm not asking you to believe it.'

'My opinion can hardly matter to you. What more have you to tell me?'

Maudie frowned, then swung round in her chair and addressed Ben.

'I expect you'll want to know what happened to me this morning?' she said.

'Wot did?' he asked. 'You sed you was comin' back ter lunch.'

'I know I did.'

'And then yer was goin' ter tell me orl abart it.'

'Yes, and I meant to.'

'Why didn't yer?'

'Because I got the wind up. When I began thinking outside I felt I was getting into a jam, and then when I thought someone was following me that put the lid on. I went right round a block to test it, and the footsteps came round after me. So then I jumped on a passing bus, and then I got off the bus and jumped on to another. Call me silly if you like—after all, I'd done nothing the law could nab me for—but once funk gets you you're done, and the funk got me this morning right and proper! I expect I'd been holding on to myself without knowing it, and all at once everything snapped. I don't expect you to understand it.'

'Lummy, I unnerstans it,' said Ben sympathetically. 'Yer starts runnin', and it's no good torkin' ter yer legs! Wot 'appened then?'

'I cooled down a bit when I knew I'd shaken whoever it was off—'

'The fog'd 'elp yer—'

'Of course. But I was already late for my job, and I couldn't face a row, and more than that I didn't want to risk going to Woolworth's where the police might know I worked and be waiting for me, so I decided not to turn up there at all and to say I'd been taken ill when I turned up tomorrow. Yes, but that didn't get me through today, did it? I was in a proper tangle, and I wanted time to work something out. So I just walked about like a fool and a lunatic, and couldn't work out anything. I'll say I was tired! Talk about a headache! . . . Well, nobody here's going to worry about that, I expect! Not but that you haven't taken it better than I thought you would, Mrs Wilby, I have to say that. Anyhow, when I found it was lunch time

I got a bite somewhere, and perhaps that put back a little of my sense—what was I running away from?—I was daft!—and suddenly I thought of the tobacconist where I got messages and wondered if there'd be one. So I went there and inquired, and there *was*!'

Ben's eyes opened wide.

'Wot! From Blake?'

'Yes. A telegram, but though it was addressed to me—well, of course, it had to be—the message was for you. It said—wait a moment.' She opened a smart, red leather bag she carried—Mrs Wilby wondered whether Mr Wilby had bought it for her—and drew out the telegram. Then she read out: '"Tell Eric take 7.12 pm train Euston to Penridge change Applewold will meet Penridge station good and important news for all no time to lose so don't fail." And it's signed O.B. There it is.'

She handed the pale pink form to Ben, and after he had read it he passed it on to Mrs Wilby. Meanwhile Maudie went on:

'I didn't know what to do at first. See, I wanted to drop it. But then I thought I'd better pass the message on, though it meant going home to do it. But I couldn't stay out for ever, could I? Anyway, I went back, and no one pounced on me outside the house as I'd expected they might, and found mother in a fair stew. She told me what had happened and how you'd left while the police were there, and she fair got my goat the way she went on, so I left her again as soon as I could, and somehow got a hunch you might have come here. Well, there wasn't anywhere else I could look for you, was there? So I came along, and this time I *was* followed again, at least I think so, once you get that feeling everybody's a policeman in disguise, but I didn't make for here till I was pretty sure I'd shaken them off again—that is, if there was ever anyone to shake off!—and—well, now you know the lot!'

And having reached the end of her narration she suddenly became conscious that she had also reached the end of her mission, and jumped up; but only to sit down again nervously to await the next step. Mrs Wilby seemed no more certain of what the next step should be, and Ben found the eyes of both women upon him.

In his view, the next step was obvious. It was the seven-twelve from Euston.

17

What Happened at Euston

The hands of the large clock pointed to fourteen minutes to seven when Ben entered Euston station. This meant that he had twenty-six minutes for reflection before the seven-twelve began its journey into the unpredictable future, and he would rather have been without them. Once the journey had started there could be no change of decision, no turning back. The policy he had advocated in Mrs Wilby's drawing-room would be set in motion with the train, and before he would have to stir again in either mind or body there would be not far short of a dozen hours of drowsy, uneventful comfort. Saying he got a corner seat. But before this temporary haven was reached these twenty-six minutes had to be endured, and he had to continue his wavering insistence that he was right.

Not that he had met with any violent opposition. Maudie indeed had hardly entered the discussion at all, sitting silent and deflated after her spate of words, and Mrs Wilby had not pressed her suggestion that Blake's telegram should be handed to the police. Ben had expected that she would, and was surprised that she did not, for there was much to be said for the suggestion. This had become more and more obvious to him as he groped his way Eustonwards to continue his own detective duty. But if the police had been informed it would have involved bringing not only himself but Maudie under their notice, and he had no relish for this until it became quite definitely unavoidable.

'And then,' he had argued, 'wot 'appens if the pleece do see this telegram? Do they tike the trine theirselves? Orl right! Say they do. Blake ain't no mug, and it ain't likely 'e'll show 'iself to a bobby 'oo gits aht o' the trine! 'E'll proberly be 'idin' somewhere, be'ind a trunk or somethink, and on'y come aht when 'e sees Eric!'

To this Mrs Wilby had responded that the police were not mugs, either, and that if they wanted to surprise a man they would hardly appear in uniform, but Ben still held out.

'Blokes like Blake,' he argued, 'could smell a copper if yer put im in a piller-caise.'

And then, quite suddenly, Mrs Wilby had yielded her point, and had agreed that Ben should make the journey alone, and had provided the money for the return fare.

So here he was. With the question of the police still worrying him, like grit in your eye. And here was a policeman, just ahead of him, so there was still time to put the police wise if he wanted to!

He paused behind the policeman—well behind—and the policeman had no notion of the imaginary conversation that was going on in the mind of the individual in his rear.

'Oi, copper!'

'Hallo!'

'I got somethink ter tell yer.'

'Carry on.'

'Yer know that chap wot was fahnd dead in the cellar yesterday in Norgate Road?'

'What about it?'

'Nummer 15.'

'Is that all you've got to tell me?'

'Well, there was two blokes fahnd 'im afore the pleece did, and one of 'em was a feller called Blake and the other was me, and a telergram come this arternoon to a gal 'e knows where I was stayin' at a shop, not where I was stayin' but where the telergram went, I bein' Eric wot 'e calls me, and it sed . . .'

No, thanks!

Now finally giving up the idea of informing the police, Ben moved towards the ticket office. Someone, not a policeman, followed him, but he remained blissfully unconscious of this. He felt a little flustered, however, when he reached the ticket office and thrust four pound notes through the aperture with the rather hoarsely-delivered words, 'Return ter Penridge.' Mrs Wilby had looked up the cost in her *ABC*, and the amount had staggered him. Fancy payin' orl that and 'avin' nothink ter show fer yer money arterwards bar bein' where yer'd got ter! It was beyond the region of Ben's simple logic. On the rare occasions when he permitted himself the luxury of travelling otherwise than on foot it was usually no farther than to the nearest ground of a local football team. All he got back from his four pounds—or Mrs Wilby's four pounds—was one shilling and twopence.

'It don't mike sense,' he murmured as he turned away.

171

'Don't you want your ticket?' called the clerk.

'Lummy, yus, I pide enough fer it!' replied Ben as he turned back and snatched it. Somebody approaching the spot ducked back as he did so.

He now had twenty-three minutes. What should he do with them? A cup of tea didn't seem a bad idea, so he made for the buffet. So, well behind him, did the somebody who had ducked back. The tea cost threepence, reducing his one and twopence to elevenpence, but in addition to this he had nearly all of the five pounds Mrs Wilby had given him on the previous day. She had financed the expedition lavishly, and had Ben known he had a pursuer he would have assumed that his unusual wealth had become known and was attracting the underworld.

The tea warmed him, but when he discovered he had lingered over it and that his twenty-three minutes had diminished to thirteen, he wondered anxiously whether this preliminary luxury had cost him the desired corner seat. Annoyed with himself, for Ben did love a corner, he hurried to his platform. It was the same platform as that along which someone else had hurried exactly twenty-four hours earlier with similar ignorance that he was being followed, and history now repeated itself with new actors.

Ben's love of a corner was coupled with a love of solitude, which after all expresses the attitude of the majority of Britishers who travel by train, and he found the desired empty compartment in a coach far up the platform and near the engine. The expected sense of peace pervaded him as he opened the compartment door, entered, closed the door, and sank down in the corner next to it facing the engine. It was now three minutes past seven, and only nine minutes remained before the train would glide out of the station. Of course, plenty could happen in nine minutes. You could fall off a roof, bounce on a pavement, and find yourself on an operating table. Or you could run a couple of miles from a Chinaman. Or, saying you played for the Arsenal, you could score half a dozen goals. Bringing the possibilities nearer home, Scotland Yard could answer a 999 call, follow a clue, dispatch a police car to Euston, and produce a policeman with an enormous hand that would hoik Ben out of his comfortable seat. But although there was always one element in Ben's composition ready to be resigned to anything, and therefore subconsciously expecting it, his mood at the beginning of these final nine minutes was beautifully peaceful. Heaven, surely must be something like this! Were there corner seats in Heaven? There must be, or how could it be Heaven. A corner seat—no one to talk to you, or to make you talk to them—a nice softness at your back—a pretty coloured picture of somewhere or other opposite, a picture seen hazily through half-closed lids—warm tea still winding its way pleasantly through one's distant lower regions—sounds growing fainter—coloured picture growing dimmer—no yesterday— no tomorrow—only this tiny little moment that belonged completely to oneself and to nobody else—now not even the moment, because now there was nothing, nothing at all . . .

The dissolved coloured picture began to resolve again. The extinguished station sounds rediscovered their voices, soft and tremendously distant at first, then gradually growing louder and nearer and harsher. A shout. Somebody being ordered to stand away? A whistle, which conjured a vision of a guard's green flag. Then, much closer, the unmistakable voice of the engine, and—at last!—that long-desired, soul-satisfying sense of movement.

The journey northwards had begun, and Ben opened his eyes wide with a sigh of contentment. And found himself staring into the eyes of Maudie Kenton.

18

Two in a Train

Oh, no! This couldn't be! So Ben closed his eyes again, as he always did to give logic a second chance. But when he reopened them logic had refused to respond, and Maudie Kenton was still there.

'Nice little surprise packet for you?' she laughed.

'Go on!' answered Ben.

It was hardly adequate, but it takes a little time to get back into your stride. She laughed again.

'We are going on, aren't we?' she said. 'All the way to Cumberland. Don't look so stunned! Not much of a compliment, I must say! You ought to be pleased.'

Ben shook his head, implying his total lack of comprehension.

'I don't git it,' he said.

'What don't you get? It's simple.'

'I don't git wotcher doin' 'ere?'

'Same as you, looks like. Going to Penridge.'

'Yer mean, orl the way?'

'Well, I'm not going to waste three pounds eighteen

shillings and tenpence! There's my suitcase on the rack.'
While Ben raised his eyes to the small, rather shabby suitcase above the coloured pictures she rattled on: 'Wicked,
what they stick you these days for fares! I nearly fainted!
Where's *your* luggage?'

'Eh?'

'Travelling a bit light, aren't you? Or is your trunk in
the van?'

Ben made an effort. 'Look 'ere,' he expostulated. 'When
are you goin' ter start torkin' sense?'

'I am talking sense,' she retorted, with a grin. He could
not decide whether she really felt as gay as this, or whether
she was putting it on. 'If you've brought nothing with you
I'll have to lend you my second pair of pyjamas. How far
is Penridge from Gretna Green? Any idea? We ought to
get spliced to save a scandal!'

Ben counted ten slowly to himself, and then tried again.

'Nah, listen, miss,' he said. 'I dunno wot's at the back
of yer mind, but I'll tell yer wot's at the back o' mine. It's
this 'ere. It ain't goin' ter 'elp matters if you git aht at
Penridge staishun alongside o' me!'

'Isn't it?'

'I arsk yer!'

'So what?'

'I can tell yer wot! Git aht at the fust stop and go back
'ome!'

'Thank you for nothing!'

'It's fer yer own good—'

'How about your own good? But don't let's worry about
anybody's good for the moment. We're both here, so let's
make the best of it. And after all, haven't you forgotten
something?'

'Wot?'

'Oscar Blake's at the other end of our journey—'

'I ain't fergot that!'

'But what you've forgotten is that I've known him longer than you have, and have more interest in him than you have, and that the telegram that is taking you to him was sent to me.

'That's fair enough,' agreed Ben; 'but the telegram didn't say nothink abart you comin' with me!'

'No, but if I choose to come along, that's my own business.'

Ben blinked, then answered: 'Orl right, but 'ere's something that's my bizziness. Yer've follered me along 'ere, ain't yer? Orl right. But wot I want ter know is—'oose side are yer on? See, when I know that, I'll know 'ow ter treat yer!'

Maudie regarded Ben quizzically. 'This is a rum business, however you look at it,' she replied, 'but as you've just said my point was fair, I'll be fair in return and say yours is, too. I don't trust many people any more than I expect them to trust me—how's that for honest?—and I'm not going to pretend I can make you out, but from what I've seen of you both at my place and at Mrs Wilby's I'll say you seem to be straight, so here's a straight answer. I'm on the side where my bread's buttered, and you can work that one out for yourself!'

'Give us a mo' and I will,' promised Ben.

'Then you'll be cleverer than me!'

But Ben shook his head. 'It's easy, miss, if yer knows wot yer aht for.'

'How about explaining that?'

'Wot I means is that if yer aht ter try and mike a bit

more by the quick way yer'll chum up with Blake agine, sayin' 'e'll 'ave yer, wich yer don't know, and see if yer lucky—'

'Is that your *own* little idea?'

'I thort yer knoo better! Yer sed I was stright, and would it be stright ter go up ter meet Blake on Mrs Wilby's ticket and then drop 'er?'

'Sorry! Go on.'

'Where was I? Oh, yus. Yer'll do that—join up with Blake—or yer'll say ter yerself like, "I've worked with Blake once and where's it got me, dirty gimes don't pay," 'cos it was a dirty gime, wer'n't it, yer carn't git away from it, miss, and where it's got yer is on the wrong side o' the pleece, with the bloke yer was messin' abart with dead, and 'is wife a widder, and so wot's goin' ter be next, and so yer'll say, "It ain't good enough, I've begun goin' stright, and I'll go on goin' stright and I'll drop aht at the fust stop and keep aht, or I'll stay along and see if I can hend hup better'n I begun." If yer git me?'

'Sakes! Is this a sermon?' asked Maudie.

'Yer mean like wot they sez in church?' replied Ben. 'Lummy, fancy me a parson!'

'Not so hard as you think! You'd get anyone tied up! But—let's work this out! We've got all night, and it's a new experience to talk this kind of stuff. You wouldn't call it straight to double-cross Mrs Wilby?'

'Would *you*?'

'P'r'aps not. But I'm to double-cross Blake?'

'Yer wouldn't, not if yer got aht at the nex' staishun.'

'But I would if I stayed here and sided with you!'

'In a way—yus,' Ben agreed.

'Well, then?'

'If you can't see it, I can't show yer.'

'Everything's worth trying once.'

'Okay. Do yer stand fer murder?'

'I didn't murder Mr Wilby!'

'No, but we're tryin' ter find aht 'oo did, and Blake sez 'e knows. Would it matter ter double-cross a bloke like Blake ter git at the truth?'

She did not answer, but looked impressed. Encouraged, Ben went on:

'And there's another thing, miss. *We* know yer didn't murder Mr Wilby, and that yer don't know nothin' abart it, lettin' alone 'avin' any concern in it, but do the pleece know it?'

'What do you mean?' she asked sharply.

'Well, they're wantin' ter see yer, ain't they—or 'ave they seen yer?'

She shook her head.

'Then we can tike it they still want ter. We dunno jest why, but s'pose they've got on ter wot yer *'ave* done, and s'pose they argies—'

'Argies?'

'Eh? That's wot yer does when yer tries ter work things aht. S'pose they argies, "She was in with Blake—it was Blake got 'er ter go abart with Mr Wilby—she might of 'ad a quarrel with Mr Wilby, and arter a quarrel anythink might 'appen, so we gotter put 'er among the succerspects till we know she's clear." Do yer git wot I mean? It won't be till we find aht 'oo did do it that yer'll stop bein' a succerspect. Sime as me.'

She looked at him with a kind of helpless admiration.

'What beats me hollow,' she said, 'is where you picked up your sense!'

'Along with fag-ends,' he answered, with a wink.

'You ought to be in Parliament, the way you can talk!'

'That's wot Churchill sed larst time I dined with 'im, but—well, it seemed a shime ter cut 'im aht.'

She took a little cigarette-case from her red leather handbag, and after extracting a cigarette and putting it between her highly-coloured lips held the case out to him. As he eyed the case—it was silver, and looked new—she remarked, with a rather twisted smile: 'I guess your thought—it's correct.'

'Mr Wilby give it to yer?' he said.

'Only the case, so you needn't worry about the cigarette. But p'r'aps you'd like to change your compartment?'

'Why?'

'Being seen with a girl like me!'

Taking the proffered cigarette, he replied: ''Ave I blimed yer? We're born like we are, and it ain't easy ter chinge. Lummy, I've tried orl me life, but I orlways come aht the sime!'

'I say, you've worked out the lot, haven't you?'

They puffed in silence for a minute while the train bore them on towards their strange goal. A young man with a weak chin came along the corridor, paused at the entrance, peered in, and then passed on.

Maudie gave a short laugh.

'He'd have changed *his* compartment, if you hadn't been here!' she remarked.

'Then I've sived yer from somethink,' answered Ben.

'Yes—I'm beginning to wonder how much you're saving me from,' she responded. 'But now let me talk for a bit, because you've got something about me wrong. It's my own fault, though—through something I said.'

'Wot was that?' he asked.

'About which side my bread was buttered. That wasn't the real reason I came—not this time. Or p'r'aps it would be more honest to say it wasn't the whole reason. One reason was those inquisitive policemen you've just been talking about.'

'Still callin', are they?'

'Yes, and I'm not keen to meet them till I know a bit more how things are.'

'Yus, but—'

'Whoa, didn't you hear? I'm talking now! When I got back from Mrs Wilby's, or just before I got back, more properly speaking, I saw a bobby coming away. I even heard him tell Mother that he'd call again later, and that if I returned in the meanwhile she was to keep me home. So what did little Maudie do? I've said you were good at guessing, but you won't guess *this*!'

'I don't need ter, as yer goin' ter tell me.'

'Yes, I'm telling you. I slipped round to the back, and I got our short steps out of the lean-to shed, and I put them on the roof of the shed, and I went up them and in through a back window. I may say I've done it before when I've come home late!'

'Did yer Ma ketch yer?'

'She didn't, or I mightn't be here. There'd have been the hell of a row, and when she knew I wasn't staying she'd probably have run out into the street calling "Fire" or something! But she didn't get the chance. I heard her below, waiting for me to come back through the front door, while I was busy packing my suitcase for my getaway. And when I'd done it I let it down to the shed roof by a rope, and then followed it down myself. Pretty smart work, don't you think?'

181

'I—dunno,' murmured Ben.

'Are you going to disappoint me?'

'It was a smart gitaway, yus. On'y—I ain't so sure abart the idea, see?'

'You think it would have been smarter to have waited and let the police badger me?'

'P'r'aps not. Not since this wasn't the beginnin' o' maikin' yerself scarce. But didn't yer leave no note or nothink?'

'What could I have said in it?'

'Won't she worry?'

'Mother? About herself. Not about me!'

'Oh! Well, wot abart Woolworth's?'

'I've got measles! Didn't you know it?'

'Yer need a doctor's word fer that.'

'Right again, as usual. But I'm not troubling about Woolworth's. That'll have to look after itself when the time comes. And as this is a real heart-to-heart, hadn't I better tell you another reason I did what I did? You won't believe it, but it's a fact. This has got on my nerves proper! I don't think I *could* sit down quiet, or sell paper and notebooks across a counter—not until I've seen this blasted thing through! You're quite right, what you said. I knew it all before, but it's helped, hearing you say it, too. Those short cuts to glory lead you bang into a wall! I've finished with Oscar Blake—I told you I had way back in Jewel Street, didn't I?—God, already that seems a week ago!—and if I can help you to clean up this mess, I'm all for it!'

She paused, rather breathless, and the train began to slacken speed. They sat silent until it had stopped and had started moving again. Then Maudie said:

'I *haven't* got out—I'm still here!'

The young man with the weak chin came along the corridor again, glanced in, and passed on.

'Yus, and so'm I still 'ere,' grinned Ben. 'That bloke's 'avin' no luck ternight, is 'e?'

19

Conference over Coffee

Roused from fitful sleep by that queer subconscious instinct that makes most of us wake up at the right time, Ben and Maudie opened their eyes as the train began to slacken speed before Applewold.

The station into which they glided was only just waking itself in the greyness of dawn, and the few passengers who emerged on to the platform after the train had stopped looked like ghosts flitting away before the full daylight caught them. Two of the ghosts, emerging from the coach behind Ben's and Maudie's, flitted swiftly into the shadow of a wall, while Ben and Maudie stood to decide the details of the plan they had agreed on in the train.

'I can't say I'm sold on the idea,' muttered Maudie.

'We ain't goin' orl over it agine, are we?' begged Ben.

Maudie had originally objected to the plan, and now looked like renewing her objections. It was that Ben should go from Applewold to Penridge alone, and that she should follow on the next train.

'How long shall I have to wait?' she demanded.

'I dunno that yet no more'n you do,' he answered.

'Suppose there are only a couple of trains a day?'

'Then I'll be on the fust and you'll be on the second. There's a porter—we'll arsk 'im.'

The porter, after eyeing them with vague curiosity and registering the private opinion that a pretty girl like this might have found a better travelling companion than a queer cove like that, informed them that the connection for Penridge would be along in two hours, and that if they had good pairs of legs they could almost walk it in the time.

'Why, how far is Penridge from here, then?' inquired Maudie.

'Not more'n fifteen miles,' the porter told her.

'Fifteen miles! No tha-nk you! That's beyond my limit for a day! How often do the trains run to Penridge after the next one?'

'There's another in just over an hour.'

'And I suppose we wait in a cold and cheerless waiting-room?'

'You can get a cup o' coffee at the Station Hotel just across the road,' the porter said, 'unless Bella's over-sleepin'.'

'If she is we'll wake her, don't *you* worry!' retorted Maudie. 'Is there a hotel at Penridge, too?'

'Ay. Station Hotel. They all seem to be called that along the line.'

Bella undoubtedly looked as though she had overslept when she admitted them. Her eyes were glassy, and her hair sprayed in all directions like a bed of untidy brown grass. 'Looks as if a cat 'ad sat in it,' was Ben's comment as they settled down in a chilly room to two large cups of coffee. But the coffee warmed them, and they were in a mood to be thankful for small mercies. 'If I took a room here,' Maudie remarked, 'I might finish my beauty sleep as I've got three hours to wait!' Then, half-way through her cup, she returned to the attack.

'You know, this waiting's going to get my goat!' she frowned.

'It'd git orl our goats if yer came along with me and upset the 'ole apple-cart!' replied Ben. 'That's wot it'd do!'

'I'm not so sure.'

'Ain't yer?'

'Why should he suspect me, any more than you think he'll suspect you?'

''E won't suspeck yer—'

'There you are!'

''Cos we ain't goin' ter give 'im the charnce! You finish yer beauty sleep, like yer sed. Or wot abart a walk?'

Maudie turned ironical eyes towards the window. The grey shroud was changing to a white film.

'Hardly the weather for joy-walking!'

'It ain't. Funny 'ow mist follers me abart.'

'Well, anyhow, it's cleaner mist up here than what we left in London. I expect this is what they call mountain mist, and we're getting it being so high up.'

'No, we're gettin' it because I'm 'ere,' insisted Ben. 'Yer don't need no other reason.' He looked at her apprehensively. 'So *that's* fixed, ain't it? You stay 'ere, and I goes on.'

'Seems so,' she sighed, grudgingly, 'and if I haven't died of gaiety, what do I do when *I* go on?'

Ben sighed, also. This was asking a bit much, wasn't it? How can you work out what you don't know?

'I reckon yer'll 'ave ter use yer dissercrashun,' he said.

'My what?'

'Eh? That means when yer does a thing wot yer thinks best at the time wot yer does it. Fer instance, if I ain't there yer might describe me like and arsk people if they'd seed me. There wouldn't be two.'

'People?'

'No, me.'

Maudie gave a short laugh. 'Looks to me as if, once we've separated, we may spend the rest of the day trying to find each other again! How about this? You heard me asking the porter if there was a hotel at Penridge?'

'Tha's right. Staishun 'Otel, sime as this 'un.'

'Well, if you're not on the platform I'll find out if you're at the hotel, and if you're not, and there's no message—you might be able to leave one there if you need to—then I'll wait till you do turn up, or a message comes along.'

'That's wot I calls brinework,' answered Ben appreciatively.

'Thanks for the applause! So for the moment that's me. Now about you. Have you decided what *you're* going to do?'

'Eh? We knows that. I'm goin' on a'ead—'

'Yes, but what are you going to do when you meet Oscar Blake? Throw your arms round his neck and kiss him?'

Ben grinned. 'I 'adn't thort of it.'

'What have you thought of? You don't want to get stuck for an idea.'

'Tha's right, on'y if yer dunno wot's ter foller the on'y idea yer can git is 'ow ter start! Ain't it? So wot I gotter do is ter start bein' friendly so's ter mike 'im tork.'

She nodded. 'And I wonder what he's going to talk about?'

'Well, one thing'd be 'is plan fer mikin' a bit, wouldn't it? That might 'ave nothink ter do with the murder, but my bet is that it 'as, and corse, that's wot I gotter git 'im onter—'oo did it, if 'e knows, and if '*e* didn't?'

'You still think he might have done it himself then?'

'Well, it wouldn't mike me fall dahn in a faint!'

'I hope not! You'll need to keep your wits—and you'll need to be careful!'

'Yer needn't worry abart that, miss,' Ben assured her. 'I won't say nothink abart me wits, but I spends 'arf me life bein' careful, and helefunts walkin' on wine-glasses ain't got nothink on me, miss!'

She smiled. 'You'd make a cat laugh. When are you going to call me Maudie, Eric?'

'Eh? Oh! Well, I'll 'ave a shot at Maudie if you'll stop the Eric. Ben's wot they wrote dahn somewhere when I was born, sayin' they wrote dahn anythink. Is there any more corfee?'

'Yes, let's fill our cups, and see where we've got to. If I'd thought this time yesterday that in twenty-four hours you and me'd be drinking coffee together somewhere in Cumberland I'd have had five fits! Don't ask me if it's a scream or a tragedy! Just as well we don't know what life's got in store for us sometimes, isn't it?' They began their second cups. 'Where *have* we got to?'

'Staishun 'Otel, Penridge,' Ben reminded her. 'Yer waitin' there ter find aht where *I've* got ter. That was it, weren't it?'

'Yes, and I believe I'm getting somewhere, too! Wait a moment—I'm chasing something—'

'Where?'

'Oh, my God! A thought! Listen. Suppose you bring

back some news. Don't say "Where?" again! To the hotel where I'm waiting.'

'Not this 'un, the other 'un.'

'Of course! Do we pass it on to Mrs Wilby or the police?'

'Lummy, 'ow do we know afore we know wot it is?' complained Ben. 'You wanter 'ave the 'ole thing done afore we starts!'

'No, but I want to know where we think we're going before we start, even if we never get there,' retorted Maudie. 'Listen, something may happen like this. You may get hold of some information but not be able to leave. Blake may stick too close to you, or you may want to stay around— either to get some more information, or because you'll want to keep your eyes on him to see he doesn't slip away again when he may be wanted. Do you get all that?'

'I git it.'

'Right! Then that's where I may come in. You'll know I'll be at the hotel—most probably—and you must find some way of contacting me—'

'Cong wot?'

'Of getting in touch with me—coming to me or 'phoning to me or sending a message somehow or other—don't ask me to work out every detail!—and then I could pass on the information to whoever we decided was best.'

'Yer mean, ter Mrs Wilby or the pleece, sayin' I carn't do nothink fer some reason we can't think of, accordin' ter wot it is and wich we want.'

Maudie blinked. 'Half a minute while I work that one out! . . . Yes, I think that's about it. He won't know I'm here—if we start keeping me dark we must go on doing it—so I'll be free to move where I want to. I could even go back to London to see Mrs Wilby, if it was necessary.'

Ben looked at her with admiration.

'Yer'd do that?' he asked.

'You keep on forgetting I'm here to help.'

'Tha's right. And like you say, I may find I wants a messidger. On'y, corse, if I finds aht 'oo done the murder, it'll 'ave ter be the pleece, won't it? No matter 'ow you and me figger like?'

'I expect so.'

'There ain't no expeck abart it. But, mind yer, if I find aht 'oo done it, that'd mean we ain't.'

'Aren't you a little ray of sunshine?'

Ignoring the gentle sarcasm, Ben continued, following his own line of thought: 'Yes, one carn't play abart with murder, it'd 'ave ter be the pleece, and if yer want the truth, I've 'arf chainged me mind and p'r'aps we orter've told 'em the lot in Lunnon. Mrs Wilby was fer it at fust, wasn't she, even though it might of meant gettin' 'er boyfriend inter trouble.' He did not notice Maudie's eyes suddenly sharpen. 'It's goin' ter be narsty if we find as it was 'im done it, but I reckon she's ready ter fice up ter that now, if she wasn't afore, and when yer thinks of it 'e couldn't be much good, could 'e, if 'e was arter Mrs Wilby afore 'er 'usband was popped orf ter mike 'er free like, that'd be as dirty as yer could git, no matter 'ow Mr Wilby 'iself 'ad be'aved, but—'

He stopped short, suddenly noticing Maudie's expression and pulled up by a realisation of what he was saying.

'*Would* you mind telling me just what you are talking about?' asked Maudie.

'Eh? Nothink,' muttered Ben.

'I see. Just something you read in a book!'

'What?'

She shook her head reprovingly at him.

'Listen, Ben,' she said seriously, 'if you've said more than you ought it's too late to draw back now—and I don't think you have said more than you ought! We're working together and you've got me on the straight path, God knows how, but never mind that, and if we find ourselves in a jam before we've finished I've got to know as much as you or I won't be able to help—in fact, I may do something to upset everything. You must see that?'

Ben frowned. The trouble was he did seem to see it. Maudie's words sounded disturbingly logical.

'Of course,' Maudie went on, watching him, 'if you believe after all we've talked about and said to each other that I'm *not* on the straight path and I'm still up here to cheat—'

'Go on!' interrupted Ben easily. 'Yer knows I don't think that.'

'Honest truth?'

'Corse, Maudie. I knows that 'owever bad yer started, yer comin' clean nah.'

Something suddenly made Maudie bite her lip. 'It wouldn't be easy not to after a dose of *you*!' she said, almost resentfully. 'You'd turn a hard-boiled egg soft! Very well! As you do trust me—'

'Ain't I sed so?'

'Then you must act as if you do. Goodness, why, here you suddenly blurt out something damned important and entirely new about a man who's been making love to Mrs Wilby—'

'Oi, not so quick!' Ben interrupted again. 'I dunno abart that! Leastwise, I dunno 'ow much. But—yus, I expeck I gotter tell yer nah, on'y doncher fergit it's orl privit like—well, any'ow, this bloke fell fer 'er, and arter Mr Wilby be'aved like wot 'e did at the cinema just afore 'e went orf ter git murdered—'

'What!'

'Eh?'

'Are you telling me that Mr Wilby was with her that afternoon?'

'Yus, that's wot I'm tellin' yer, and 'e be'aved so funny she thort 'e was drunk or somethink, see, 'e'd joined 'er arter it started and chuckled or somethink in the dark, so she got fed up, 'oo wouldn't, and left 'im there—'

'At the cinema?'

'Lummy, corse at the cinema, they wasn't at a cricket match . . .'

'Go on!'

'I'm tryin' ter. She left 'im at the cinema, afore it was over, so 'e must 'ave left jest arter, but 'e didn't go 'ome, we know that, but she went 'ome, and 'avin' 'ad enuff like she was goin' orf with 'im, not Mr Wilby but the other bloke, or leastwise she meant ter, when along I comes and stops 'er gettin' in the taxi, and arter she 'ears wot I told 'er, see, I told 'er afore the pleece did, 'ave yer got it? Then she chinges 'er mind like, and telerphones to 'im and finds 'e's gorn away sudden, and so—well, that started 'er wunnerin', but she ain't told nothink abart this ter the pleece, nobody knows it bar me, and barrin' nah you, so if we find aht that it's 'im and that Blake knows it's 'im, wot do *we* do?'

Maudie needed a few seconds to absorb what she had just been told, and then she answered:

'But I thought you'd decided that we would have to tell the police?'

'Yus,' replied Ben, 'on'y I wish I was sure Mrs Wilby wouldn't wanter know fust. See, she engaiged me fer this job and is payin' me fer it.'

'Who is this other man?'

''Oo is 'e?'

'Yes, what's his name?'

'I dunno.'

'Didn't she tell you?'

'If she 'ad I'd of knowed.'

'Did she say what he was?'

'No.'

'Or where he lived?'

'No.'

'Then how would you know he was the person Blake meant if he mentioned anybody?'

'Arsk me another! But I've seed 'is pickcher.'

'What! Did she show it to you?'

'No, I see it on 'er mantelpiece the fust time I called, but it 'ad gorn the second time, so I reckoned she'd 'ad enuff of it.'

'Or didn't want the police to see it, p'r'aps?'

'Well, that's an idea, miss.'

'But *you* saw it, you say?'

'Yus.'

'You're sure it was this man? It wasn't Mr Wilby?'

'It wasn't Mr Wilby, I've seen Mr Wilby, and yer could tell it was the other bloke by the sorter way she sorter kep' on sorter lookin' at it.'

'Then you'd recognise him if you came across him?'

'Tha's right.'

'It might be useful if I could, too. Will you describe him?'

'Lummy, ain't yer arskin' 'em? I never was no good at discripshuns.'

'Have a shot!'

'Well—'e 'ad a moustache.'

'So have millions of others.'

'That ain't my fault.'

'A big moustache or a small one? Light or dark?'

'There yer've got me.'

Maudie sighed. 'Do try and be more helpful! Can't you rake up a squint or something?'

'Lummy, 'e 'adn't no squint,' replied Ben, ''e was a good-looker, like some o' them blokes, yer might say, 'oo sings love-songs on the pickchers. Pity abart this weather, ain't it?'

Maudie looked at him in surprise.

'What's biting you all of a sudden about the weather?' she inquired.

'Well, it's bad fer the sheep.' Her surprise grew as Ben continued with loud vehemence: ''Oo'd be a farmer? But, corse, mist ain't so bad as the snow wot buries 'em.'

Had the strain of the situation been too much for him and sent him loony? That was Maudie's thought, but before she could express it she received a violent kick under the table.

'Well, I better find Bella and pay the bill,' said Ben.

He left his chair, and she watched him cross the room and open the door. As he closed the door again, after poking his head out into the passage, he remarked loudly: 'Thort I 'eard 'er ahtside, but I must of bin mistook.' Then Maudie got on to it.

'But you did hear someone?' she murmured, keeping her own voice low.

Ben nodded.

'Yus, and I thort they was stoppin' and listenin',' he replied, 'but let's 'ope that was a mistake, too! Any'ow, ain't we torked long enuff? 'Ow abart that beauty sleep? Yer've got a hour and a 'arf, and it may be the larst chance yer'll 'ave fer a bit, miss.'

'"Maudie" still sticks in your throat, doesn't it, Eric?' she answered.

20

Re-enter Blake

A countryman who shared with Ben a compartment from Applewold to Penridge proved disturbingly talkative. His conversation was harmless enough, and in another mood Ben would have been willing to exchange the time of day and state of the weather with him, but Ben's need during these final few miles of his long journey was silence for contemplation of the ordeal ahead, and such silence was denied him by the countryman's wagging tongue.

'Be yew from these paarts?' was the countryman's opening.

'Not me, I'm from Lunnon,' replied Ben.

'I be from Naarfolk,' stated the countryman. 'There bean't no mountains in Naarfolk. Do yew know Naarfolk?'

'I bin ter Yarmouth.'

'Ah, a rare fine place, Yarmouth,' said the countryman. 'I'd a sight sooner be in Yarmouth than where I be goin' so I would!'

And then Ben had to learn where he was going, and that he was on a visit to a sister who had married a Cumberland grocer and who had seven children and a goat. The village she lived in was eight miles from the station, so how he was going to get there if no one met him he had no idea. Ben had no idea, either, and he couldn't have cared less. But, impervious to his companion's lack of interest, the countryman rambled on. He hoped the beer was good in Cumberland, as good as it was in Naarfolk, because good beer cheered one, and dang it!—one needed cheering in this sort of weather. Mist was the something limit, weren't it? Of course, yew got mist in Naarfolk, but that was sea mist, that was, and sea mist was more friendly. Mountains weren't friendly. They got on top of yew. No, he would never have come up here but for his sister and the seven children and the goat. Chew-chew, they called it. The goat. Because of the noise it made when it chewed. What had brought Ben up?

Ben pretended not to have heard the question the first time, but when it was repeated he replied:

"Ollerday.'

'Oh! Yew be hikin'?'

'Tha's right.'

'Yew better been in Naarfolk fer that.' How much longer was he going on? "Tis easy hikin' in Naarfolk, there bean't no big hills. Hills, ay, in some parts, there be some round Trimingham tu make an old 'un puff, ay, but no real big 'uns. And there be holiday camps at Runton, in the summer 'tis a sight, sure. No, yew never get me hikin' among mountains. Mountains ain't friendly.'

He glanced out of the window at a high peak. Ben himself felt a little oppressed by the towering skyline, although most of it was obscured by coiling clouds creeping slowly and with seeming stealth down to the valleys. The peak at which the countryman was glancing was the only one

197

visible, and even that became blotted out a few moments later. Ben hoped that the countryman's conversation would be blotted out, also, but this was not to be.

'What I say is,' resumed the countryman, 'yew go up mountains too slow and yew come down 'em too quick! Ay! And when 'tis misty like now, yew doan' know where yew be comin' down tew! But I got a cousin, now, he lives at Thetford—yew ever been tu Thetford? and he was tellin' me once . . .'

The cousin lasted for the rest of the way to Penridge. Indeed, the old man from Naarfolk was so voluble that the train stopped at Penridge before either of them realised it, and when realisation came they both leapt out in a panic.

This was not a good preparation for Ben's next ordeal, and he hoped the countryman would not continue to be a nuisance and would speedily take himself off. No one else had got out of the train, and the platform was deserted but for themselves and a distant porter. There was no sign of either Oscar Blake or the countryman's sister.

'Wimmen!' muttered the countryman, gazing around in disgusted disappointment. 'Yew can't depend on 'em no more'n the weather!'

Ben stooped down, pretending to be busy with a loose boot-lace. It was an anxious moment, because women, once started, could become an endless subject. With anyone possessing a knowledge of Ben, or watching him closely, the ruse could not have succeeded, because normally Ben did not care whether his boot-laces were loose or not, or even if he had any at all, and his present technique was to untie the laces as soon as he had tied them up so he could tie them up again. But the countryman, apparently, observed nothing irregular, being too concerned at the absence of his sister—the absence of the seven children and the goat was less disturbing—and soon he began to drift away towards the distant porter. Out of the corner of his eye Ben watched the two men meeting and conversing, and then he saw the countryman drift away completely through the little grey brick ticket office.

Good! Ben had got rid of one little trouble before the next, many sizes bigger, arrived!

Completing his drawn-out work on his boot-lace, Ben straightened himself as the porter approached him leisurely.

'Lost your ticket?' inquired the porter.

'Eh? No, I was jest lookin' ter see as I'd tied me boot-laice proper,' answered Ben.

'Oh! Then could I have your ticket?'

Ben groped in his pocket, and suddenly his expression went glum.

'Lummy!'

The porter grinned.

'What's that sticking out of the side of your shoe?' he asked.

Stooping once more, Ben found his ticket. It was by no means the first time his boot had formed the terminus of some possession's tortuous journey through his pocket holes.

'I reckon you was born lucky,' remarked the porter as he took the ticket, tore it across, and gave Ben back the return half. 'It would have cost you a pound or two if you'd had to pay all over again.'

'I'm lucky orl right,' returned Ben. 'I'm knowed as the 'Uman 'Orse-shoe.'

'You might have brought us along some brighter weather, then!'

199

'It weren't no brighter in Lunnon when I left.'

But Ben was not here to discuss the weather, and he glanced around at the deserted platform, while the porter watched him curiously.

'Expecting somebody to meet you, like that other one?'

'Eh? Well, I thort there might be some 'un.'

'There was a man here five minutes before the train came in, but he seems to have gone away again.'

'Wot was 'e like?'

'No need to describe him,' said the porter, turning his head towards the booking office. 'There he is, come back.'

Ben twisted his head galvanically, and saw Oscar Blake standing in the doorway, regarding him with half-amused, half-cynical eyes.

Lummy! Yus! There he was. Large as life. If not larger. Now fer it!

Blake walked towards him.

'Morning, Eric,' he said.

'Sime ter you,' replied Ben.

Blake paused, glanced around casually, and then inquired, 'All alone?'

'Did yer expeck me ter bring the family with me?' retorted Ben.

'I didn't know you had a family.'

'Well, I ain't.'

'I'm relieved,' smiled Blake, placing a large hand on Ben's shoulder, twisting him round, and beginning to walk with him back to the ticket office. There was something unpleasantly compelling in the pressure of Blake's hand. 'Not because you haven't a family, Eric, but because I find you just the same as when we met the day before yesterday.'

'Go on!'

'What?'

'Was it on'y the day afore yesterday?'

'That's all, so perhaps you haven't had much time to change. But, to tell you the truth, Eric, when I thought about you after we had separated I could hardly believe you hadn't been a dream. Now I find that you are indeed real flesh and blood. How has the world been treating you?'

''Ow's it been treatin' *you*?'

'Ca' canny, eh? Well, perhaps you're right till we can talk in private. I expect we've both got plenty to tell each other.'

'Yer've sed it. Where are yer goin' ter tike me?'

'Where do you suggest?'

'Are yer stoopid or jest pertendin'? 'Ow do I know? I never bin 'ere afore. 'Ow abart where yer livin'?'

'That's an idea,' answered Blake blandly.

'Then I votes we hacts upon it.'

'A little later, perhaps. Where I am living has another guest at the moment. You may meet this guest presently—but not, I think, till after our little chat.'

Ben took a chance and, lowering his voice, he asked sepulchrally:

'Yer don't mean the bloke wot done it?'

'Done what?' inquired Blake.

'Corse, yer'd never guess, would yer?'

'I might have a shot when we get inside.'

'Inside where? Nah we're comin' ter it!'

'As you say, we are now coming to it.'

Blake, with his hand still on Ben's shoulder, had kept him walking all the while, through the ticket office, out into the open, and across a yard. Ahead of them now loomed a building not dissimilar to the hotel in which Ben and Maudie had conversed. Above the grey brick porch were the same words: 'STATION HOTEL.'

Ben's steps grew slower.

'What's the matter?' asked Blake.

'Are we goin' in there?'

'Why not?'

The reason why not was that in about an hour's time Maudie would be going in there, too! But it was hardly a reason Ben could give to Blake.

'Well—a bit public like, ain't it?' he said uneasily.

'It's not opening time yet,' Blake replied, urging Ben forward by an increased pressure of his large hand—nuisance, it's being so large. 'And, besides, I can get a private room. The boss is an old pal of mine.'

Ben didn't quite like the sound of that, either, and as they went in through the porch an old tune began to worry through his mind. It worried him because he didn't know why it had come into his mind or what it was. Then, suddenly, the answers to both questions came to him, worrying him even more. The tune was that of '"Will you come into my parlour?" said the spider to the fly.'

The boss who was said to be an old pal of Blake's met them in the hall.

'Ah, you've found your friend,' he said to Blake.

'He's come along,' replied Blake. 'Wonder if we could have the same room you gave me yesterday?'

'Don't see why not. You know your way?'

Blake nodded. 'And could you send along something a bit livelier than coffee? You know. On the house. And no questions answered.'

The proprietor winked, and Blake winked back.

'Straight ahead, old boy,' said Blake to Ben, 'and round the corner on the right.'

He gave Ben a shove forward. The proprietor lowered his voice and whispered in Blake's ear as he passed by.

'You certainly do pick 'em up!'

'I'm a Christian all right, all right,' answered Blake.

The proprietor gazed after them as they went along the passage, then shrugged his shoulders and went to fetch something a bit livelier than coffee.

Round the corner on the right were six steps, then another turning on the left, and then a door. Behind Ben, Blake reached out with his hand and gave the door a shove. It swung inwards, and another shove, this time on Ben's back, took him into a bare room with a bare, stained table and some bare, stained chairs, illuminated by a small and very dirty window half-obscured by ivy . . . Blast that tune!

'Well, here we are,' said Blake. 'Sit down.'

'Reg'ler 'ome from 'ome, ain't it,' commented Ben, as he sat.

'I don't suppose you expected cushions?'

'I expeck wot I get.'

'Damn good motto! Don't tune up for a moment. I'll be back in a jiffy.'

Blake ran from the room, closing the door after him. Ben was surprised not to hear a key turn. Though, after all, why should Blake imagine he would run away the moment after he had arrived? And why *should* he run away? He'd come up here to do a job, hadn't he? Very well, then! The one thing was to get this first part of the job done before Maudie turned up. If Blake bumped into Maudie, what would happen then? It might prove a spanner in the works! And what had Blake wanted this room for yesterday? And who was this other guest at the place where Blake was living? . . . Will you come into my parlour? . . . And where . . .?

The door opened, and Blake returned with a small tray adorned with bottles and glasses.

'All set,' said Blake, putting the tray down on the table. 'So now for the low-down!'

'Yus, and you start,' suggested Ben.

But Blake shook his head as he poured out the drinks.

'No, visitors first,' he replied. 'I want to hear what happened to you after I left you know where! Let's have the lot. Don't miss anything out.'

Don't miss anything out! Ben meant to miss a great deal out, and the tricky question was just how much. After thinking a moment, and fortifying himself with a first swallow of Cumberland beer—if the countryman was going to strike the same brand he'd find it all right!—Ben began cautiously.

'I expeck yer knows a bit?'

'Never mind what I know,' retorted Blake. 'You keep talking as if I didn't know anything.'

'It'd saive time—'

'Then don't you waste it! I've not seen anything in any paper up here—you can have that much.'

'Okay.' Ben took a second swallow, and gained a little confidence. 'Yer remember givin' me that address—'

'Of course I remember!' interrupted Blake. 'If you want to save time cut out the frills and make it snappy! Did you go there?'

Ben fought back.

'Corse I went there!' he returned. 'Wot abart *your* frills? 'Ow'd I get your messidge ter come up 'ere if Maudie 'adn't give it ter me, and would she give it ter me if she jest passed me in the street and we 'adn't ever met afore?'

'Carry on, carry on, don't start losing your wool!' exclaimed Blake impatiently.

'I'll keep mine if you keep yourn,' answered Ben. 'I 'aven't come orl this distance fer a barkin' match, I come ter be friendly. 'Ow far 'ave I got?'

'You haven't got anywhere, unless you count the Kentons' doorstep. What happened when they opened the door to you?'

'They wasn't too pleased at fust. Yer see, Maudie—she's a tart, ain't she?—Maudie didn't know nothink abart your goin' orf like yer did, and that mide 'er 'uffy. Is she sweet on yer?'

Blake's eyebrows went up, and he laughed.

'What makes you think that, you mug?'

'Mug yerself! I got an idea yer'd been pretty thick together—'

'Did she say anything?'

'Abart wot?'

'About—us?'

'I don't git yer,' blinked Ben innocently.

'Oh, yes, you do! You must have had some reason for thinking what you've just said?'

'It was the way she went on, but mind yer I was on'y guessin'. She's close, that one! Kind o' gal, I should think, yer'd never get ter tork, not with a red-'ot poker.'

'Did you try to get her to talk?'

'Wasn't my bizziness.'

'Let's have a straighter answer?'

'Orl right, 'ow abart this 'un. You told me that if I went to the Kentons and waited, I might do a bit o' good fer meself. Well, if I'd spent me time pokin' inter bizziness wot wasn't mine, and you got ter 'ear of it, would I be 'elpin' meself—?'

'You bet you wouldn't, sonny!'

'Orl right, then, so stop arskin' me questions like I was a mug. Yer note ter Ma Kenton sed, "No questions," so I reckoned that went fer me, too.'

Pleased with himself, Ben finished his glass and poured himself out another, while Blake watched him thoughtfully.

'How about their side?' came Blake's next question. 'Did *they* ask questions?'

Ben responded diplomatically: 'Yer must fergive 'em if they arst a bit. Yer don't 'ave a strainger suddenly plarsted on yer withaht bein' a spot curious, do yer?'

'All right. They asked questions. And how much did you tell them?'

''Ow much was I supposed ter?'

'Can't you answer any question of mine the first time?'

'That's your fault fer arskin' such rum 'uns. 'Ere's one fer you. Was I supposed ter tell 'em abart the murder or 'ow you and me fust met?'

'By God, you weren't!'

'Well, so I didn't,' returned Ben, accepting the cue, 'and 'ere's somethink fer yer ter mike a note of. Yer sent me orf ter the Kentons, but yer didn't tell me 'arf enough wot I was ter do or 'ow ter act when I got there. Tike Maudie ter the pickchers, that was orl yer sed, so I 'ad ter do orl the thinkin' fer meself. I didn't tell the Kentons abart the murder—mind yer, if it *was* murder, we gotter fix that yet, ain't we, when we come ter *your* part? And I didn't tike Maudie ter the pickchers. I'm leavin' that ter you. But, corse, nex' mornin', when the paipers comes aht, there's a bit abart the body bein' fahnd in the 'ouse in Norgate Road, and that hupset 'em—'

'Why should that upset them,' demanded Blake sharply, 'if you hadn't said anything?'

Lummy! That was a slip, that was! Or wasn't it? Taking another drink, Ben plunged.

'If yer want the truth,' he said, 'I wunnered the sime thing. Maudie was the one that was hupset the most. See, they give 'oo it was—Mr George Wilby, that's right, ain't it, like we fahnd on 'is card—and they give the address in Drewet Road—Nummer 18, wer'n't it?—see, Mrs Wilby idenchified the body—'

'Oh! Did she?'

'Eh? Yus, corse! So I thort Maudie might know something abart the Wilbys, but—well, wot I sed, Maudie's a fair oyster and when I arst 'er wot was bitin' 'er, and wot was a dead body, we'll orl be one some day, she—she . . .' He stumbled as his inventive powers broke down for a moment, then got an idea and went on: 'She called me a nime and then rushed up to 'er room, and I didn't see 'er agine not till she went orf ter Woolworth's, that's where she works, Woolworth's.'

'I see,' said Blake.

'Good! That saives a lot o' trouble!'

'But she comes back for lunch.'

'Oh, yer knows that?'

'You're not forgetting I've been staying there?'

'Tha's right, so yer 'ave.'

'What did she do when she came back to lunch? Did she say anything then?'

'Not ter me.'

'And her mother?'

''Er mother! She ain't got no more sense'n 'er parrot!'

'What did you think?'

'Wotcher mean?'

'About Maudie's outburst?'

'Blimy if I knows wot yer arskin' orl this for! Wot did she do? Wot did 'er mother do? Wot did I think? Well, if yer want it, wot I thort was that she'd bin up ter somethink that was ter do with the Wilbys, though I couldn't fit you in, 'cos when you come acrost that card on the corpse yer didn't seem ter reckernize the nime, or yet the pickcher of the woman. Any'ow, 'ow many more times 'ave I gotter tell yer that wasn't my bizziness, so I lets Maudie alone and keeps on waitin' like, and when she comes to me with yer messidge I ses to meself, "Okay, Eric, yer bin a good boy, and 'ere's yer prize," and so I leaves 'em and along I comes and 'ere I am. And—well, that's the lot, so nah I reckon it's your turn!'

But Blake did not seem to think so.

'Not just yet, old boy,' he answered. 'There's a bit more before I've had the lot. You haven't told me yet just what they put in the papers. It's a bit out of the world up here, and even when the papers do arrive we don't get the London editions. Did you bring a paper up with you?'

'No.'

'That's a pity. What did they say?'

'Ain't I told yer? Jest that the body was fahnd, and then 'oo it was arter it 'ad bin idenchified.'

'Who found it?'

'Mr Attlee.'

'Don't play the fool!'

'Well, I arsk yer, 'oo fahnd it! The pleece, o' corse.'

'Not so much of the of course! You and I found it, didn't we, and we weren't the police? Was that of course?'

'Wotcher gittin' at?'

'I want to get at who found the body after we did . . .'

'Lummy, ain't I told yer? The pleece—'

'And how they got to know? You and I know how *we* got to know—just by chance—'

'Was yourn by charnce?'

'Oh! And what does that mean?'

'Nothink if yer don't think so.'

'All right. Leave that. But it'd be funny if a policeman came upon the body by chance if he wasn't looking for it! It might have stayed in that cellar for days before anybody found it. Were they suspicious for any reason, or did anybody else put them on to it? Did the papers say anything about that?'

'Oh, I git yer,' answered Ben, thinking hard. 'No, they didn't say nothink abart that, leastwise not in the paiper I saw. Corse, there might of bin more in others. Yus, some'un else might of come acrost the body and told 'em, but wot's it matter?'

'I don't ask questions that don't matter,' retorted Blake. 'Damn it if I know whether you're the world's biggest mug or not! Was there any mention of any clue?'

'If there was, I missed it.'

Blake looked exasperated, then gave it up and tried something else.

'How did you get up here?' he asked.

'Well, it was a bit of a walk,' replied Ben, 'so I come on a efilunt.'

'Try again.'

'Well, 'oo's the mug this time? I come on a trine.'

'Fancy that! Now see if you can answer the question properly. How did you pay for your ticket? I seem to remember I only left you a pound. P'r'aps you've got a large banking account.'

'Listen,' said Ben. 'If yer didn't think I could rise the money, wot was the good of arskin' me ter come?'

'I'm asking now *how* you did it, you damn fool! I couldn't telegraph the money! How did you? Any reason for not telling me?'

Ben had a very good reason for not telling him, so he quickly invented another.

'Orl right—but it don't go no further?'

'This is a private conversation.'

'Okay. I 'ad ter pick a pocket.'

'Really?'

'Yus, and orl o' cause o' you, so doncher fergit it!'

Blake smiled. 'I won't—and thanks for the tip. I'll have to look after *my* pocket! I thought p'r'aps Maudie had lent it to you.'

She would have if Ben had got that idea first. He wished he'd thought of it.

''Ow many more questions?' he complained. 'I'm gittin' dizzy!'

Blake got up from his chair and walked to the window. He stood there for a full minute while Ben regarded his broad back and wondered what he was thinking. He also wondered how long this interview was going to last, and whether they would be through with it before Maudie turned up. A clock on the mantelpiece did not help him, for across its cracked face the hands stood immovably at thirteen minutes past five.

At last Blake turned, and came back to his chair.

'You're up here because you want to make a bit of money—is that right?' he began.

'There ain't no other reason,' answered Ben. 'Yer told me there might be a job, and that's wot I'm 'ere for.'

'Well, if you'll do all I say, and ask no questions, you're in for a nice little pile.'

'Wot do yer call a pile?'

'Would fifty quid interest you?'

'Fifty quid?'

'That's what I said. It might work up to as much as a hundred, or more. It all depends on how I work it, and whether you carry out my instructions to the letter.'

'That sahnds OK ter me. Wot's the instructions?'

'I want you to go back to London—'

'Wot, when I've on'y jest come 'ere—'

'With a letter. It'll be sealed, and if you break the seal you'll not only lose your pay, but you'll be for it.'

''Oo's the letter to?'

'Mrs Wilby.'

Ben blinked. 'Yer don't mean—as I'm ter call on 'er?'

'That's what I do mean. How can you give her the letter if you don't call on her?'

'Oh! Well, wot's in the letter?'

'You'll learn that later.'

'Oh! Well, why not nah?'

'Don't ask questions, Eric. Just do as you are told, and remember what you'll lose if you don't. She will give you a reply, which will also be sealed.'

'When yer say sealed, do yer mean jest stuck dahn?'

'I told you not to ask questions, but that's a damn-fool one! Sealed with sealing-wax, and if the seal's broken when you return to me with it, your game's up. And I may as

211

well tell you that—not being a damn fool myself—you'll waste your time if you do break the seal, because there won't be any money. Not this time.' Blake paused, looked at Ben hard, and then continued: 'You can know this much, Eric. My letter will contain certain information, and all I'm asking for this trip is her reply. When I get that—if the reply is what I expect—we'll get cracking.'

Ben rubbed his nose.

'Do I—git yer?' he asked.

'I can't say before I know what you've got,' replied Blake.

'Will the letter I'm ter tike 'er say 'oo done it?'

'It will, Eric.'

'And then yer goin' ter bleed 'er?'

'What a nasty word! But you have the idea.'

Ben rubbed his nose again.

'Wot I don't see,' he said, 'is why Mrs Wilby should give yer money fer not lettin' on 'oo killed 'er 'usband?'

'There's a lot you don't see, Eric,' Blake answered, and drew the debated letter from an inside pocket. There was a heavy smudge of red seal over the flap. 'This letter will give her more information than just who did it. Don't try and puzzle it out. Just accept the fact that Mrs Wilby will probably be willing to pay all she's got—and she has plenty, though Mr Wilby had gone beyond his last bean—and that the information won't be worth a cent to you until I give it to you myself, after you've come back here with her reply. How much money did you net in that little pickpocketing job?'

'Eh?'

'And did you buy a return ticket?'

'Yus! No! Wot?'

'Let's have the truth. I can easily turn out your pockets if I want to.'

'I bort a return,' said Ben quickly, 'and I got enuff ter git another back 'ere agine.'

'Then take this now, and see you don't lose it,' said Blake, handing him the envelope, 'and if you wonder why I'm trusting you, I'll tell you. It's because I'm taking no risk, and because I'm satisfied you know which side your bread's buttered. That's all. There's nothing more.' He looked at his watch. 'You can get a train back in twenty minutes. See you get it. You'll be in London tonight, and you'll go straight to Mrs Wilby. Sleep where you like, but keep clear of the Kentons, make sure you're not followed, and return here on the first morning train. It gets in at seven-thirty. Come straight here, and wait for me. And now, Eric,' concluded Blake, jumping up suddenly, 'I'm off to never mind where.'

The next moment he was gone.

21

Ben Listens to the Impossible

'Loony, that's wot I was, yer carn't git away from it,' Ben admitted afterwards when trying to describe his actions during the next sixty seconds, 'but, see 'e'd suddinly gorn *bing!* And I didn't wanter lose 'im, but I 'ad ter git that letter ter Maudie, didn't I, and 'ow was I ter do it and ter foller 'im at the sime time? It 'ad orl 'appened too quick, 'im doin' the vanishin' act, and I 'adn't 'ad time ter work nothink aht. So when I lef' the room meself wunnerin' 'ow ter work it, and gits another surprise by bumpin' inter the country bloke wot was torkin' ter me in the trine, and when 'e sez, "Wot, are you in trouble, too?" it came over me suddin could I mike any use of 'im? So I sez "Yus, are yer stayin' on 'ere?" and 'e sez, "Yus, my sister ain't turned up, so I gotter waite till she comes," so then I gits me idea and jumps on it like a mouse on cheese, yus, and fergittin' that sometimes the mouse gits caught, and so any'ow I sez, "Well, I'm expectin' some'un, too, on'y I carn't waite, she'll be 'ere soon on the nex' trine from Applewold." "I see," 'e sez, "and yer wants me ter give 'er a messidge?"

Well, I arsk yer, wasn't that 'andin' it ter me on a plite? "I want yer ter give 'er this letter," I sez, "and ter arsk 'er ter tike it ter where she'll know, would yer?" "'Ow'll I know 'er?" 'e sez. "Wot's 'er nime?" "Miss Kenton," I sez, and 'ands the letter ter 'im quick. 'E took it, sayin' 'e was orlways glad ter 'elp anybody, and while 'e was lookin' at it with wot I thort was a funny expreshun I 'opped it afore 'e could chinge 'is mind. I told yer it was loony, I mean a letter like that, and givin' it ter a strainger, but wot with wantin' not ter lose Blake so's I could foller 'im, me brine was orl of a wobble, that's a fack, and any'ow that's wot I did, and even when 'e calls aht, "'Arf a mo," I never stopped, and was aht o' the 'otel in a blink!

'Yus, and I was on'y jest in time, and if I'd stopped fer 'is 'arf a mo' I'd of lost Blake! But there 'e was, at the bottom of the 'ill, and 'ad turned a corner and was aht o' sight the momint I clapped me eyes on 'im. There was three laines away from the staishun, and if I'd bin a second laiter I'd of 'ad ter guess.

'Did I run dahn that 'ill? Lummy, I was at the bottom afore I started!'

And again Ben was only just in time, for the next stretch before two more turns was only a short one, and he reached it just as Blake was once more vanishing round the turning to the left. After that the going was easier. The lane narrowed, and although it contained many twists it now offered only its own direction, which was mainly uphill. Ben gained the impression that he was wriggling up a mountain.

The mist, which increased with the gradient, had both its virtues and its vices, for while it forced Ben to keep closer behind his quarry than he cared for lest the back he was following should dissolve, it also served as his own protection. Once, indeed, he would probably have met his Waterloo without it. Blake stopped, and turned his head. Ben saw it coming round, and just had time to go flat, as in an air-raid, so that Blake's gaze went over and beyond him. Ben's prostrate form may have looked to Blake, if he saw it, like a vague shadow, but it was a shadow that sweated while it pasted itself to the ground. 'Lummy, that was a fair let orf,' described Ben, 'and when 'e goes on agine and I 'ops up I goes dahn agine 'cos me legs 'adn't quite got over it like.'

He managed to keep standing at the second attempt, but another bad moment followed at the next twist of the lane. Blake had stopped again, this time to light a cigarette, and Ben nearly walked into his back. The match which Blake tossed behind him landed on Ben's sleeve.

The strange uneasy journey continued without further incident until a rough stone wall was reached just before the narrow lane petered out into a steep track. The wall ran along the right-hand side of the lane, and a small gate came into view rather unexpectedly, for the region seemed too remote and isolated for human habitation. The gate led to the bare untidy garden of a tall square cottage, and without pausing Blake passed through. But Ben paused, and all at once ducked below the wall. He did not now have only Blake to guard against. There might be eyes at windows!

Because of his precautionary manœuvre he did not see Blake enter the cottage. He merely heard a door open and close. He waited for a minute, then raised his head cautiously till his eyes were just above the level on the wall top. Beyond the intervening mist the cottage looked dead. He had never seen a cottage less inviting. But some sort of life must go on inside it, and somehow or other Ben had got to find out just what that life was.

Allowing another minute to go by, and discovering that it produced no catastrophe, Ben became bolder, though he still kept low as he groped his way to the gate. The gate afforded him less protection from watching eyes, if there were any, and he kept his own eyes fixed on the windows for the possible unwelcome appearance of a face. There were wide gaps between the rotting wooden slats of the gate. Indeed, two of the slats were missing, forming a gap wide enough for a small 'un like Ben to slip through.

And all at once he did slip through, urged by a new panic. He had been concentrating on the view ahead, but his panic was due to a sound behind, and before he had time to think an entirely new situation had developed which left him gasping.

The sound behind drew closer, causing him to slither swiftly aside and wedge himself between the wall and a bush. As he did so the cottage door flew open and Blake came rushing out. 'I'm done—'e's spotted me!' thought Ben, in black despair. But Blake did not make for the bush, he made for the gate, and then Ben realised that he had spotted someone else. He heard a mad scramble, and gathered that the person who had been approaching the gate behind him had turned and fled, with Blake after him; and in a few seconds the sound of the chase died away.

Lummy! What now?

The answer was painfully obvious. It was the open cottage door. Ben accepted its most unpleasant invitation, lurched away from the bush, and sped through. A woman's voice called down shrilly from the top of a flight of stairs.

217

'Who was it? Did you catch him?' Then the tone suddenly changed, becoming sharp and angry. 'Ah! Would you? Get back, or you'll know what's coming to you!'

Ben did the right thing. He did not wait. If he had waited he would have stayed stuck at the bottom of those stairs, for obviously he would find nothing but trouble at the top, but before hesitation could weaken him he raced up three stairs at a time, and when he arrived he found trouble in plenty. On a small landing were two people. One was an old woman holding a revolver. She was bony and hard-visaged, and even in that first swift moment Ben recognised her likeness to Oscar Blake. The other was a man standing in a doorway. His cheeks were pale, and he looked desperately ill, but in spite of his pitiable condition Ben recognised him, also. He had not, after all, been at his best in their one previous encounter.

Ben's startlingly rapid ascent had a second virtue. Surprise is an invaluable weapon, and Ben had undoubtedly delivered one. The old woman stared at him as though he were something that had popped out of an impossible dream, and before she could recover from her shock he had dashed the revolver out of her hand and dived after it as it fell to the floor.

The woman, partially recovering, dived with him, but Ben got there first. Seizing the weapon he brandished it at her, and she backed tottering to a wall. Beside her was a second open door leading, Ben gathered from his glimpse, into a back bedroom.

'Git in there!' gasped Ben.

'Who are you?' the woman gasped back.

'That don't matter—git in there!' he retorted, and waved the revolver perilously.

The woman shrieked. 'Be careful—it's loaded!'

'Yus,' shouted Ben, 'and yer in the wrong plice if it goes orf! Git in, git in, I ain't tellin' yer agine!'

Terrified, the woman slid backwards into the room. Ben slammed the door on her, and as he did so he beheld a sight that nearly made him weep for joy. It was the key, obligingly on the outside. He turned it with a sigh of relief.

Then he turned to the man standing in the other doorway. The man had not moved. He just looked dazed.

'Quick! Let's 'ear! Do I git yer aht of 'ere, or wot?'

The man did not answer, but he swayed slightly, and all at once Ben realised that, however desirable it might be to get him away, it would be impossible. The man's legs were beginning to sag, and he seemed to be losing whatever strength had brought him to the door.

'Come on, yer better sit dahn or somethink,' said Ben. 'I'll 'elp yer.'

Making a dive at him and seizing him as he looked on the point of falling, Ben managed to totter with him into the room and to deposit him on a chair. Then he took another dive back to the door, slipped the key from the outside to the inside, locked it, and returned to the chair. And then Ben nearly collapsed himself.

'Gawd above!' he gasped.

For was this not the man he had seen dead on the cellar floor in Norgate Road?

For several seconds they just stared at each other, each with utter lack of comprehension. It was the man who spoke first, and what he said did nothing to clear up Ben's confusion. Indeed, it only added to it.

'Haven't I—seen you before?' faltered the man.

That, surely, should have been Ben's question!

'Yer couldn't of,' answered Ben, with an absurd attempt at logic. 'Yer was dead!'

This assertion was of no use to anybody. The man passed a hand across his forehead, and then whispered, with fear in his eyes:

'What do you mean—dead?'

'Well, dead's dead, ain't it?' replied Ben. 'Or—wasn't yer?'

There was another short silence. The man suddenly glanced towards the door.

'It's locked—no one can git at us,' said Ben, 'and the old lidy's locked in the other room. And, see, I've got *this*!'

He thrust the revolver under the man's nose, as though he might gain comfort from smelling it.

'Let's try and git this a bit stright,' went on Ben, as the man seemed incapable of keeping the conversation going. 'Where I saw you dead was on a cellar floor in Lunnon. I saw the bloke wot's jest gorn aht o' this cottage there, too. 'Is nime's Blake. Is the old lidy 'is ma?' The man nodded. 'I thort so. She's got the sime sort o' fice, but let's git back ter you. Yer was dead when I saw yer, wotever yer are nah, so 'ow come yer saw *me*? Corpses don't see nothink!'

'That—wasn't me, on the cellar floor,' gulped the man. 'How did you come to go there?'

'It wasn't you?'

'No.'

'Lummy, then where was it yer thinks yer saw me?'

The man passed his hand across his forehead again.

'It was in a street, not far away—we—'

'Bumped inter each other!' exclaimed Ben, as recollection came back. Why, of course! When Ben had first seen the corpse he recalled that there had been something vaguely familiar about the face, despite the damage to it. Now at last he'd got it! Or hadn't he? 'Then yer *wasn't* the corpse! Yer was that bloke wot bowled me over. And then yer 'oofed it quick, leavin' me ter tork ter the pleeceman—'

'Policeman?' repeated the man, dully. His muddled mind could only follow slowly.

'Yus, tha's right. The bobby come along jest arter. And—'arf a mo'!' Ben's eyes narrowed as the details of that strange incident grew clearer in his mind. 'Guv'nor, this ain't the time ter mince matters! And don't fergit, I got a gun!' He waggled it, to confirm the obvious statement. 'Are yer a crook?'

'No,' answered the man hoarsely.

'Yer ain't? Okay. But 'ow was it, then, that when you and me bumps inter each other yer drops a jemmy? It come aht o' yer pocket! Tha's wot got me runnin' away meself when the bobby spotted it on the pivement, yus, and I kep' runnin' till I bunked rahnd to the back o' that 'ouse in Norgate Street where I fahnd the corpse wot I thort was you! Yus, and where Blake follers me soon arter. See, the bobby thort the jemmy was mine, and you wasn't there ter let 'im find aht it was yourn.'

'But—it wasn't mine!'

'Oh, I see. Yer was jest carryin' it abart fer fun!' exclaimed Ben, rendered sarcastic through desperation. 'And yer ain't a crook. And yer ain't the corpse. And yer ain't Mr Wilby—'

'I am Mr Wilby,' said the man.

Ben walked to the window and opened it. The room was going round at such a dizzy rate that he had to put a part of himself outside to escape going round with it. The part he put out was his head. He also needed air.

There was yet another advantage in his action, for he found himself overlooking the garden and the gate, and was able to assure himself that Blake was not yet returning. What was keeping Blake away so long, and who was the person he was chasing? Well, Ben had enough to work out without trying to solve that one, so he left it; and when he had sufficiently revived he brought his head back into the room, closed the window again, and crossed to the door. Unlocking it, he stepped out into the passage and tiptoed to the door opposite. He wanted to reassure himself that it was still locked. Putting his ear to it, he listened, and after a few moments heard breathing. He also heard a sudden, emotional muttering. 'Blast the bloody—!' The last word was unprintable. Even in his worst moments, Ben never used it himself.

He tiptoed back to the other room, relocked the door, and continued with his interrupted conversation with the man who was calling himself Mr Wilby.

'Nah, listen,' he said. 'Yer Mr Wilby, yer tell me. Orl right. Let's 'ave it, and mike it as snappy as yer can, 'cos I don't hexpeck we'll 'ave orl day fer it, and Blake may be back at any momint. I'm goin' ter the winder, and I'll let yer know if I see 'im. Wot I wanter know is 'ow you're Mr Wilby, and if yer are then 'oo's the corpse, and 'oo killed 'im?'

But this time the man preceded his answers by asking a question himself.

'What I must know first,' he returned, showing a grain more spirit, 'is how *you* come into this?'

'Well, that's fair enuff,' agreed Ben. 'See, arter findin' the corpse, and workin' aht with Blake 'oo it seemed ter be by wot was in the pockets, I didn't like the way Blake was

actin', so I goes orf on me own and tells Mrs Wilby yer
was dead, and she engaiged me ter 'elp 'er find aht 'oo
killed yer. Is that enuff ter go on with?'

'Yes,' answered the man slowly. 'Yes . . . I see.'

'Well, I'm still 'opin ter,' retorted Ben. 'Was it Blake killed
the corpse?'

'No,' replied the man. 'I killed him.'

22

The Truth at Last

A wave of indignation surged through Ben's astonishment at this latest outrageous information.

'I come up 'ere,' he complained emotionally, 'ter find aht 'oo murdered yer, and nah yer tellin' me yer done it yerself! I expeck the next thing yer'll tell me will be that I was the corpse!'

Roused by Ben's outburst to emotion himself, the man who claimed to be Mr Wilby responded tartly:

'Kindly choose your words more carefully!'

'Wozzat?'

'The word I used was killed—not murdered. And please control yourself. If I lose my own control there is no knowing what may happen—I shall certainly be in no condition to tell you what you want to know! You could never realise all I have been through, but you might at least make some guess at it from my present state! A nightmare—no, worse than nightmare, for you wake from nightmare! I have been ill-treated, threatened, starved— even drugged! And yet you expect—'

'Tike it easy, sir, I bin through a bit meself,' interposed Ben, now speaking soothingly, 'but corse it carn't be more'n a flea to a helefunt alongside o' yourn, I knows that. Drugged yer, did they? Tha's bad! But doncher worry, sir, there'll be no more o' that.' Ben prayed that he was speaking the truth. 'Jest fergit wot I sed, wotever it was, and nah let's 'ear orl abart it. I'll be watchin' at the winder, but I can 'ear through me back.' He went to the window as he spoke. 'And yer might begin, sir, if yer would, by sayin' 'oo the corpse really *was*?'

Now more composed himself, Mr Wilby replied:

'He was my brother.'

'Go on! Was 'e? Lummy, but that'd expline 'ow yer was so alike, wouldn't it?'

'We were so alike that as boys—we were twins—we used to play jokes on our friends by pretending to be each other, but I soon stopped this when I found that Daniel was beginning to use my identity to get himself out of scrapes and I received thrashings for what *he'd* done! And Dan was always getting into scrapes—small ones at first, big ones later. Indeed, they got so big that they mounted to pick-pocketing, thieving, even forgery and housebreaking. But I won't talk about it. After he'd been had up twice my father packed him off to Australia and forbade any mention of his name. We were ashamed of him, ashamed! . . . Mrs Wilby never knew of his existence.'

He paused, and Ben asked, with his eyes trained on the garden and the gate:

'Yer mean, yer didn't say nothink abart 'im when yer married 'er like?'

'I saw no need to,' replied Mr Wilby; 'but I wish to God now that I had. She belonged to a good and wealthy family—a better one, I'm afraid, than my own—and I found it difficult enough to be accepted without mentioning a crooked brother who—I then thought—would never turn up again. I was a clerk in a Midland bank before I came to London, but my wife believed in me, and if it hadn't been for her I doubt whether I should have risen even as far as I have.' He paused again, and, unseen by Ben, looked astonished at himself. 'Really—I don't know why—I didn't mean to tell you all this.'

'Tha's all right, sir,' Ben reassured him. 'When yer worked up yer spits orl sorts' o' things aht, doncher, and when people tells me things, I on'y remembers wot I'm s'posed ter.'

Mr Wilby turned in his chair, and regarded the silhouette of the back of Ben's head against the window.

'I believe I'm beginning to understand,' he said, 'how my wife came to engage you for this business.'

'Then yer unnerstands more'n I do,' returned Ben.

'It's because you're a good fellow.'

'Go on, orl yer seein' is party manners. Let's git back ter yer brother. Corse, 'e *did* turn up agine?'

'Yes—a few months ago.'

'Did yer know 'e was comin'?'

'I thought—he might. It was like this. One day I had a letter from him. I don't know how he found my address. He wanted money from me, and said there'd be trouble if I didn't send it to him. Mrs Wilby saw the envelope with its Australian stamp, but I put her off—perhaps that was the moment I should have confided in her—and of course she didn't press the matter. Not that time.'

It was odd listening to Mr Wilby's story, for on the previous afternoon Ben had heard it from Mrs Wilby's angle, and he

recalled all she had told him about the letter, and that Mr
Wilby had said it was only an advertisement.

'Did yer answer it?' he asked.

'No, I burnt it,' replied Mr Wilby. 'I tried to believe that
nothing more would happen, and that it was just Dan's
bluff. But the thing got on my mind, and I soon found
myself watching for the postman.' (Mrs Wilby had used
those very words.) 'For a while nothing more did happen,
and I began to get less jumpy, but then one day I got
another letter from Dan, and this time it was from
Southampton. Oh, I expect I behaved like a fool! I'm not
cut out for this sort of game! An envelope bearing the
Southampton post-mark would have meant nothing to my
wife—why should it?—but of course I recognised the
writing and it gave me such a shock that I seized the letter
and—and tried to hide it. Mad! Though I now know it
would have made no difference in the end. My wife grew
suspicious—naturally. She asked questions, and I gave her
stupid answers, saying it was just a business letter. To my
relief she suddenly dropped the matter, but you can imagine
the relief didn't last, and now I began listening for the
telephone bell as well as watching for the postman. Every
time the bell rang I hurried to get to the 'phone first.' (Mrs
Wilby had used those words, too.) 'And one morning, the
call I was dreading came.'

''Arf a mo'!' said Ben.

Mr Wilby waited, wiping his forehead with his sleeve as
he did so. How unreal all this is, he thought! Is this I, a
bank manager, sitting here in a bedroom in Cumberland,
telling intimate details about myself and my wife to a
stranger? But the odd thing was he did not feel that he
was telling anybody at all. He was just thinking aloud,

talking to a wall . . . saying things that had been bottled up inside him for weeks and weeks and weeks . . .

'I thort I saw some'un, but it weren't,' said Ben. 'Okay, sir. I expeck that there 'phone call was from yer brother?'

'Eh? Yes—that's right. It was Dan, and if he'd 'phoned two minutes later he'd have missed me, for I was off to the bank. I shut him up quick and arranged to meet him at three in the afternoon, and rang off before my wife came down. By a lucky chance she was upstairs, so heard nothing.'

('Didn't she!' thought Ben. 'She 'eard more'n you knew!' But he offered no comment.)

'We met at a hotel,' went on Mr Wilby, 'and I received the biggest surprise of my life. I'd expected fireworks, but instead Dan was friendly—almost sentimental! He said I'd misunderstood him, and that although he was hard up he worked his way over because he wanted to see me again and get in touch with old days. I remember him saying, "Well, George, and now I have seen you, and that's that, and I'd go back again and never worry you again if I had the dough for the fare, with just a little bit over for a fresh start. Would you go as far as that, or are you strapped?" God, he was a clever rascal—and I was the mug. He got out of me my exact financial position, learned that my wife was the one with the money, learned all he could about us, in fact—and got just exactly what he wanted—what he wanted *that* time. I'd come ready, and I gave him a hundred. I considered it worth it. And when he took the money he said, with a laugh—I remember this, too, every word, because I thought of it so often afterwards—he said, "You know, George, even after all these years, you and I are still just as we were.

228

I, the naughty one, broke, and you the simple, good one, in a nice soft job—and still alike as two peas, if I shaved off my beard and moustache. I believe—I've been studying you, George, while we've been talking—I believe that with a make-up box and a little ingenuity, I could pass myself off as you again, as I used to in the old days—remember?" I laughed back. I felt drunk with relief. And that evening I explained my happiness to my wife by saying that my shares had boomed, and took her to a theatre. The two days that followed were almost the happiest of my life. They say the greatest happiness is relief from pain. Well, mental agony is just as bad as physical, and I was getting my release from that. Then, on the following Sunday—Dan 'phoned again. Mrs Wilby was in the room. He said, "Bring fifty pounds to me tomorrow night at 15, Norgate Street, or you're for it. I'll wreck your life, and that's a promise. Nine pm." I slammed down the receiver and told my wife it was a wrong number. She didn't believe me . . . She's never believed me since.'

They were wrenched back from the past to the present by a shrill shout. It came from the room in which the old woman was locked. Ben left the window and ran out into the passage, which echoed with the din the woman was making. She was banging as well as shrieking.

'Shut that row!' bawled Ben.

'Open the door, let me out!' the woman bawled back. 'How much longer am I to be kept in here?'

'Nah, listen!' roared Ben. 'If I open the door it'll be ter shoot yer with yer own gun, so the on'y way ter sive yer skin is ter keep quiet, see?'

'You won't have any skin when my son returns!'

229

'That's where yer wrong, Ma! Yer son 'as returned, and I got 'im locked and bahnd in another room, waitin' fer a pleeceman!'

The lie went home. The woman gasped and was silent, and Ben returned to Mr Wilby, to resume his vigil at the window.'

'Okay,' he reported. 'She was jest a bit excited like, but p'r'aps yer'd better git a move on. I s'pose yer went ter Norgate Street?'

'I did,' answered Mr Wilby.

'And was yer brother there?'

'He was—though when I saw him I seemed to be looking at my own self. He'd done what he suggested. And I guessed at once what his game was. The old game, on a much larger scale. "I want all the money you've got on you," he said, "bar your fare home, or I'll be seen about with a tart, and your wife will think it's you!"'

'Lummy!' exclaimed Ben, as light dawned. 'Yer don't mean—?'

'Mean what?'

'Go on, sir!'

'You've got on to it, then? Yes, that was Dan's game. He had got into touch with some cheap girl, and whenever I refused to fork out he went about with her—to night clubs, to public occasions—was even photographed with her—and always in some uncanny way he timed the occasions when I wasn't at home and could not prove an alibi. How he got his information of my movements I don't know—'

'I berlieve I can tell yer that!' interrupted Ben. 'It was through Blake. I'll bet 'e 'elped watch yer and find aht things, it'd be jest 'is line. See, it was Blake got 'im the gal, too!'

'Blake,' repeated Mr Wilby, thoughtfully. 'I wonder? I haven't been able to place where he came in.'

'Of all the dirty tricks! So it was never you at all, eh? Yus, but when it got as 'ot as orl that, why didn't yer come clean with the 'ole thing ter Mrs Wilby?'

'Because I left it too late,' replied Mr Wilby miserably. 'Because I behaved like a weak fool at the start, when there was little to lose. I'd have had to admit to a lie—I'd said I had no living relative—and somehow the thought of Dan and his crookedness always scared me. And then things got to a point where I lost everything! My wife only taxed me directly once or twice, and she listened to my denials without saying a word. I could not prove my words—I—I was completely discredited with her. To have expected her to believe the real truth by then would have been too fantastic. Another man might have found some way out—I couldn't.'

Ben nodded solemnly.

'I reckon it'd bin a bit fer 'er ter swaller,' he agreed. 'But killin' yer brother, even if 'e deserved it—'

'Wait, wait! My God, he deserved it, but I've still to tell you about that! You don't suppose I killed him deliberately?'

'I dunno wot way that is, sir,' answered Ben, 'but yer say yer killed 'im.'

'Yes, but if I had killed him deliberately—that is, on purpose—if I'd set out to kill him, that *would* have been murder! Listen. That damned cellar was our regular meeting place. On that—that frightful afternoon no meeting had been arranged until about a couple of hours before-hand. My wife had mentioned that she was going to a film at the Odeon, and I decided to take her to the afternoon

231

performance. She'd meant to go alone, and was surprised when I showed her the two tickets I'd bought in advance. I thought she'd refuse to go with me. She didn't, and I wondered whether we were going to have a happy afternoon at last. And then came that final order of Dan's to meet him at Norgate Street, and I had to tell my wife that some sudden business had turned up and that she'd have to go to the Odeon ahead of me, and that I'd join her there as soon as I could.

'Can you imagine the state I was in? No—nobody could! I was certainly ripe for murder, and I meant to have some sort of a showdown this time or die. Perhaps my condition was partly the cause of what happened, but Dan had been drinking and was in one of his worst moods, and when I told him I had to join my wife at the Odeon and threatened him with violence he brought out a revolver—the very one, I shouldn't be surprised, you now have in your hand—and said he'd go and join her himself! Then, threatening to shoot me if I didn't do all he told me, he forced me to change clothes with him, and after that he bound me in a chair and gagged me. And then he went off. God knows how long I was left like that! I passed out, and when I came to I found him grinning at me. He'd been to the cinema, he said, and had sat next my wife, and she'd never guessed it wasn't I beside her. That may be true or not— I've only his word for it. "And now," he said, "I'm going to unbind you, because you're going to commit suicide with my little gun, and you couldn't shoot yourself if you were tied up, could you?'

Mr Wilby moistened his lips, and then concluded his story.

'My mind was dazed, and I felt as weak as a rat. I felt

quite powerless while he once more drew out his revolver. I remember asking him what use I'd be to him dead, and his answer was that as I'd been sucked dry and looked like being a nuisance I was no more use to him living and so he was going to make an end of me before clearing out of London with a pal . . . I don't think he really meant it. I think he was just trying to frighten me. He succeeded too well, for when I found myself free . . . Suddenly it happened! My fear gave me strength, and I threw myself upon him. We both went down. We rolled over and over. We became a couple of frenzied wild animals. I heard a shot, and thought I was dead. But it was Dan who was dead—and it was I who had the revolver in my hand . . . After that, my mind went blank. I don't remember anything between then and stumbling into you.'

He stopped speaking, and there was silence for several seconds while Ben revolved what he had just heard in his mind. It all fitted—yes, it all fitted. It fitted into the story he had heard from Mrs Wilby's lips. Each story was like a large piece in a jigsaw puzzle which, when joined together, made a picture. Suddenly thinking aloud, continuing his hitherto silent thoughts, Ben said:

'Yus. I'm gettin' it. You killed yer brother in wot's called self-defence like, and then Blake comes along, mikes 'imself scarce when I comes along, and then comes back like he'd not bin there afore. But 'e got on ter it, too, puttin' two and two tergether, and I dessay he went back agine arter I'd left the fust time, 'cos things was dif'rent a bit when I 'ad a second look, as if 'e'd tried a bit more ter mike 'em seem wot 'e wanted when the body was fahnd. Corse, 'e took the gun. And—'arf a mo', I'm gettin' something else. Didn't yer say yer brother meant ter leave Lunnon with a pal? Ain't that wot yer sed 'e sed? Well, wouldn't the pal of bin Blake, wot 'ad got the gal fer 'im? See, I 'appen ter know Blake was leavin' Lunnon, too. They was comin' up 'ere ter 'is mother's—thinkin' Lunnon a bit too 'ot, p'r'aps, eh?—and it was time ter try some new gime. That jemmy in the pocket of the coat yer was wearin' of yer brother's give away that 'e was orlready busy on other things. Well, don't it? But there's one thing I ain't got on ter, sir. 'Ow did *you* come up 'ere? That's got me fair beat!'

'The explanation is simple,' replied Mr Wilby, 'although you may not understand the whole of it. I had on my brother's clothes—you know that—and his ticket to Penridge was in his pocket.'

'Well, I'm blowed!' muttered Ben. 'Yer brother used yer cinema ticket, and you used 'is railway ticket! But—wot mide yer use it? Did Blake come along and mike yer?'

Mr Wilby shook his head.

'No, and this is the part you may not understand. I'm not sure that I quite understand it myself. But—you can imagine—I was in a terrible condition. I was weak and dazed, and when I found I'd killed my brother after that terrible tussle—well, that finished me. My mind gave out. The encounter with you brought me out of my first coma—'

'Where's that?'

'Woke me up. I'd killed a man. The police would want me. I couldn't go home to my wife. I seemed cut off from everybody and everything. And that ticket was there in my pocket, waiting to be used. With no will-power left, I just accepted what chance or Fate seemed to be offering me. And when I got to Penridge, Blake got out of the same train—I hardly remember it—and brought me here. And I've been kept a prisoner, without news, ever since.'

'I see—so *that's* 'ow it was,' said Ben. 'Blake trailed yer.
'E'd proberly fixed ter meet yer brother on the trine, but
when you turned up—yer didn't reckernize 'im—'cos yer
wouldn't, would yer? Lummy, I wunner if 'e reckernized
you? Which one did 'e think yer was, and which did 'e
think the corpse was when 'e was lookin' at it with me?
You and 'im 'ad never met, 'ad yer?' Mr Wilby shook his
head. 'Well, there yer are. I dessay 'e thort at furst it *was*
you wot was dead, and that yer brother 'ad killed yer—and
then 'e finds aht it was t'other way abart, and 'e lies low
and sez nothink till yer git ter Penridge, and then carts yer
orf ter see if 'e can mike a bit more aht of yer. And, I'll
bet, that letter ter yer wife—'

'What letter?' interposed Mr Wilby sharply. When Ben
did not answer—he was wondering just what answer to
give—Mr Wilby went on: 'Yes, and there's something I still
don't understand. You say Mrs Wilby sent you up here—'

'No, not exackly,' Ben corrected him. 'I'm workin' fer
'er, but it's by mikin' Blake think as I'm workin' fer 'im.
See, it's a double-cross, on'y I reckon we're orl aht in the
open arter this! Afore yer tole me wot yer tole me, yer
wife tole me 'er side of it, so nah I've got the lot the nex'
thing we gotter do is ter git yer tergether agine—ter
git—yer—'

His voice trailed off. While talking he had kept one eye
on the window and one hand gripping the revolver, for at
any moment Blake might return after his long and inex-
plicable absence and the fireworks would begin, but all at
once the watching eye became glazed. Then it closed again.
Then it opened again.

''Ave I gorn barmy?' he asked.

For what he saw arriving at the gate below was not

Blake, but Mrs Wilby, Maudie, the countryman, a constable, and a small smutty-faced boy.

His legs gave way beneath him, and as he sat down on the floor there came a loud report.

'No, I ain't barmy,' he decided, as blackness swooped upon him. 'I'm dead!'

23

Completion of the Job

When Ben came out of the darkness to make the gratifying discovery that after all he was not dead, he found himself lying on a hard and lumpy sofa in the parlour, with Maudie sitting beside him.

'Wot's 'appenin'?' he muttered muzzily.

'Let's see first what's happening to you,' she answered. 'How are you feeling?'

'I dunno yet,' he replied, as he began pressing various parts of his anatomy to see if they hurt. 'That's funny! I carn't find nothink! 'Oo was it tried ter pop me orf?'

'You!' smiled Maudie. 'As far as we can make out you sat down on your gun.'

'I never!'

'It had gone off, and nobody else fired one.'

'I'll be blowed!' gasped Ben. 'But if I didn't 'it meself wot give me the black-aht?'

'I should think anybody would get a black-out sitting down on a loud bang!' retorted Maudie. 'Well, I must announce the good news—I was told to give a shout as soon as you came to.'

'Yus—well, don't shaht jest yet,' said Ben. 'I'd sooner come to a bit more afore we git the crahd in! And, lummy, wot a crahd! 'Ow did yer orl git 'ere? And 'ow did I git on this sofa? Did I walk dahn in me sleep?'

'No, you were carried down when we found you'd missed yourself—there were rather too many people upstairs, and we thought Mr and Mrs Wilby might prefer to kiss and make friends without having you rolling about the floor while they did it.'

Ben gave a pale smile.

'Yer know, I likes the way yer torks sometimes, Maudie. Sorter gives yer a larf when yer wants it. 'Oo was it carried me dahn?'

'The detective.'

''Oo?'

'The 'tec.'

'Go on, 'e wer'n't no detective. Jest a bobby.'

'Not that one, silly! The other one.'

'Wot other one? I don't git yer.' Then, suddenly, he did. 'Yer don't mean—yer don't mean that country bloke—?'

'Who else? But, of course, you haven't heard about that yet, have you?' She grinned at him. 'I like seeing your mouth open—that's just how mine went when I saw him and Mrs Wilby at the Applewold hotel! It was just after you left me there. They were on our train—'

'Wot, follerin' us?'

'That's right. Do you remember, Mrs Wilby wanted to get in touch with the police yesterday afternoon, and you persuaded her not to—or thought you had.'

'Wot I thort,' said Ben correctively, 'was that she was goin' ter stick aht abart it, but she chainged 'er mind.'

'That's where you're wrong—she didn't change her mind! At least, not completely. She agreed—this is what she told me—she agreed that you ought to come up here yourself and that it would be best for you to meet Blake alone, but she wasn't happy about the risk, and she 'phoned up the police as soon as you and I left her house. They sent along a detective, and she decided to come up here with him.'

'Well, if that don't beat the band!' exclaimed Ben. ''Ere was I expectin' ter come up 'ere orl by meself, and fust you pops along, and then Mrs Wilby and a 'tec! 'E diddled me proper, that 'tec did, torkin' like 'e was a country bloke. But why didn't you and Mrs Wilby come along from Applewold with 'im?'

'Because that might have made too big a crowd at Penridge, and as we weren't necessary the detective thought it would be better if we followed on the next train—which we did. I'd better call him in now to tell you the rest.'

But as she spoke the parlour door was pushed open, and the countryman-turned-detective popped his head in. He darted a swift glance towards the couch, and then smiled.

'Good! You don't look as though you were dying,' he said, now without a trace of Norfolk accent.

'Every way's bin tried on me,' answered Ben, 'but it seems like there ain't no way o' doin' it.'

The detective laughed. 'Am I forgiven?'

'Lot o' good it'd be me sayin' yer wasn't. But if yer didn't wanter let on ter me in the trine, yer might of at the inn?'

'Well, you can't say you gave me much time,' the

detective reminded him. 'Anyhow, I did something better.' He turned to Maudie. 'How much does he know?'

'I'm in the middle of it,' she replied.

'Then perhaps you'll finish it? Just the facts—the frills can come later. The constable has taken Mrs Blake to the police station, and now I've got all I require from Mr Wilby I want to get to the station myself as soon as I can. There's plenty to do.'

'Okay, I'll carry on,' said Maudie. 'Only what do *we* do?'

'I'm going to try and send a conveyance along. You'd better wait for it and all come back together. Mr Wilby is in no condition to walk—oh, and by the way, I wouldn't disturb them upstairs for a bit, if I were you.'

''Nuff said!'

'Think we're mugs?' added Ben.

The detective might have responded with a polite denial, but instead he regarded, first Ben and then Maudie, with a speculative eye. His response, when it came, was not a complete compliment.

'From what I've heard and from what I've gathered,' he said, 'you may be, but as none of us are foolproof—or perfect—I'm facing the risk. Is that enough?'

'Suits me,' Maudie answered. 'Where's Tommy?'

'Tommy? Oh, Tommy went back with the constable. He's having the time of his life—and incidentally deserves it. I've told him he'll probably be knighted. Well, I mustn't wait any longer—sometimes you find mugs even at a police station! Carry on.' He threw Ben a grin. 'I reckon it be toime fer me tu get back tu Naarfolk!'

Ben grinned back as the door closed and he was gone. ''E's orl right, that feller,' he commented. 'Fer a 'tec.'

'Yes, I'd go out to supper with him if he asked me,'

replied Maudie, 'though I owe him one for making me tell you his own bit of the yarn!'

'I'd sooner 'ear it orf you.'

'Why?'

'Are yer fishin'?'

'Course I am!'

'Then 'ere's one fer yer 'ook. You and me 'ad a funny start, Maudie, but nah we seems ter git on.'

'In another minute *you'll* be asking me out to supper!'

'Doncher believe it! I eats with me fingers.'

'Well, however you eat, I'd sooner have you than the last man I went out with! Guess who it was? We had our picture taken.'

Ben frowned at her. 'Fergit it!'

'You might tell me how?' she suggested grimly.

'Easy, Maudie. 'Stead o' thinkin' back, think above! Doncher know wot's 'appenin' in the room on top of us?'

'I see what you mean. But a lot they've got to thank *me* for!'

'Well, yer never know,' returned Ben. 'I ain't one o' them fizzikolergists, or wotever yer calls 'em, but sometimes a 'usband and wife need a sorter shike up. Bang 'em apart, and then they bangs tergether agine. But 'ow abart yer gittin' on with the rest o' wot's 'appened? Don't fergit, I'm still in the dark 'ow yer orl got 'ere, and wot's 'appened ter Blake. Yus, and why this 'ere Tommy—that'd be the small boy, wouldn't it?—why 'e's going ter be knighted?'

Maudie nodded. 'Where was I up to?'

'I've fergot.'

'Wasn't it where the detective got in the train with you for the last part of the journey?'

'Yus, that was it, and played 'is trick on me by pertendin'

ter be wot 'e wasn't! Did 'e come orl the way from Lunnon in them clothes?'

Maudie brought her mind back. 'No, he got the inn-keeper to lend him a rough suit, and it was while he was getting into it that Mrs Wilby told me how she had 'phoned up the police and got him to come along. They spotted us on the train, of course, and—I may as well admit it—Mrs Wilby thought at first that I was up to fresh tricks when she found me with you. You were wondering that for a bit yourself, you may remember.'

'But yer *wasn't*!'

'No, not that time—'

'And there ain't goin' ter be no nex' time!'

'Well, there's nothing like being hopeful! Anyhow, we're talking of this time now, so we'll let the next time rip. After you and the 'tec went off, Mrs Wilby and I had our little heart-to-heart—she's all right, Mrs Wilby is—I'm telling you—'

'Yer don't 'ave ter.'

'And then we followed on the next train, and joined up with the detective on Penridge platform. And then—get your mind steady—things *happened*! This is the bit the detective ought to be telling you himself.'

'You're managin' orl right,' Ben assured her. 'Keep goin'.'

'Well—you know that letter from Blake—the one he gave you that you gave to the detective to give to me to take to Mrs Wilby—what a rigmarole! Anyhow, here was Mrs Wilby right on the spot to receive it, so there was no need to go trapesing after her all the way back to London. She opened that letter in the station waiting-room. Guess what was in it?'

'P'r'aps I could,' answered Ben, 'but you tell me.'

'It said that Mr Wilby wasn't dead, and that he would be returned to her intact for five thousand pounds—five thousand!—and that if the sum wasn't forthcoming, Mr Wilby would be returned to the police instead, and charged with murder!'

'Gawd! Wot a skunk!' growled Ben.

'You've said it! Pretty low! But am I one to talk? Of course, Blake thought you would give her the letter, and she was to tell you just Yes or No, and whichever reply you brought back to him, he would act according. I expect Blake didn't want to reappear yet in person, and that's why he had you up, to act as go-between. The letter wasn't signed, it was written all in capitals, and there was no address.'

'Yus, 'e'd go corshus,' nodded Ben. 'That's 'ow them blackmailers works. And corse 'e wasn't goin' ter arsk 'er ter fork aht the five thousand ter *me*! 'E'd 'ave ter give 'er time ter arrainge things and git the cash, and then 'e'd see as no one else could git 'old of it fust. Proberly 'e meant ter pay me orf with tuppence! Well—wot 'appened then?'

'Mrs Wilby fainted.'

''Oo wouldn't?'

'It was certainly some shock! But luckily she recovered almost at once and got a grip on herself, and then we all went to the inn and waited.'

'Fer me?'

'For Tommy.'

'Wot! The nipper?'

'Do you remember asking the 'tec just now why he hadn't told you who he was at the inn when you gave him the letter, and he said you hadn't given him time?'

'Yus. See, Blake 'ad jest gorn off, and if I'd 'adn't follered 'im quick I'd of lorst 'im.'

'Yes, and when you bolted like you did, the detective guessed the reason for your hurry, and so instead of holding you up and wasting valuable time he—as he put it himself to you—did something better.'

'Wot was it?'

'He got hold of a small boy who was hanging around to follow *you*!'

''E never!'

'I'm telling you.'

Ben rubbed his eyes. 'Coo! Wot a gime!'

'And after he'd done that he went to the station to meet Mrs Wilby and yours truly with the letter, and then carted us back to the hotel to wait for Tommy's return, like I said. We had to wait some time, and while we were waiting the 'tec got busy and 'phoned to the local police station, and a sergeant and a constable came along. I call that pretty smart work on the 'tec's part, because you see it meant that we were all set by the time the boy returned. You see, he returned with Blake on his heels.'

'Wot!'

'Yes—Blake ran plumb into the arms of the law!'

Ben's mind reverted to the moment when Blake had dashed out of the cottage and he had dived behind a bush to avoid him. But it had not been Ben Blake had spotted, it had been this little nipper—and the little nipper had won the race back to the hotel!

'So that's why 'e never come back!' he murmured. 'If that ain't a fair knock-aht! . . . And then wot?'

'The rest is easy,' concluded Maudie. 'Blake lost his head, and the sergeant hauled him off to the police station for questions while the rest of us came on home. And now, as you've heard, Ma Blake's been hauled off, too. I don't know what they'll be charged with, but after the police have got all their evidence—and you and I'll be roped in for statements, I expect, and yours will be prettier than mine!—there should be at least two charges for them to answer—blackmailing and kidnapping.'

'Yus, the pleece'll 'ave 'em on those, if on nothink else,' agreed Ben. 'They kep' Mr Wilby locked up, and they knocked 'im abart, and they drugged 'im. Yer'd think that's enough ter go on with! Corse,' he added, after a pause, 'they won't 'ave nothink on Mr Wilby.'

'I hope not,' Maudie answered.

''Ow can they? 'E on'y killed 'is brother in wot's called self-defence, and 'e didn't mean ter do that—like I didn't mean ter sit dahn on me gun. 'E ain't done murder no more'n I'd of done suissicide. Why, lummy, 'e was bahnd and gagged afore the flare up!'

'Well, you seem to know, Ben, so what will the police have on *me*?'

'They won't 'ave nothink on you, Maudie,' he retorted. 'Yer carn't be 'ad up fer goin' abart with a bloke! Orl there'll be on you is wot yer 'ave on yerself—if yer see wot I mean?'

'I see what you mean,' said Maudie.

A few moments later they heard steps on the creaky stairs, and Mrs Wilby came into the room. She was pale but composed, and Ben realised that this was the first time he had seen happiness in her eyes. But there was also some anxiety in them as she glanced quickly at him.

'Orl alive, mum,' he reassured her. 'There's nothink wrong o' me.'

'Thank heaven for that!' she exclaimed, and then turned to Maudie. 'Miss Kenton, would you go up to my husband?'

Maudie looked scared. 'What does he want me for?'

'Don't be worried. Perhaps he wants to show you how much better he is than his brother—and I think I'd like you to find that out, too. Would you mind?'

'Yes! No! Of course.'

She jumped up, and left the room rather flurriedly. Mrs Wilby turned back to Ben.

'One reason I sent her up,' she said gravely, 'was because I wanted a few words with you. You know that everything's all right now between me and Mr Wilby?'

'I knoo it would be, mum,' answered Ben, 'once yer got torkin'.'

'And you know that we owe it mainly to you?'

Ben shook his head.

'No, mum—or if I 'ad anythink ter do with it, it was just the charnce that took me inter that there cellar. But it'd of come right, any'ow.'

'You think so?'

'Well—don't you?'

She did not answer at once, and suddenly he guessed what was in her mind. It was something which recent events had made him forget. After a few seconds she asked:

'I suppose Miss Kenton has told you everything?'

'She tole me orl she knew,' replied Ben guardedly.

'But there was something she didn't know, wasn't there?'

'Was there?'

'Something that only you and I know.'

Ben nodded. 'I knows wot yer means, mum,' he said; 'but I've fergot it.'

'I shall forget it, too, Ben,' she replied; 'but before I do I have to tell you the end of it. You remember, don't you, that I was worried about the sudden absence of—that friend?'

'That's right, mum—but corse we knows now that it wasn't fer—well, fer wot we thort it might be.'

'Yes, but now I know more than that. I know why he went away. He went to Paris to make certain arrangements, and he telephoned from Paris just before I left London yesterday evening. He asked me to join him there.'

'And you told 'im "Nothin' doin'," didn't yer?'

Mrs Wilby smiled.

'I told him something stronger than that,' she answered. 'He's gone out of my life—and Mr Wilby has come back into it.'

Ben smiled back.

'It's like I orlwise sez, mum,' he responded. 'Everythink comes aht okay so long as yer 'angs on. That's right, ain't it . . . Oi! There's our car.'

THE END

Also available

Ben Sees It Through
J. Jefferson Farjeon

With his usual knack of getting into trouble, Ben the tramp finds himself hunted by the law and the lawless.in this breathless adventure of murder and blackmail.

Returning home to his Cockney roots after a trip to Spain, Ben meets a mysterious stranger on a cross-Channel steamer and is promised a job. On arrival at Southampton they take a taxi. Ben gets out to post a letter, but on returning to the cab finds the stranger has been murdered! Pursued by a mysterious foreigner, Ben escapes his clutches, only to find the police are now after him and the whole political establishment is in danger.

'Ben is here more Ben-ish, and consequently more likeable than ever.' LIVERPOOL POST

'Ben will once more delight all readers by his adorable Cockney insouciance and nerve.' SATURDAY REVIEW

Also available

Detective Ben
J. Jefferson Farjeon

*Ben the tramp, the awkward Cockney with no home and
no surname, turns detective again—and runs straight into
trouble.*

Ben encounters a dead man on a London bridge and is
promptly rescued from the same fate by a posh lady in a
limousine. But like most posh ladies of Ben's acquaintance,
this one isn't what she seems. Seeking escape from a gang
of international conspirators, Ben is whisked off to the
mountains of Scotland to thwart the schemes of a poisonous
organisation and finds himself in very unfamiliar territory.

*'Jefferson Farjeon is a master of the particular art of
blending horrors with humour.' SUNDAY TIMES*

'Ben is a sheer joy.' GLASGOW HERALD

Also available

Number Nineteen
J. Jefferson Farjeon

Ben the tramp's uncanny knack of running into trouble is unsurpassed in his final hair-raising adventure taking place at No.19, Billiter Road.

On a grey afternoon he was destined never to forget, Ben sat down on a park seat and proceeded to think, not of cabbages and kings, but of numbers, lucky and unlucky. But it wasn't Ben's lucky day, or that of the nondescript-looking stranger sitting at the other end of the bench— murdered before his very eyes! That was the prelude to the most uncomfortable and eventful twenty-four hours Ben had ever spent in an uncomfortable and eventful life.

'Few authors of detective stories are so persuasive as Mr Farjeon.' TIMES LITERARY SUPPLEMENT

'Mr Farjeon discovered some time ago a good recipe for an entertaining story by mixing humour with thrills.' DAILY TELEGRAPH